BY AMANDA EYRE WARD

Lovers and Liars

The Lifeguards

The Jetsetters

The Sober Lush (with Jardine Libaire)

The Nearness of You

The Same Sky

Close Your Eyes

Love Stories in This Town

Forgive Me

How to Be Lost

Sleep Toward Heaven

LOVERS AND LIARS

LOVERS AND LIARS

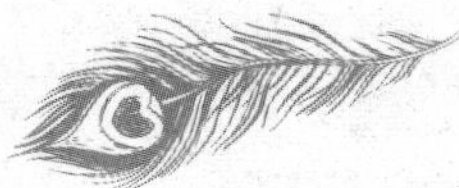

A NOVEL

AMANDA EYRE WARD

BALLANTINE BOOKS
New York

Lovers and Liars is a work of fiction. Names, characters, places, and incidents are the products of the author's imagination or are used fictitiously. Any resemblance to actual events, locales, or persons, living or dead, is entirely coincidental.

Published in the United States by Ballantine Books, an imprint of Random House, a division of Penguin Random House LLC, New York.

Ballantine Books & colophon are registered trademarks of Penguin Random House LLC.

Grateful acknowledgment is made to Darren Sardelli for permission to reprint "Recess! Oh, Recess!" from *Galaxy Pizza and Meteor Pie* by Darren Sardelli, copyright © 2009 by Laugh-A-Lot Books. Used by permission of Darren Sardelli.

Library of Congress Cataloging-in-Publication Data
Names: Ward, Amanda Eyre, author.
Title: Lovers and liars: a novel / Amanda Eyre Ward.
Description: First edition. | New York: Ballantine Books, 2024.
Identifiers: LCCN 2023052723 (print) | LCCN 2023052724 (ebook) |
ISBN 9780593500293 (hardcover; acid-free paper) |
ISBN 9780593500309 (ebook)
Subjects: LCSH: Sisters—Fiction. | Destination weddings—Fiction. |
Truthfulness and falsehood—Fiction. | LCGFT: Domestic fiction. | Novels.
Classification: LCC PS3623.A725 L685 2024 (print) |
LCC PS3623.A725 (ebook) | DDC 813/.6—dc23/eng/20231117
LC record available at https://lccn.loc.gov/2023052723
LC ebook record available at https://lccn.loc.gov/2023052724

Printed in the United States of America on acid-free paper

randomhousebooks.com

2 4 6 8 9 7 5 3 1

First Edition

Book design by Alexis Flynn

For Kara Cesare,
Brilliant editor, true friend—
When I walk with you into the woods,
I know we will find our way home.

CONTENTS

LOVERS AND LIARS

TOGETHER
WITH THEIR FAMILIES
Sylvia Peacock
&
Simon Rampling
INVITE YOU
TO THEIR WEDDING
Sunday, July 13, 2025
at 11 A.M.
Mumberton Castle
ENGLAND
Civilians, Morning Dress (or Lounge Suits)
Serving Officers, Serving Dress
Ladies, Morning Dress with Hats

PROLOGUE

SYLVIE

On the night before her wedding, Sylvie Peacock could not sleep. She walked toward her window, where she could see the outline of Mumberton Castle. Moonlit treetops were a silvery ocean. The dawn songs of goldcrest and thrush would begin soon, but in the deep of the night: only silence. What was she doing in Northern England on the grounds of a crumbling castle? How had the last glowing embers of hope led her here, of all places, preparing to marry again?

Despite the castle's grandeur, Sylvie missed the Coconut Grove Elementary School library where she worked, missed the thrum of a second-grade class choosing their weekly books, missed the smells of peanut butter and paper. Another chance at love had been intoxicating, but now Sylvie just wanted to go home to her rescue greyhound, Willie, and her bungalow on Hibiscus Street.

Sylvie moved toward an ornate armoire and touched her wedding dress, which she had picked out with the help of her best friend, Florence. They had spent a humid morning in bridal boutiques—Grace Loves Lace, Ever After Miami—before ordering Cuban sandwiches and strong coffee at their favorite café and finding the perfect dress on eBay: a long, swishy affair with a big bow in the back, a *bustle,* and pockets. Sylvie liked to tuck a tiny notebook and pencil in her pocket in case someone recommended a book she'd want to read later.

When she'd married for the first time, she was so young: twenty-five! Sylvie's dress had been short and breezy, nothing more than a white sundress, really. She'd worn gold sandals, held a bouquet of wildflowers—swamp mallow, coral honeysuckle, Carolina jessamine. Alexander had called her his mountain girl even as they married in a bayside ceremony.

Alexander had been dead for ten years, yet Sylvie was still surprised every morning not to find him in the music room where he'd been choir director. Under his tutelage, the kids had sung David Bowie and the Beatles.

The new choir director taught the kids a Taylor Swift medley and Katy Perry's "Firework." When Sylvie heard music down the hall, she would stop whatever she was doing (securing book flaps with library tape, ordering more spine stickers) and let the sweet voices wash over her. She would reflect, in answer to the Katy Perry lyrics: *Yes. Sometimes I do feel like a plastic bag drifting through the wind. Wanting to start again.*

Sylvie's gown was smooth against her fingertips. She thought about her sisters, Emma and Cleo, both now in England for her wedding. They had been strangers for so long. And yet, who else could understand the riot of uncertainty inside Sylvie: the shards of loneliness; a longing for her father's cigar-and-soap smell; her terror of love's entrapment?

When they were children, the Peacock sisters would climb the rocks behind their house to escape their mother. Sylvie was the smallest but insisted she did not need help summiting Skull Rock. She would glance back periodically, to make sure her sisters were protecting her from anything, from everything.

At the top, the three girls made a nest of tangled limbs. Sylvie sat in Emma's warm lap as Emma played with Sylvie's crimson hair. Cleo's head rested on Sylvie's shoulder. It seemed they were the only people in the world—they had each other, and joy, an endless Montana summer. The sisters pointed out stars and told stories about how they would fall in love and marry in the Bitterroot Mountains.

Sylvie had once believed her sisters would always be beside her, watching out for her. She'd counted on their protection. She could still close her eyes and remember feeling safe, sandwiched between them. Now, she knew that her sisters—and Simon—were liars.

In her pajamas, Sylvie sat down at a small desk Simon had placed in the corner of the room for her. She reached into the *New Yorker* tote bag she used as a purse, rummaged until she found a Bic ballpoint.

Sylvie ripped a clean page from a tiny notebook. She wrote:

I'm sorry, Simon.
I'm going home.
It's over.

TWO MONTHS EARLIER . . .

PART ONE

A LIBRARIAN IN LOVE

1
SYLVIE

Sylvie was in love.

She knew that everyone would think—her mother and sisters would surely think—that she was marrying Simon for his money. And, OK, Sylvie knew she would *not mind* being rich. And who didn't dream of a wedding in a fairy-tale castle?

Sylvie's sisters never answered when she called, no matter the time of day. Sometimes she would text, *Hey, anyone free to chat this weekend?* Mostly they would not reply. At all! It was hard to convince herself they were just distracted. It seemed as if something was very wrong between the three of them. Sylvie worried there was a secret her two older sisters were keeping from her. What could it possibly be?

Sylvie dialed Emma's landline. Emma, the only one of the three Peacock sisters who had stayed in their childhood town in Montana, had a wall phone with a rotary dial, a curly cord, and a satisfyingly heavy earpiece. Sylvie decided the news of her whirlwind engagement should come through the wall phone. She bit her lip as it began to ring. One, two, three, four . . . after ring number five, Sylvie gave up.

Next was Cleo, who lived in Brooklyn. Cleo was always too busy to talk and prefaced even her calls *to* Sylvie with "I don't have time to talk but . . ." Cleo never answered and didn't answer now. When her assertive, somewhat bossy message came on—*Leave a message for Cleo Peacock after the tone*—Sylvie cut the line.

Should she call her mother, Donna? Sylvie paused. Whenever she called Donna, Sylvie hung up the phone miserable. Her mother had named her after Sylvia Plath. No, she would not call her mother just yet.

Sylvie decided to send a text. "I deserve this," she told herself as she composed a note with her thumbs on her tiny iPhone keypad. Her heart hammered in her chest.

What about Alexander? said the voice in her mind.

"Alexander is dead," she responded. She added, to her sisters, to her father in Heaven, to her mother in the Margaritaville Retirement Community, to herself, "I am not a gold digger. I am a librarian."

Her finger hovered over the "Send" button.

2
CLEO

Sylvie's insane text arrived while Cleo was in therapy with Dr. Benjamin. Cleo's longtime therapist had retired, and she was trying out someone new. When Cleo's phone dinged, she glanced into her open-mouthed Gucci tote bag. Cleo was a criminal defense attorney—she could turn her phone over on a table and she could jam it into her bag, but she could never—ever—turn it off.

"Cleo," said Dr. Benjamin schoolmarmishly, "I prefer my patients to silence their cellphones as soon as they enter—"

"Look," managed Cleo, grabbing her phone. "Dr. Benjamin, *look*!"

Dr. Benjamin took the cell and examined Sylvie's words with narrowed eyes. "This is a text message?"

"It's from my baby sister, Sylvie," said Cleo. "Sylvie's first husband died ten years ago, when she was twenty-five. Sylvie never moved on. She's been in the same house, in the same librarian job, just living the same life without Alexander for a decade. I've been worried about her for *ten years.* And then, a few months ago, she meets some guy online. A rich guy named Simon. An *alleged* rich guy. And look, now she says she's getting married." Cleo stopped and took a deep breath.

She opened her mouth to say more but couldn't think of anything else to say.

Dr. Benjamin's brow furrowed. He looked eighteen years old, Cleo thought. His fresh Ph.D. was framed on the wall behind him.

"And you mentioned that you and your sisters are estranged?"

"I wouldn't say *estranged*."

"What word would you use?"

Cleo tilted her head thoughtfully. She had large green eyes and freckles; as a kid she'd been nicknamed "Pippi Longstocking" until she'd cut her own hair with her mother's pinking shears at age nine. She'd worn it short ever since. Cleo was a size four with long, lean muscles from private Pilates sessions.

"I'd use the word *busy*," said Cleo. In truth, when Alexander had died, they had all been engulfed in shock and grief. Tragedy brought some families closer, Cleo guessed, but in their case, the opposite had been true.

At Alexander's funeral, Sylvie had asked her big sister, "Why do you think he went for a drive that night, Cleo? Did I do something to make him go for a drive that night? What could I have done to make him go? What did he mean by needing some air?"

Cleo had held her tongue between her teeth. She should have told her sister the truth right then and there, let the chips fall, allow Sylvie to understand who Alexander had truly been. But Cleo couldn't do it—she couldn't add to Sylvie's pain. Her entire life, Cleo had devoted herself to protecting her sisters.

So she'd said, "Sylvie, I have no idea."

Since then a feeling of doom came over Cleo whenever Sylvie called: Every conversation, no matter how anodyne, was now heavy with betrayal. And in terms of Emma, Cleo had lent her a great deal of money for her fledgling business, writing two giant checks to Sweet Nothings, Inc., which (let's be honest) was surely a pyramid marketing scam preying on disenfranchised stay-at-home mothers. After the second payment, Cleo had said, gently, that she couldn't send any more. Emma had seemed to be avoiding Cleo after that.

"I'm not implying there's anything wrong with being estranged," said Dr. Benjamin. "At times, it can be healthy to have space from your family of origin."

Sometimes, Cleo was caught off guard by flashes of memory. Brooklyn children on bikes would remind her of the way the Peacock sisters had careened around their childhood streets in a row, unstoppable. A photo of a snowy mountain could conjure the feeling of Sylvie's hand in Cleo's on the chairlift after a day of learning with their skis in "pizza pie" stance. A fancy pot de crème made Cleo think of the way she and her sisters had always counted the dehydrated mini marshmallows in their hot chocolate packets to make sure they were fairly distributed. They had shared everything: snow pants, toothbrushes, turtlenecks, knee socks, shampoo, hair bands, barrettes. In fact, Cleo's favorite barrette belonged to Sylvie. It was made of braided ribbon that fell from the clip into her hair, deep blue and pink.

Benjamin's office was brightly lit—the opposite of her old therapist's office, which had been filled with yolk-yellow light from a ceramic lamp. As her mother had taught her, Cleo crossed her legs at the ankle, knees pressed together. The pose was a remnant of Donna's drama-school training. Cleo's right hip twanged and she vowed that she'd allow her daughter to sit however the hell she wanted.

If she ever had a daughter.

Was she going to have a child? Cleo was thirty-nine: Her dwindling fertility was one of the issues that had brought her to Dr. Benjamin in the first place. At this point, she probably *couldn't* have a child. She wasn't sure how she felt about this.

Also: Cleo was pretty sure she was in love with her best friend, Isaac, and not her longtime, live-in boyfriend, Danny. This was another dilemma she hoped to hash out with Dr. Benjamin.

"How does your sister's engagement make you feel?" queried Dr. Benjamin.

Cleo closed her eyes.

"Can you name your feelings right now?" said Dr. Benjamin. "For example, fear . . . concern . . . curiosity?"

Cleo looked at him steadily. "I feel," she said, "an overwhelming sense of futile anger and the sense that I am wasting four hundred dollars."

Dr. Benjamin remained calm. Cleo imagined he was thinking *transference,* and maybe he was right. Because who was she angry at, really? Her mother, who had decided to name her after a suicidal Egyptian queen? Her father, beloved Police Chief Peacock, who had been so kind and selfless that it had set them all up for failure as they searched endlessly for a man like him? Sylvie, for jumping into love so suddenly it left Cleo questioning her choices? New York, and how it was making her into a brittle veneer of the lush girl she'd been when she arrived from college? Her other sister, Emma, for seeming so settled and at peace, her entire life an affront to Cleo's meticulously planned escape from Montana? Herself, and if so, why?

"You're angry," said Dr. Benjamin.

"Yes," said Cleo.

Dr. Benjamin nodded. He clasped his fingers together, rested them on his belly. He continued to nod. Cleo raised her eyebrows. "What do I do?" she asked.

Dr. Benjamin looked at her quizzically. "It seems like Sylvie is healing. Perhaps you're jealous of her?"

Cleo exhaled forcefully, as if she'd been punched. Dr. Benjamin's words seemed to ring in her ears. How could she be *jealous* of Sylvie, who had endured more than anyone should be able to survive? Sylvie was a victim, the family tragedy. If Sylvie was happy, what would that mean for the rest of them? Cleo felt—inexplicably—a wash of fear. She wanted a cigarette desperately, though she had quit smoking years before.

She looked at Dr. Benjamin, suddenly thankful for him, after all. She needed help, and here he was.

3
EMMA

-$24,039.50

Emma could not believe her baby sister's text message. Too late, Emma understood that Sylvie's incessant phone calls had not been the entreaties of a lonely librarian becoming a bit of a whack job, but attempts to share her joy. Emma had waited and waited to have a nice stretch of time to talk (and one iota of energy to listen to poor, sad Sylvie) but the time had not come.

Instead, a text message about a wedding in a castle, followed by a second, jubilant request: "RSVP!"

Emma's husband, Rich, strode into the kitchen, flanked by their sons. In Missoula, Montana, the sun was low by afternoon; a rogue flash of light fell on Rich's hair, making it golden. His round face had been ruddy when they were teens, and years of beer and tour skiing had made his nose and cheeks permanently ruby-colored, especially when he was chilly.

"I just got some news from Aunt Sylvie," said Emma.

"Is it bad news?" said Rich.

"It's *good news,*" said Emma.

"Oh, OK!" said Rich. "Lay it on us! I'm ready for some good news, how about you, G?"

"Bet," said their thirteen-year-old son, Guinness, collapsing into one of the rickety chairs that surrounded the kitchen table. Guinness, defying his name, was towheaded, his hair almost translucent. The beer he'd been named after was stolid and thick, but Guinness was fragile, partial to wearing fleece pajama pants to school with T-shirts he ordered from eBay promoting long-ago events: JAZZERCIZE PICNIC, '89! 1999 WILSON FAMILY CRUISE! Guinness's mysterious stomach pains fueled Emma's insomnia—they'd reached the end of tests that insurance would cover, so all night, most nights, Emma searched for an answer to what was ailing her sweet firstborn.

"*Bet* means yes, right?" said Rich, who enjoyed looking up teenage phrases on urbandictionary.com.

"Bet," agreed Guinness.

"Aunt Sylvie's getting married! And the wedding is in a castle!"

Rich rubbed his eyes. Emma knew he was thinking about how much the trip would cost. Sylvie hadn't mentioned *where,* exactly, the castle was located, but it was sure to be an expensive journey from Missoula, Montana. Rich touched his longish beard. He hated shaving, but deigned to trim his graying beard every Sunday.

"Will there be *knights*?" said ten-year-old Jameson. Unlike his brother, Jameson was chubby, his red hair curly and thick. Jameson refused to cut his hair and was starting to look like a frumpy middle-aged woman, with his shoulder-length curls, silver Croc sandals, and roomy clothing.

"Knights in shining armor," drawled Guinness in his weird teen monotone. "Dub. I could see Gram in a crown. Not gonna lie, the knights will be scared of *her*."

The two boys, secure and loved enough to see their grandmother, Donna, as a joke rather than a gorgeous, poisonous villain, began laughing. None of them had seen Grammy Donna since she had abruptly ditched Emma to move to a luxury Arizona condominium the year before.

"Did you even know Sylvie was engaged?" said Rich.

"I never called her back," said Emma mournfully.

"Sweetie," said Rich, encircling her in his arms.

She resented his pitying tone. She resented Sylvie's exciting future with whoever Simon Rampling was. She resented the fact that *only she* had done the right thing, had stayed in freezing cold Missoula and married and had kids. *She alone* had helped with Donna's chores, brought adorable grandchildren to be with their grandmother on every holiday, never going *anywhere,* because Rich's job as the Hellgate High School shop teacher could not afford them fancy vacations.

When Emma was eleven years old, her mother, Donna, told Emma about her affair with their next-door neighbor, Noah. (Until this moment, Noah had been the random dad next door, a married man and father of one of Sylvie's classmates.)

Donna needed Emma's help in covering up for her "evening walks." During these excursions, which were presented to Emma's dad as "mother-daughter stargazing," Donna and Noah had sex in a field near their homes and Emma lay in the grass nearby wanting to disappear. She was too scared of her mother's wrath to run home.

Donna had once had shining, brassy hair. She was curvy and proudly so—she favored sweaters with deep V-necks and even rested her fingers around her cleavage when she spoke, using her long, fluttering fingernails to draw attention to her breasts. Her waist was kept trim with Jane Fonda workout tapes. Even in her later years, her creamy skin seemed to glow and she wore bright pink gloss on her lips, putting it on in the morning before she made coffee, reapplying it until she was in bed for the night (she kept it on the bedside table). Donna wore eye makeup (shadow and liner), heavy mascara, big (if not expensive) jewelry. She bought (and misplaced) golden hoop earrings of various sizes and never removed a circular locket with a photo of her long-dead father inside.

"Shall we do a little stargazing, sweetheart?" Donna would say, entering the living room smelling of Chanel No. 5.

Emma would be watching TV with her father and sisters. She prayed inside her mind for someone to protest her leaving, for anyone to notice her misery, her inner screaming.

"Emma? Darling?"

"OK," Emma would say.

"My little nature girl!" Donna would coo. They would exit the house hand in hand. Donna would drop Emma's fingers as soon as they were out of sight.

Some nights, in the grass, Emma would pray for God to make her disappear for real. She wished, it's true, to die, if only to end the anguish of the summer nights she was forced to lie still and hear her mother betraying her beloved dad.

God just left her in the field. A part of her was still there, feeling those itchy blades of grass under her legs.

Now, Emma was always surrounded by her family—their house was noisy, messy, filled with sports equipment, the smell of food cooking, laundry, and laughter. But it was the same Montana night outside, the same brittle sky that had proven to be empty of salvation.

For a time, Emma thought she could make perfume. She'd always been fascinated by the way fragrances could change her mood: from the sick-but-thrilling panic she still felt when she smelled her mother's favorite, Chanel No. 5, to the way she could close her eyes and name the calming source notes of motherhood—citrus (like the Lemon Pledge she used to polish); Moroccan oud for its deep, dark earthiness; the mint note of Irish Spring soap. She took online perfumery classes, keeping notes on her French teacher's lectures, buying scarves at the Goodwill to tie jauntily around her hair like Mathilde did, closing her eyes to create "perfume briefs" and later the scents she'd imagined for a line she would start called "Peacock Perfumery."

Even after it became clear that she couldn't make a living in Missoula selling perfume and she joined a work-from-home company called Sweet Nothings instead, she thought about the world through the lens of fragrance, storing memories and labeling emotions by scent.

With her perfumes, Emma could speak without saying a word.

Emma's Sweet Nothings Team Leader, Cassidy Rose, smelled like candy, a saccharine sweetness. When Emma had joined the company, Cassidy Rose's fragrance made Emma feel alive, successful. Now, any fragrances with raspberry notes made Emma feel ill.

Because, thanks to Cassidy Rose, Emma had lost every cent of her family's savings. Rich would not be able to retire from his job at Hellgate High School and start a company making wooden furniture. Emma had burned through every dollar in their bank account buying Sweet Nothings lingerie, lotions, lube, and other sex toy products and amassed a debt of almost twenty-five thousand dollars. She was keeping this heartbreaking secret from her husband as every day—every hour—her debt grew more alarming. Failure smelled fermented: faintly rancid, cloying, deepening to a metallic scent of doom.

4
SYLVIE

The Monday after Sylvie's engagement was glorious and ordinary—a dawn walk with her rescue greyhound, Wilhelmina ("Willie," for short), along Hibiscus Street, a stop for coffee, settling Willie in the shady yard with a fresh bowl of water, parking in the teachers' lot at Coconut Grove Elementary School. The only thing out of place was a massive diamond ring—formerly Simon's mother's ring—encircling Sylvie's finger.

Sylvie was five-three, and wore her long auburn hair twisted up and held with a clip, chopsticks, or—in a pinch—a pencil. She had light blue eyes, almost-invisible lashes, and unruly brows. Her nose was long and thin, elegant, and her chin was a little bit pointy. Sylvie could do with a department-store makeup consult or a YouTube tutorial. She kept meaning to make time to investigate eye and lip liners, but ended up reading instead. Long walks with her dog kept her from the ravages of the Russell Stover chocolate samplers she loved and bought herself at Publix.

Since Sylvie had discovered her body as a source of pleasure (thanks to Simon) her color was rosier, her eyes aflame, as if continually surprised by her happiness and her thoughts of Simon—

his mouth, his strong shoulders and thighs, the way he encircled her waist in his hands, thumbs slowly moving across the bare skin of her stomach, her breath quickening.

Before entering the library, Sylvie twirled her engagement ring to hide the stone. At lunch, she secured the diamond with her thumb as she entered the teachers' lounge.

Phillip, the assistant principal, greeted Sylvie by hoisting his ham-on-wheat. Florence stood by the kettle, pouring hot water into her Cup Noodles, making sure not to splash her sensible blouse. Sylvie had thought about calling Florence when she texted her sisters about Simon's proposal, but something had held her back. She wanted to savor the secret, and also to postpone the questions she knew would come about her whiplash engagement.

The microwave beeped, and Beck, who taught third grade and seemed to be growing a goatee, removed a bag of popcorn. He ripped it open and the disgusting, mouthwatering smell of synthetic butter filled the room.

Sylvie mustered her courage. "I have a weekend update," she said.

"Please tell me it's about Simon," said Florence. "When are we meeting this sexy beast?"

Phillip pouted. "I've been on Scruff for *years* and I have *never* matched with a Brit." He reached his hand into Beck's popcorn bag and Beck slapped it. "Please, just a handful?" said Phillip. "My diets are making me insane."

Sylvie couldn't fathom why Phillip was on a diet. He was tall and willowy; his pressed clothes fit his skinny frame perfectly. When he wore short sleeves and chino shorts, his arms were ropy and his calves breathtakingly defined: On the weekends, he ran for hours along the Miami coast wearing a red cap and mirrored, wraparound sunglasses.

Beck tilted the bag toward Phillip.

"Well," said Sylvie. "Well . . . Simon asked me to marry him."

All sounds stopped in the teachers' lounge.

Florence looked up, a fork of noodles halfway to her mouth.

Beck stopped chomping his snack.

Phillip splayed his hands across his rib cage, widened his eyes, raised his eyebrows, and made a weird pout with his lips.

Nobody spoke.

Sylvie knew they all cared for her and wished her the best. And Simon *was* the best. She loved his accent and his birding and his broad chest and the way he smelled. Once, Simon had said, "I saw a Flame Robin in Tasmania and her feathers glowed just like your hair." Sylvie (like both her sisters) had hated her orange locks . . . until that moment.

After getting engaged on Friday evening, Sylvie and Simon had spent the weekend making love and reading. Simon slept with his arm across Sylvie and his face nestled in the crook of her neck. Sometimes, she woke to kisses below her ear, down her neck, and she rolled toward Simon. . . .

Finally, Phillip broke the silence. "Oh. My. God," he said. He placed his Shakeology container on the table. "I'm so excited," he said, not sounding excited in the least.

"Um, Sylvie, just wondering . . . have you heard about internet scammers?" said Beck.

"Yeah, a *bird photographer*?" added Phillip. "That doesn't sound like an actual job. No offense."

"He just finished an assignment for *Audubon,*" said Sylvie. She had to admit that she had no proof Simon wasn't just a nut job *pretending* to be on assignment for *Audubon.*

Her friends shot one another worried glances, as if Sylvie couldn't see. Florence shook her head, ringlets bouncing. "Isn't this a little quick, Syl?" she ventured. "I haven't even met him yet! And I'm your best friend! Aren't I?"

It was a little quick.

It was *a lot quick,* Sylvie knew it. But she didn't honestly care.

The deadening fog she usually felt had been lifted a bit. For ten years, everything had seemed leeched with gray, but now there was some color. And it was such a relief! What happened next had to be better than where she'd been. No one who hadn't felt the weight of grief would understand. Good idea versus bad idea was not a part of her formula anymore. Less grief won; it always won, and that was that.

"I thought you would be happy for me," said Sylvie, her voice cracking.

Phillip rushed to hug her, and Florence rose, joined in. Beck, uncomfortable with touching and being touched, patted Sylvie on the back. "I deserve something good," said Sylvie.

"Nobody's saying you don't," said Florence.

"She does deserve something good," noted Beck.

When she returned to her library, Sylvie had four minutes before the second graders arrived; she scrolled through her phone, seeing that she had a voice message from Simon:

"Hey, Syl, it's me. You're my fiancée! I told my father. We call him Mac, by the way—he's Scottish, and met my mother when he moved to Mumberton as a young veterinarian. She asked him to come to the castle and castrate their bears! Which he did, and they fell in love.

"Anyway, Sylvie, my dad started crying. In a happy way. I haven't heard him excited about anything since he was diagnosed. Before then, even. He's speaking with the wedding team right away. Did I tell you Mumberton has a wedding team? It's really just Louisa, the librarian, and her friends down at the Ratty Arms pub. But anyway, thank you. I just wanted to say thank you. I know this is rushed. But it was so wonderful to hear my father . . . to give him something to look forward to. I'll ring you later. It's Simon, did I say that already? I . . . love you. It's Simon, your fiancé."

The second-grade teacher, Kendall, rushed into the library, trailed by twenty-three seven-year-olds. "You're getting married," she cried, crushing Sylvie in a warm embrace, and the kids began hooting and screaming.

That night, Sylvie went home to Willie. Sylvie was sure Willie had been abused in her previous life as a racing greyhound—she was awful around other animals—barking, growling. Willie had emotional damage—that was just the way she was.

Sylvie could relate. Since Alexander's death, Sylvie had maintained a cabinet of pills to help her sleep: Lexapro, Lunesta, Trazodone, and (in a pinch) Xanax. Her doctor called it "hypervigilance," this constant feeling that something awful was about to happen. Because something awful *had* happened, and *could* happen at any time. How were you supposed to go back to peacefulness once you knew?

Well, pills.

Sylvie made herself pasta. She sat at the table she'd once shared with Alexander, shook out a linen napkin from a set they'd received as a wedding gift. Alexander's place was empty, as it had been for ten years, since that night when he'd stood up in the middle of watching Thursday night *ER* and said, "I'm going for a drive, Syl. I need . . . some air."

She had wondered about those two words for a decade.

Some.

Air.

What had he meant by that?

After her meal, Sylvie sat on her porch swing. Every time a person walked by, Willie barked and barked. Some people looked annoyed or scared, but Willie was on a leash. Simon called and then Florence called, but for some reason, Sylvie didn't answer. She just wanted to be still. She was exhausted. Even joy, it seemed, made her tired.

But in the bed she'd once shared with Alexander, Sylvie couldn't sleep. She took half a Xanax, but a familiar fear flooded her body anyway, competing with the pill's velvet calm. Willie, who would tear apart anyone who tried to hurt her, curled beside Sylvie, breathing slowly. The Florida moon cast a beautiful blue light on her coverlet. Eventually, Sylvie slept. She did not dream.

PART TWO
FOLLOW THE MONEY

1

CLEO

"Gin?" asked Isaac, Cleo's best friend from law school. He was now a journalist and a professor at Columbia, and had summoned Cleo to his Upper West Side apartment to discuss what he had found out about Sylvie's fiancé's money.

"Is it five yet?" said Cleo.

Isaac peered out his window. "Looks sort of dim, don't you think?"

"Could be rain," said Cleo, her lips curling into a smile.

"Nah," said Isaac, not taking his dark brown eyes off her. Isaac, forty, was a former squash star who still played a few times a week. He was tall—over six feet—and balding quite a bit. He often touched the remains of his ash-colored hair, ran his thin fingers along his temples and around his ears to the nape of his neck, where he let the hair grow a bit long—his sole affectation. Isaac's lips were full and he had thick eyebrows and permanent five-o'clock shadow stubbling his cheeks.

He was very handsome, objectively, and Cleo did sometimes think of Isaac during sex with her boyfriend, Danny. She also thought of Isaac's lips more than was normal for a friend to think about a platonic friend's lips.

Isaac's mother, Hannah, loved Cleo like a daughter, she had told her years before. But her only child, Isaac, had to marry a Jew. "You got that, Cleopatra?" said Hannah.

"Sadly, yes, I've got that."

"It's a pity," Hannah had said.

Cleo glanced at her watch: 5:01. She narrowed her eyes and evaluated the dimness of the evening. "Yes, give me gin," she said.

"You're going to need it," said Isaac.

"So this Simon guy is sketchy," said Cleo. "I *knew* it."

"Simon's ex-wife is from a very interesting family," said Isaac, pouring gin into what appeared to be a glass from a 1970s Happy Meal. "A family that needs to put money into things like . . . for example . . . an ancient castle in England."

"Money laundering," said Cleo. "From drugs, or what?"

"Remember the class 'Oligarchs and Thieves'?" said Isaac.

"I always wanted to take that class," said Cleo.

"Why didn't you?" said Isaac, handing Cleo her drink.

"Didn't seem like it would be applicable to my life," said Cleo. She lifted her drink. "Guess I was wrong."

"When Simon divorced, he got a massive payout. We're talking many generations of wealth. So what is he being paid for, exactly? By the way, his ex-wife lives on Madison now, with Simon's daughter, Penelope."

"Sylvie mentioned that Simon had a daughter," said Cleo. "I had no idea she lived on Madison Avenue!"

"Where else?" said Isaac.

"So who owns this castle Sylvie's planning a wedding in?"

"Simon's family has lived in Mumberton Castle since the year 1205. But now Mumberton Castle is owned by Black Bear Partners, LLC."

"A shell company," said Cleo.

"One of many," said Isaac. "A bank account made of castle stones."

Cleo sighed and shook her head. Isaac's home was dim and cozy, crammed with castoffs from his parents' apartment, located across Eighty-eighth Street. Every time Isaac's mother redecorated, Isaac was blessed with another piece of furniture, most of it overstuffed and printed with flowers and/or jungle animals. When the apartment above his rented office went on the market, Isaac's parents bought it for him. Completely focused on work, he'd let his mother fill that apartment with hand-me-downs as well. Isaac still used the TV he'd watched as a teenager, with a built-in VCR, though he had somehow added streaming services to the giant appliance for watching true crime shows with takeout from 88 Noodle or the reopened Popover Cafe. (He kept a stack of to-go menus in a pile on his coffee table anchored by his TV remote.)

Once in a while, Isaac would date, and his girlfriends ran the gamut from rail-thin aspiring models to brilliant academics, including Rosanne, an art history professor who almost married Isaac, but eventually did not. Once in a while, there'd be a boyfriend. No one ever stuck: Work was Isaac's great love, as it was Cleo's.

Cleo took a long sip of her gin and set out the snacks she'd picked up on the way over: pickles, crackers, a block of sharp cheddar.

"I have a cheese board!" said Isaac.

"I'm sure you do," murmured Cleo. Isaac rummaged for a bit and found a wooden slab with the words TELL ME YOU LOVE BRIE carved into it.

"Et voilà," he said.

"Your mom!" said Cleo.

"I know," said Isaac. "I'm lucky. How's the toxic Donna?"

"Toxic," said Cleo. "As usual. And I guess I'm going to have to see her at this wedding in a castle."

"OK, let's talk about that."

"I want you to know I got a new therapist," said Cleo.

"Thank God," said Isaac, who saw his own therapist, also located on Eighty-eighth Street, twice a week.

Cleo slipped off her shoes and rubbed her big toe on the arch of her foot. "I'd rather discuss felonious Simon. Where are his accounts?"

"Cayman Islands," said Isaac.

"Of course. So Simon Rampling is filthy rich and free and clear from his ex-wife's family?" said Cleo.

"Very rich, seemingly filthy," said Isaac. "Yes."

After a few Happy Meal glasses of gin, Cleo and Isaac decided to track down Simon's ex-wife, Thisbe Rampling, née Barber. They donned their sneakers, planning to walk across Central Park with a water bottle of gin, hoping to find hot dogs along the way. Cleo rummaged in Isaac's hall closet for a disguise, grabbing a dark trench coat and the dingy tennis cap Isaac used for racket sports. Isaac sipped his gin daintily and watched Cleo, one ankle crossed in front of the other. "Why, may I ask, do you need a disguise?"

"She can't know *who we are*," said Cleo conspiratorially.

"She *doesn't* know who we are."

"Right," said Cleo, tossing a Yale sweatshirt toward Isaac. "Turn it inside out," said Cleo. She found sunglasses and put them on. "Let's go," she said.

"You are way too drunk for this expedition," said Isaac.

"I am *just the right drunk* for this expedition," she asserted.

The sun was setting as they walked toward Central Park. The hot dog vendor was still open, and Cleo perched Isaac's father's Ray-Ban sunglasses in her hair like a headband as she savored her dinner: two hot dogs with ketchup and cheese. "I guess I don't need the sunglasses," she said, sheepishly.

"Yeah, and they're prescription," added Isaac.

"This is delicious," said Cleo, biting into the hot dog.

"I feel like we should add Sprite to the gin," said Isaac. "But we have a full bottle of gin and if we buy a can of Sprite, it will also be full."

"OK," said Cleo, "let's buy *two* cans of Sprite, and pour out half each, then add the gin and get rid of the water bottle."

"You're a genius," said Isaac.

They sat on the steps of the Met to finish eating their hot dogs. It grew cool as the sun set, and Cleo wrapped the trench coat around her shoulders. They sipped their gin-and-Sprites. "I'm all for spy games," said Isaac, "but why is investigating your sister's fiancé *your* problem?"

Cleo sighed. "I'm not great with boundaries," she admitted.

"Are you jealous?" ventured Isaac.

"Christ, that's what my new therapist asked me!" said Cleo.

"It is a fair question," said Isaac, gently.

"I have Danny!" said Cleo miserably. "Why would I be jealous of Sylvie marrying some British billionaire?"

Isaac remained silent.

Cleo rose. "Let's nail this perp!" she said, finishing her can and tossing it into a trash can. Isaac followed as Cleo walked toward the address they had found for Thisbe Rampling: The Bellemont on Madison and East Eighty-sixth. "The Bellllllle-mont," drawled Cleo, making the name of the building sound even snootier than it already sounded when you pronounced it normally.

"It's newish," said Isaac when they reached the building.

"I do love the limestone," said Cleo.

"I have a friend here," said Isaac. "It's gorgeous inside."

"OK, so the property records showed her in 5C," said Cleo.

"Sold at sixteen million three." She gazed up at the stunning building. "I mean," she said, "it's not the penthouse. If I had a billion dollars and could live in the penthouse of the Bellllllle-mont, I would be so happy."

"I don't know if that's true," said Isaac.

Cleo nodded and shrugged. "Fair," she admitted.

"We done here?" said Isaac.

"What do you mean?" said Cleo. She removed Isaac's father's sunglasses from her hair and put them on. "We're going in."

"We are *not* breaking and entering," said Isaac.

"Of course not," said Cleo. "We're *delivering*." She scanned the street, spotted a Starbucks. "Wait right here," she said. Isaac pursed his lips, seeming equally charmed and weary. Cleo reemerged with a bag. "It's a mug," she said.

"We're delivering a Starbucks mug to Thisbe Rampling," clarified Isaac.

"Yup."

They nodded at the doorman as he pulled open beautiful metalwork doors and ushered them into a small but tasteful lobby. "I have a delivery for 5C," said Cleo to a mustachioed man behind a black granite desk.

"I can take that," said the man, obsequious but firm.

"Need a signature," said Cleo. "I'll wait."

He picked up a phone. Cleo walked to a low-slung orange couch and draped herself across it. Isaac sat in a matching orange chair. Cleo grinned at him wickedly.

"Ma'am," said the concierge. Cleo turned her head to the side and raised an eyebrow, listening, but did not rise.

"She says you can leave it right here at the front desk. I'll sign," he said.

"No," said Cleo. "I'm not getting fired over this. She needs to sign or come pick it up another time."

"What exactly is the delivery?" said the man, peeved.

"How would I know?" said Cleo.

He exhaled showily, and Cleo put the glasses back on. A silver-haired gentleman Cleo recognized but couldn't put a name to entered the lobby with a very young woman on his arm. He nodded to the concierge and they swept past the desk toward the elevator bank.

A bird-boned woman appeared, wearing striped men's pajamas and thick eyeglasses. She blinked and looked around, as if the room were too bright. "Mrs. Rampling," said the concierge. "They're right there." He pointed, flaring his nostrils distastefully, as if showing Simon Rampling's ex-wife a pile of garbage.

Cleo stood up. Isaac remained seated. "Can I help you?" Thisbe Rampling said. "Rodge says there's a delivery?"

As Cleo approached, she noticed that Simon's ex-wife smelled like La Mer face cream, the same kind Cleo herself used now that Danny had upgraded their skin-care regimens. Thisbe took off her glasses, rubbed one eye with her fingertips, then put her glasses back on. Cleo had expected Thisbe to be glamorous, someone who looked like one of Cleo's fancy NYU friends, but this woman looked . . . normal. She looked like a weary mom.

"My sister is marrying your ex-husband," she said.

Thisbe's polite smile disappeared.

"I'm just . . . my sister's been through so much. I want to know . . . is Simon . . . good?"

"Cleo!" cried Isaac.

Thisbe stared at Cleo for a moment as if she was going to answer, to tell Cleo what she needed to know. Was Simon good? Was *anyone* good?

Alexander had not been good.

Thisbe blinked rapidly. Her brow furrowed and her eyes widened—was she scared? She was. She seemed scared. She whirled and ran to the elevator.

"The police will be here in one to two minutes," said the concierge. It seemed this was not the first time he'd had to protect his high-net-worth clientele.

Cleo was motionless, clutching the Starbucks bag. Isaac grabbed her arm and hauled her out into the street, hailing a cab and shoving her in seconds before a police car arrived, sirens wailing.

"What the *fuck,*" said Isaac when the cab was speeding across the park toward his building.

Cleo folded her shoulders inward. She tilted her head from Isaac, clutching her hands together in her lap. Thank God she was wearing the ludicrous Ray-Bans; they would shield her tears from Isaac. She did not turn to him, and kiss him, and tell him that she loved him.

2

EMMA

-$28,959.51

It's a Sweet Nothings
Love Fest Party!
May 30 at 6 P.M.
Sunridge Home for Seniors
Missoula, Montana
Unit 306
(Harriet McDowell's Place!)
Wine & Snacks Provided
HOSTED BY:
Emma Peacock Catalfamo
Sweet Nothings Executive Fuchsia Level Ambassador

Selling lingerie to octogenarians wasn't how Emma had planned to spend the last few years before she lost the bloom of youth, but here she was, approaching the Sunridge Home for Seniors with the new "Tantalizer Supreme" in her passenger seat. Rich's truck handled the mountain roads with ease.

Being a Sweet Nothings Ambassador was very stressful. Each month, she had to sell eight hundred dollars of product to remain at the Executive Fuchsia Level, which gave her a thirty percent commission on her sales. (If she'd manifested better, she'd have a downline of salespeople she would have recruited; their sales would add to her total.)

For the last few months, Emma had bought her own stock at retail cost from herself. Cassidy Rose (who would add to *her* total whenever Emma bought anything) had patiently explained that paying for Sweet Nothings product Emma had already purchased was an investment—*an investment in Emma*. It seemed counterproductive to buy products *from herself,* but without these sales, Emma couldn't have reached eight hundred dollars of sales for April and would have been demoted to Beige. Going back to Beige Brand Ambassador meant that she'd have to pay the three-hundred-dollar signing fee again if she wanted to keep working for Sweet Nothings.

Cassidy Rose was vibrant and charismatic. Emma felt like an infatuated teenager around Cassidy Rose, growing warm in her presence. Her eyes were gray, shot with yellow. She had perfectly highlighted hair. Sometimes, Emma wanted to kiss Cassidy Rose, and sometimes Emma just wanted to *be* her.

"Your job is to empower *every woman in this town,*" Cassidy Rose had said, raising her cute eyebrows and looking serious. When Emma ran out of her own friends to call, she thought of her mother's best friend, Harriet, whom Emma hadn't spoken to in years. Luckily, Harriet was game. "Nothing here to do," Harriet had said. "Why not, I guess? Are we talking about—what, sex toys and such?"

"Well . . ." said Emma, "well, no, it's not sex toys. Well, I mean, I *do have* those items, of course, but Sweet Nothings is all about connection and um, loving yourself. Inside. Um, feeling . . . empowered."

"Did you say something about free wine?" said Harriet.

With her new Discover card, Emma had bought one box of red wine and one of white, then transferred the cheap stuff into bottles from the recycling bin that belonged to wealthy oenophiles down the street. She rinsed the bottles first, of course, buying 150 corks on Amazon for $16.99 and putting the bottles in boxes from Missoula Liquors. Hiding in the shadows of the alley behind her house on recycling day, cold raindrops hitting her cheeks with painful pinpricks, Emma felt she had taken a wrong turn.

Maybe she should have left town, like her sisters and even her mother. But now she had her boys—she just had to move forward. Even if moving forward meant crouching in alleys, ruining the Ugg boots her mother had given her when she fled to Arizona, and jamming used wine bottles in her eldest son's hockey bag.

"Welcome, Harriet and friends!" cried Emma. Harriet's retirement condo was pretty, and Emma had hung Sweet Nothings panties over the electric fireplace for ambience. "Let's start by talking about foreplay!" she said, trying to sound as confident as Cassidy Rose in their Boss Babe training sessions. Reciting the script she'd memorized, Emma said, "Foreplay should be your *second* favorite 'F' word!"

A woman in a lumpy cardigan tittered. Emma thought the woman looked familiar. She squinted, and the woman winked. Oh my God, it was her middle school gym teacher, Mrs. Randolph. "Pheromones," she managed, holding up the Hot 'N' Heavy lotion. "Pheromones help with your happy and your horny!" The words had sounded hilarious when Cassidy Rose had spoken them, but now Emma just felt gross. She was supposed to make everyone cup their hands into "hand-ginas" next, then squirt various warming lubes into them. Mrs. Randolph watched her. No—no way. She wasn't doing the hand-ginas.

"If you're single as a Pringle, you can buy this for yourself!" she said weakly.

"May I try?" said Harriet kindly. Harriet had always made Emma feel wonderful, even when they were small. She'd roll her eyes when Emma's mother told her to lay off the cookies, Donna holding her nose up with her finger to simulate a pig nose. Harriet would say, "Oh, Donna, hush!"

"Yes, of course," said Emma, passing her the lotion. "Thank you, Harriet."

Harriet, a muscular woman with shoulder-length gray curls, squeezed a peach-colored daub and rubbed it into her hands. She brought them to her face. "Mmm," she said. "Smells delicious. Here, try!" She held the bottle out to her friends.

Emma quickly opened her box of scented lotions. "Everyone! Please!" Emma said, passing around shea-butter massage oils and the heart-shaped warming pack that you rubbed until it became hot. She handed out catalogs and order forms.

Harriet's friends, tentatively and then with gusto, asked straightforward questions, and, gaining confidence, Emma answered them. She decided *not* to say (as Cassidy Rose had suggested), "Great Head lube reduces the gag reflex in the back of your throat and masks the taste of semen . . . so no more yackin' while you're snackin'!"

Instead, when Sally Pope, who had run the post office until her retirement, said, "Emma, honey, do you have any lotions for . . . well, making things less dry down there?" Emma passed her a selection of lubricants. Emboldened with a bit of her boxed-then-bottled wine, she even held up an illustration of a woman's privates, explaining the places women enjoyed being touched. "I'm sure you know all this," she said, though she wasn't sure at all.

* * *

After the Love Fest Party, Emma parked outside her home, the one she and Rich had moved into when Rich's parents passed away and left them enough money to scrape together a down payment and secure a big loan with an adjustable interest rate that had rendered them worried each month as soon as the higher interest rate kicked in. Still, they were fortunate: Much of Missoula had been bought up by landlords who charged so much that many of Rich's teacher colleagues had been forced to move out of town and face long commutes.

Their front living room faced the street, and Emma could see her husband sitting on the couch, a boy on either side of him—Jameson leaning on Rich's shoulder, Guinness sitting upright. All three needed haircuts; Emma made a mental note to get out her clippers. The boys were too old for stories, and yet it looked as if Rich were reading to them.

Emma took a moment to scroll through her phone. Sylvie had posted a picture of herself with someone Emma didn't recognize. Emma's baby sister looked radiant, holding up a margarita glass. Underneath the photo, Simon had commented "Cheers!" Emma stared at the picture for a while, feeling strangely dislocated by the thought of Sylvie's happy life with these strangers. If this was Sylvie's family now, who was Emma?

Donna's move to Arizona had made Emma feel unmoored, despite the fact that Donna was mean to Emma and her family.

In the Missoula Free Box, Emma had once grabbed a book called *Parent Yourself: A Twelve-Step Healing Plan for Motherless Daughters*. After reading the first two chapters, Emma tossed it. She was too busy taking care of everyone to be able to examine why she took care of everyone.

She liked taking care of everyone!

Inside, Rich stood and stretched. The boys rose as well, hugged their dad. Emma wanted to feel delight, watching them. She knew she should feel delight. Instead, a list of things that needed doing scrolled in her mind: apples for lunches, make the minimum payment on the credit cards, call back the dentist and explain a bounced check . . . but how? What was the explanation for a mother who bounced checks for dental cleanings?

Emma opened her order forms and tallied the night's total. She had sold one hundred and twenty-seven dollars of Sweet Nothings product. She ignored taxes these days, preferring to get through one week at a time. She would handle tax day next April.

Her phone rang—it was Cleo. "Hey!" said Emma. "You'll never believe where I've been this evening. Remember Mom's friend Harriet?"

"Em," said Cleo, sounding weird, and maybe drunk. "We need to talk about Sylvie's fiancé. This Simon guy is not what he seems. He has secrets, Em. Deep, dark secrets."

Emma kept the engine running. "Tell me everything," she said.

3
SYLVIE

The first time Sylvie Peacock saw Simon Rampling's name, he had posted a poem on the Checkoutmyshelves app, a sort of Instagram for book lovers. Every time one of her contacts posted a new book cover, Sylvie's phone made a trilling sound that gave her a dose of dopamine. Sylvie rarely hit the double-heart icon that signaled the book lover should get in touch, but Simon had intrigued her from the start.

The poem he'd posted was called "Recess! Oh, Recess!" by Darren Sardelli:

Recess! Oh, Recess!
We love you! You rule!
You keep us away
from the teachers in school.
Your swings are refreshing.
Your slides are the best.
You give us a break
from a really hard test.

Sylvie recognized it immediately—it was from *Galaxy Pizza and Meteor Pie,* one of the books checked out most often from her library. Published in 2009 by Laugh-A-Lot Books, the book was out of print, and Sylvie had repaired the library copy a few times already.

She was inside her cramped office, preparing to help supervise the lunchroom, when she saw Simon's post. On a whim, she double-hearted it, then left her phone on her desk and went to the cafeteria, wearing her apron with the scissors in the pocket so that she could cut open kids' yogurt tubes and packages of gummy fruit snacks. Her apron also contained a plastic knife to open banana tops.

After lunch duty, during which she opened endless containers of chocolate milk, stopped children from standing on their chairs and/or screaming, and helped custodians wipe up spills, Sylvie returned to her desk. She unwrapped her egg salad sandwich and peeked at Checkoutmyshelves. Simon had double-hearted her latest post, a stack of her favorite detective novels.

Before Simon, Sylvie had dated. But when a guy finally said, "You have *way* too many issues," Sylvie had to agree. She was a child from a rough home *and* a young widow. It was a lot.

Sylvie scrolled through Simon's account. He often tagged the Miami Public Library, posting covers of books of bird paintings, cookbooks, literary fiction (Ann Patchett and Alice Munro), books about travel (Pico Iyer's *The Lady and the Monk: Four Seasons in Kyoto* and Paul Theroux's *Dark Star Safari*), and many, many murder mysteries.

A reader! Sylvie had been searching for a reader. Checkoutmyshelves was filled with men who posted *Infinite Jest* and *Cloud Atlas* and *Gravity's Rainbow* with comments like "Can't wait to discuss!"

First of all, they didn't want to *discuss,* which implied they wanted to listen to someone else and not just tell their date about what they believed to be the key takeaway of *Infinite Jest:* that the woman who kills you in this life will be your mother in the next life. And none of these people had read *The Pale King*, which was Sylvie's favorite David Foster Wallace novel (her favorite essay was obviously the one about the cruise ship, though "Consider the Lobster" was awesome, too). When she read David Foster Wallace, Sylvie found a sacred space. His words had reached her during her anguish after Alexander's death. But she didn't want to share this space, to decimate it with idle chitchat.

Sylvie didn't want to *discuss* books. She wanted to *read*, and was happy to hand a book over when she was done with it, but she was in it for the escape, the loss of her pained self, the silencing of her brain as she inhabited others'. Who cared what the themes were? It was all in the feeling.

In life, Sylvie was ill at ease. Sure, in her library she sometimes felt OK, but only while reading did Sylvie feel peaceful. She yearned for this feeling; she craved it. Often she spent her waking days waiting for the moment that she would be on her couch, a book open, her dog beside her. The spell of reading felt like coming home. Her childhood had been sharp with secrets, scary at times, poisoned with hidden emotions. As soon as the words on the pages of Nancy Drew mysteries began transforming into a blanket of oblivion, Sylvie had understood that reading was her getaway car.

The pleasure of submersion, embraced by the stories of a great writer—this was her addiction. A great plot with OK sentences was adequate. Poised, elegant sentences were her favorite, whether or not they hurtled her along a gripping narrative arc. If the sentences were lean and smart, Sylvie would follow them anywhere. She had no problem with speed-reading, either, if the mood struck her. She didn't want to reflect. She just wanted to read and be loved by someone who would sit next to her and shut the hell up. A reader. She yearned for a *real* reader, and otherwise, she'd just as soon be alone.

But here was Simon.

They messaged back and forth all afternoon, Sylvie taking breaks to do her job, reading to her kids in the Book Nook and then helping them find books, checking them out with her special wand and its satisfying beep.

In her library, all children were equal. Not all the students spoke English at home, but this didn't matter when they exclaimed over bright pictures of pirates (J 904.7), dinosaurs (J 567.9), or Halloween crafts (J 745.594). Some parents remembered library day each week—sliding the plastic-clad books into monogrammed backpacks—and some children looked at Sylvie with genuine fear when they'd forgotten. She had a loose policy and usually hit "Override" when a kid was blocked from overdue fines. Her library's treasures were meant to be held close, brought home, paged through, loved . . . maybe even lost.

Every year she had to pay for missing hardcovers, spending a glorious day going wild at Books & Books. She couldn't think of a better use for the dregs of her tiny salary.

Late in the day, on the day she first met Simon, he sent a long note, telling her he was a wildlife photographer, originally from Northern England. His full name was Simon Bettencourt Rampling, and Sylvie immediately penned *Sylvia Peacock Rampling* in calligraphy across her mind. This was a childhood habit and completely ridiculous—humiliating, even.

That said, Sylvia Peacock Rampling *did* have a nice ring to it.

Simon was leaving Miami in the morning to head to the Santa Ana bird sanctuary on the south Texas coast (it was golden-cheeked warbler season). Shooting a feature for *Audubon,* he would be gone for three weeks.

Although Simon was the first man Sylvie had wanted to talk to in a while, she felt a bit relieved that he was headed out of town—it took the pressure off. As the days went by, they messaged about books, then began to open up to each other about other things—his divorce and sadness about his young daughter, Penelope, moving with her mother to New York; Sylvie's widowhood. The poem "Recess! Oh, Recess!" was Penelope's favorite, as it turned out. It was remarkable how quickly Sylvie and Simon grew close—she began calling him in the evening as she walked Willie, eager to hear about his day photographing birds on the swampy Gulf Coast. His accent was entrancing. When he said he'd like to fly home and have her over to his place for dinner, it didn't even seem weird.

Simon lived on Indian Creek Island, a posh address. An armed guard stopped Sylvie before she was allowed to drive past the imposing gatehouse, making sure she was on his list. (There she was—Sylvie Peacock.) Following Simon's directions, she drove past enormous modern mansions, then reached a metal gate. Simon had told her about the gate; she punched in a code and drove down a dirt road. Every inch of this land was worth a fortune.

She was unnerved, trying to reconcile Simon's home address with the man she'd come to know—a man who loved to sleep outside, nestled in the "Cat's Meow" sleeping bag he'd bought himself as a UMiami undergrad, after moving from an area so far north it was almost Scotland.

Sylvie drove for ten or so minutes, turning a bend and reaching a vast expanse of waterfront property. There was a small dock with a canoe, a hammock slung between two live oak trees, and a smallish ranch home. Simon came outside as she parked. "Sylvie," he said.

She ran toward him. (Later, she would reflect and think, *Did I really jump out of my car and run toward Simon? Yes, I did!* It was so unlike her that Sylvie felt proud of herself.)

Her attraction was immediate. As someone who spent much of her time alone or in stories, Sylvie was unnerved by the pulsing of her blood. She reached him and her breath caught in her throat. His arms went around her for the first time and he drew her close. She felt his broad chest, her own body responding, a heat, a thawing.

Simon kissed her. His lips were warm, hungry. His smell was just right: It made her want to press closer. Sylvie felt dizzy with desire, but this pleasure was immediately cut with guilt.

Alexander!

She stepped back.

Simon composed himself. He was, like Sylvie, thirty-five years old. He was taller than she'd expected. Due to his bookishness and birding, she'd assumed he would be skinny, a nerd. But Simon was broad and strong. Sylvie had never even dated a man who looked like this—she'd always chosen intellectuals, and they, like Sylvie, tended to ignore their physicality, choosing an afternoon reading over a visit to the gym.

But Simon was clearly an athlete: His body was present, vibrating, reminding Sylvie of her own. Even as she stood apart, Simon's kiss shot through Sylvie. She wanted more. Sylvie had not thought about her body in a long time. It was fine, she went for walks, but this—*this*! She felt alive.

Would he kiss her again? Would she kiss him? Sylvie realized she was staring at his mouth. She moved her gaze down, quickly noting the way his soft T-shirt fell over his wide chest, and his fitted pants (oh my God, she was thinking about what his pants were hiding, *did he wear boxers or briefs,* could she have sex with him right here in the driveway, but the oyster shells looked rough . . .). She made her eyes move to his feet, clad in Havaianas flip-flops.

OK. She could stare at his toes. But even his toes were sexy—tanned, the hairs on them golden from the sun.

"Can I show you around?" said Simon, breaking the sexy silence.

"Yes!" she said, overly enthusiastic, though all she wanted was to lie down on the oyster shell driveway and say *Take me.*

Sylvie did not lie down on the oyster shell driveway and say *Take me.* Overwhelmed, she reached out and grabbed Simon's hand. He hesitated and she felt desire, hot and strong between them. It was real: This was a real thing. Sylvie's skin ached for his touch. "Show me around," she managed.

("You should have said *Take me!*" said Florence later. "Though I agree, those shells might have scratched a bit.")

Simon led her inside his rancher: whitewashed walls, terracotta floors, and a wooden table covered with a simple yellow cloth. Large windows framed a rose-colored sky. Sylvie inhaled, smelling cumin, garlic, and chicken.

"Are you hungry?" said Simon.

Sylvie nodded, locking her eyes with his. She wanted to kiss him. She wanted to be underneath Simon, to be open to him. She wanted to feel him inside her—Sylvie ached, on fire. She tried to breathe. He stepped close. Sylvie waited until he was three inches, one inch away, and then she moved her mouth to his mouth. Simon kissed her back, lightly and then less so. She circled his neck with her arms and they couldn't stop (and Sylvie didn't want to stop, not ever). By the time Simon lifted Sylvie and she wrapped her legs around him and he carried her to his room to get a condom, Sylvie was naked, her dress abandoned on his kitchen floor tiles.

("Whoa," said Florence later. "Much better than the driveway.")

Later, they returned to the kitchen. "My housekeeper made these enchiladas. She was worried I'd disappoint you with spaghetti and tinned Bolognese sauce," said Simon.

Housekeeper? Sylvie had once hired Merry Maids but felt so guilty afterward that she'd overpaid them and never called again. She cleaned one room of her house every weekend day, watching HGTV as she scrubbed and swept.

Sylvie explored as Simon tossed a green salad with sliced pears, cherries, and goat cheese. All four walls of the living room were lined with shelves crammed with books: paperbacks, hardcovers, new, old, faded, and bright. Sylvie knew many of the books but hadn't seen some. The books were alphabetized by author. Sylvie peered at the spines, eyes widening.

Did Simon shelve all of his books together? It seemed so.

Simon alphabetized the nonfiction, which Sylvie disliked intensely.

("Sheesh," said Florence, shaking her head. "Good thing Simon got you in the bedroom before you saw his library.")

Sylvie sorted her books by theme, author, and geographic area, a way of being a rebellious librarian. She often drank wine and rearranged her books or just looked at them and thought about things like where she wanted to go, stories she'd like to live inside, or alternate means of categorization.

Not that she thought the Dewey decimal system should change—no!—she just liked to move ideas around in her mind, considering ways that books could be grouped together, inspired by an exhibit she'd seen by the artist Ai Weiwei. Sylvie loved how he created new narratives by rearranging formerly discrete objects, like making giant snakes out of children's life vests.

In Simon's living room, Sylvie spotted an Eames chair—she'd long coveted an Eames—even on Craigslist, they sold for thousands. On the mantel was a framed quote from Beatrix Potter's children's book *The Tale of Johnny Town-Mouse:*

One place suits one person,
Another place suits another person,
For my part, I prefer to live
In the country like Timmy Willie.

That was weird.

But not as weird as shelving the fiction and the nonfiction together and alphabetically.

Next to the quote was a photograph of a little girl: Simon's daughter, Penelope. "Isn't she beautiful?" said Simon, coming into the room.

Sylvie nodded. She put her arm around him and pulled him close. "And the Beatrix Potter quote?"

"I feel very guilty about not living in England with my father. But it doesn't suit me. Beatrix reminds me that it's OK to know what suits."

Sylvie smiled. Not so weird, after all.

While she had been snooping around, Simon had set a picnic table in the yard. They settled at table, sharing a bench—Sylvie in her underwear and Simon's T-shirt, Simon in his boxer shorts.

("Really?" said Florence later. "OK. I'd pegged him for a tighty-whitey type.")

Sylvie gazed over the water as she ate, and they fell into an easy banter. Sylvie wanted to ask about the alphabetization *of non-fiction,* but decided to wait—the Dewey decimal system was an important topic for her.

They watched the bay in silence. Sylvie leaned against Simon and she felt sheltered.

It seemed like a dream: They made love and were quiet and sat next to each other with books, and after a few blissful months, Simon asked her to marry him. The proposal was sudden. They were reading in a shared hammock and he put down his book and said, "Sylvie? I love you. I want to marry you. This is rushed but OK, my dad is sick. It's worse than anyone thought. He told me last night that he's . . . dying. My dad is dying, but somehow that makes me feel like I want to marry you. I want you to be mine forever. I want to marry you with my father there, at my side. Sylvia Peacock, will you marry me?"

Sylvie's mouth dropped open. Her finger rested on the last sentence she had read of *The Witch Elm,* Tana French's thriller. Her mind was still partially in Ireland, where a skull in a tree trunk had just been discovered.

"What?" she said. As a gesture to the momentousness of the occasion, Sylvie closed her novel, not even marking the place.

"My dad has cancer," said Simon. "We've never been close, but still, I—"

"I'm so sorry, Simon."

"And everyone's so sad. *I'm* so sad. And I thought, about three minutes ago, what if I brought Sylvie to Mumberton Castle, and we had a big wedding, and everyone would be happy, most of all . . . me."

"Me too," said Sylvie. Willie the dog, also crammed in the hammock, looked at Sylvie. The thought of a wedding and going to England and Simon being hers forever and her sisters and mother having reason to be *relieved* for once instead of worried about her, and meeting Simon's father, and Sylvie never having to be alone again . . .

Sylvie's happiness was too much. To save herself, she went numb.

Once, Sylvie had googled "why do I float above myself sometimes dizzy" and learned that what happened to her was called "disassociation." A strong emotion came and her mind just . . . fled. Good or bad emotions—it didn't matter—she sliced a hole in the fabric of reality and slipped out, finding peaceful nothingness while her body remained in the world.

Sometimes it wasn't nothingness. Sometimes Sylvie escaped to a place decorated in calm colors, a hammock by a mysterious sea, or the rocks behind her childhood home—the bright Montana sky above. And when the strong emotions faded, she could swim back to consciousness.

Sylvie fought against her comforting escape now, trying to root herself in this moment.

Say yes, Willie seemed to say with her soulful brown eyes.

The universe was singing. Willie was sending a telepathic message. Even the ghost of Alexander (also in the hammock, of course, because he was always, always with her) seemed to nod his spectral head.

"Will you marry me?" said Simon.

4
CLEO

Although Cleo's Codependent No More app counseled her to leave Sylvie alone, to "keep her side of the street clean," to just say, "not my circus, not my monkeys," and stand by as Sylvie married a liar, Cleo's sense of duty was too strong. She wanted to save her sister and protect her from heartbreak, even if Sylvie seemed to bring it upon herself, to be honest. Cleo would amass a dossier against Simon Rampling that was irrefutable; fly to England in time to make her case; and then escort her fragile sister back to Miami.

When Cleo opened Cleo Peacock, LLP, on the Upper East Side, she wanted an office that announced she was the best. All of her (male) bosses had had traditional offices with enormous wooden file cabinets and huge, macho desks with a zillion drawers and squeaky (if very comfortable) leather chairs. Cleo had told her designer to go "one hundred percent minimalist," spreading her fingers wide as she imagined clean lines. "I want a powerful female vibe, none of the heavy, leather stuff."

The designer had done her bidding. Her desk was gold with a metallic brushed finish. It had no drawers, which had seemed perfect when the designer showed her the design but necessitated Cleo using the bookshelf behind the desk as a catchall: The top shelf was littered with cough-drop wrappers, pennies, business cards, and pens—all the junk that should have gone in a desk drawer. Cleo had called the designer to complain, and the designer had lined her desk and the shelf behind her with plants to hide the detritus and silver bowls to hold some of it. Cleo had to admit it looked cool, but if she ever replaced her five-thousand-dollar desk, she'd get one with a fucking drawer, or even go old-school with the right-hand-side bank of many drawers, some with locks and room for a bottle of Merlot and some gossip magazines.

She had no trash can. "Trash cans are clutter," the designer had said coolly. Every damn day, Cleo filled silver bowls with napkins and deli sandwich wrappers, and every morning, they were emptied and gleaming again.

Law was a jigsaw puzzle. Cleo's job was to move the pieces, not to assess guilt or innocence. Perhaps this was why the case of Sylvie's fiancé, Simon Rampling, fascinated her. For one, he hadn't hired her, so she could draw any conclusion the evidence led toward, as opposed to turning off the part of her brain that cried out *Guilty!* For another, it was a chance to atone. Cleo had failed her sister once—unforgivable, though of course she yearned for forgiveness—and she was not going to fail her again.

Heading home after work, Cleo found herself in front of Nordstrom, examining a bandeau top and matching shorts printed with what appeared to be carousels. French carousels, bien sûr. Where would Cleo—or anyone—wear such an outfit? Probably not to a wedding in a castle.

What *would* Cleo wear to a wedding in a castle? Something long . . . and diaphanous . . . Cleo imagined an elaborate "sister of the bride" headpiece, like one of the characters in the musical *Six*, about the wives of Henry VIII.

Cleo hadn't seen *Six* but she'd seen the billboards, and the

Tudor gowns were fabulous. The thought of tomboy Sylvie getting married in Tudor finery in a castle was so absurd it made Cleo suddenly furious. If *anyone* should be married in a long, velvet, ermine-lined cape . . . it was Cleo. She was without a doubt the most queenly of the Peacock sisters!

Cleo lifted her chin, continuing through Rockefeller Center. She imagined Donna as the spiteful, withered queen mother; herself as the reigning queen in her most powerful and majestic years; Emma as a kindly lady-in-waiting (she was such a *mensch,* even though Emma would never know the meaning of the word, since Jews in Missoula were few and far between); and Sylvie as the flyaway-haired princess, twirling on the castle . . . grounds? Lawn? Whatever, Sylvie was the carefree baby. Even though she was a widow. She was still the adorable child.

Cleo smiled, thinking of herself in a crown or one of those regal pointed hats with a veil floating off the top. But then her mind returned to the present day: She was going to be late again for dinner with her boyfriend, Danny.

Danny would be in the midst of preparing a complicated meal, a dish that would have required a trip to some hidden market or artisan butchery, an expensive knife Cleo could afford but felt resentful about buying anyway. Some nights, to be truthful, she just wanted a yogurt, but she did her best to find enthusiasm. She knew Danny made elaborate meals because he felt like a failure, his novel-in-progress indefinitely stalled. Danny thought they were trying to have kids, imagined himself a stay-at-home dad, but Cleo was still on birth control pills, which she hid at work.

Danny was also hiding something: a giant engagement ring, which he had bought with Cleo's credit card. She knew a proposal was imminent and wished she was glad. Instead, she felt trapped and uneasy.

Danny was lean and ripped, every inch toned to perfection from his afternoons at Barry's Boot Camp. He wore his dark hair long and used a hair dryer to create pleasing waves that framed his high cheekbones. His hands, feet, and penis were large and thin. Unfortunately, the more objectively fat-free and perfect he became, the less Cleo wanted to make out with him. Cleo had once noticed him looking at himself in the bureau mirror as they were having sex. She had opened her eyes and seen him, atop her, watching his own body.

Once in a while, a stranger on the subway or in a shop would hold Cleo's gaze flirtatiously and she would feel powerful, but she never took it further than this. She was too honest to cheat, and too busy to end things with Danny.

Danny was almost as critical of Cleo as her mother had been. But when Cleo pleased Danny, she felt euphoric, blissed-out for days.

He was harder to please than he used to be.

Danny followed her location on his phone as she progressed home to Brooklyn. He was, he said, worried about her being mugged. He dropped questions into their evening conversations, like "Hmm, by the way . . . just wondering . . . were you, like, looking at magazines at the bodega on Forty-ninth? It seemed like a long time to grab milk, haha!"

Haha indeed.

What—did he think she was sequestered in a bodega bathroom, having a quickie with a stranger . . . or murderous client? *As if.* In truth, she'd been leaning against a refrigerated case, paging through gossip in the *New York Post*. Did he know this, too? Did his phone *see* what she was doing? When she read gossip at home, Danny looked at her sternly. He left her books he wished she'd read on her bedside table: *The Wind-Up Bird Chronicle*, *My Struggle: Book 1*, *Gravity's Rainbow*. In a tiny act of rebellion, Cleo read erotic romance on her iPad, stories about cowboys and handymen and Parisian chefs in *très chaude* kitchens who took their shirts off.

Cleo reached the subway entrance and couldn't make herself

go down the stairs, though commuters jostled her on either side. Around Danny, Cleo felt invisible. She wasn't really herself with him, more like a shape-shifter who *responded* to him. Cleo gravitated to people who made her feel like Donna made her feel. She understood what she was doing cognitively; she'd read *Narcissistic Mothers and Their Legacy of Blame and Shame.* Danny watched her like Donna had. He required her to adjust herself to his needs and whims. He was as messed up as she was, so it felt as if she could rewrite the story of her life if she could change him.

Cleo had escaped from her family; she'd made it. Here she was in motherfucking Times Square on a beautiful day in a skirt worth a thousand dollars! And yet she was so lonely. Cleo wished she could just stop by for dinner with Emma's family . . . or meet Sylvie at the park to see her dog run. Maybe, in saving Sylvie, Cleo could change her patterns, make up for what she had done a decade before—what she had done to Alexander.

5
EMMA

-$31,002.70

“Emma,” said Rich, not very quietly. Emma opened one eye. Rich stood at the foot of their bed in a Costco towel. His hair was wet from the shower and he smelled of the tropics because Suave Tropical Coconut was the cheapest shampoo at Albertsons.

“What time is it?” said Emma, pulling a pillow over her head. Her day loomed—endless—in front of her. She rolled to her stomach.

Emma took after her father in more ways than one: their shy grins, stocky builds, and ability to eat dessert without getting *too* pudgy. Emma was named after Flaubert’s Madame Bovary, which . . . what was there to say? Her mother, Donna, had held baby Emma, peered into her newborn face, and named her after a fictional character who, at the end of her tale, eats arsenic. Emma’s father had not objected. What did this mean? Emma would have to ask her sister Cleo, the only one of them in therapy.

Emma had dainty feet and elegant ankles. She bought a new shade of nail polish almost every time she went to the Dollar General. Even if no one saw her toes (hidden by wool socks from October through March) Emma made sure they were painted.

In a way, her unseen Dollar General toenails were a metaphor for Emma's entire life. She went seemingly unnoticed no matter how hard she tried to shine, muffled as if covered by a wool sock. Cleo was the superstar, Sylvie the family tragedy—the only role left for Emma was the ghost destined to haunt the middle, a ghost trying to be the glue that would hold the whole broken family together. But how could a ghost be glue? A ghost is intangible! Thus, Emma's anguish.

"I got you a present!" said Rich. The uninhibited glee in his tone gave her the strength to remove the pillow and face him. Rich handed Emma a package wrapped with wrinkled Christmas paper: jolly Santas waltzing with jolly polar bears.

"It's June," said Emma, scrutinizing the Santas. "Isn't it June?"

"Almost summer," sighed Rich. Summer in Missoula was the sweet prize for making it through gloomy winter: weeks of fishing, biking the trails around town, hiking, and camping trips. Huckleberry jam on homemade bread and lazy afternoons napping while the boys ran all over town, wild. The fragrances of thyme and juniper.

Emma unwrapped Rich's package carefully, folding the paper for later, unveiling a small plastic figurine. "You got me . . . a toy soldier?" she said.

"Sweetie! It's a knight! In shining armor!"

Emma blinked a few times, willing herself to understand. "What?"

"I bought tickets to Sylvie's castle wedding!" crowed Rich.

"What?" said Emma, alarmed. Their checking account was overdrawn and their retirement account was negative thirty-thousand-some dollars, a staggering debt made possible by a revolving magic show of minimum payments and new lines of credit. "With what credit card?" Emma managed.

"Card?" said Rich. "No, I called Jane's Travel downtown! She's planning it all *as we speak.* I can work another year, so what? We can't miss Sylvie's wedding and that's that. As the kids say, YOLO! That means, *you only live once.*"

"Rich . . ." said Emma. She was going to have to borrow from her mother. She was going to have to get another card. Acid rose up her esophagus and her head began to pound.

"Here are the details from Jane. It's going to be the best trip ever!"

"Oh, Rich," said Emma. She grew teary looking at Jane's careful itinerary:

Jane's Travel

Catalfamo Family UK Tour and SYLVIE'S WEDDING!!!
VACATION BRAINSTORMING
(Just some ideas for you!)

Arrival LONDON Heathrow

- London Eye Ferris Wheel?
- James Bond Jet Cruise on the Thames River

Car hire to Mumberton Castle

- Steam train through Murthwaite Halt
- Hadrian's Wall with guide in Ancient Roman costume
- Wordsworth's Dove Cottage tour
- Shopping! Ambleside Luxury Sheepskin & FAMOUS Grasmere Gingerbread MADE BY HAND and the lady is wearing the cutest bonnet on the web page!
- Osprey Viewing Excursion with Boat Ride on Bassenthwaite Lake
- Cumbrian Heavy Horse Clydesdale Ride on fell or beach, weather dependent (IT RAINS A LOT THERE!)
- Predator Experience at Witherslack Hall Farm
- Beatrix Potter House Tour

Bachelorette Party (they call it "Hen Night" over there in England FYI!!!): Drunken Duck Inn in Ambleside? LET'S DISCUSS!

Suggest bringing layers, including a rain jacket or umbrella and rubber boots (they call them "wellies").

Emma, Call me ASAP!
Jane XXOO

"I told her you'd call this morning," said Rich. "OK, I'm off to work. I love you, honey."

"I know," said Emma.

"We're going with the boys to England!" said Rich.

"I just can't believe it," said Emma.

"Well, believe it, baby. Maybe a vacation can get your mind off your sex toys."

"It's not just toys," said Emma, reflexively.

"Right, sorry. Maybe a vacation will get your mind off your sexual empowerment products."

"God, that sounds nice," said Emma. In the dim recesses of her overloaded head, she remembered that one of her credit card bills had come with a blank check. Was it in her office trash can or the garbage bin at the top of the driveway?

If she disappeared in the wilds of Northern England, would the creditors find her? First, she could hold her babies' hands as they walked around Piccadilly Circus. They could stay in a castle. And then she could just take . . . what? A bottle of Benadryl? Six bottles of cough medicine? She imagined writing a check to Jane's Travel, going to England, and just enjoying the last days before Rich knew she was a liar.

Or maybe Sweet Nothings would . . .

After all, Cassidy Rose said . . .

She believed she was a Boss Babe and . . .

Emma put her head in her hands.

"Why don't you look happy, Em?" said Rich.

Emma's brain short-circuited. She just . . . went blank. All the maneuvering, the credit limits, the debt, the fact that she had spent their savings, *Rich's* savings, the money he'd planned to use to retire and create the life he wanted—it all disappeared. It was too much. The possibility of fixing things, of returning to some semblance of normality, was gone. Emma was going to lose everything; it was just a matter of time. Cassidy Rose was not her friend. Cassidy Rose had played her. There was no other option than to ride the wave.

"I'm so happy!" she said. And in a feat of mental gymnastics she could never hope to understand, Emma *actually felt happy*.

"Hooray!" said Rich.

PART THREE
STRANGERS ON A TRAIN

1
SYLVIE

A man in a silk top hat and a bright blue three-piece suit (accessorized with a red tie, red handkerchief, and a tiny red rose on his lapel) opened the door of Sylvie and Simon's London taxicab with a flourish. "Welcome to Brown's Hotel!" he said.

"Oh, Simon," said Sylvie, jet-lagged, shielding her eyes against the bright sun and grabbing his hand.

"My favorite hotel in the world," said Simon.

"Welcome in," said the bellman, tipping his top hat.

Sylvie turned to gather her bags, but two porters were already taking them from the taxi and another pair of men swung open wooden doors with ornate glass panes. Sylvie, pressing smooth her rumpled sundress (it had seemed so chic in Miami), tried to appear accustomed to opulence. She stepped from the taxi and walked across tilework spelling out the hotel name beneath her silver Birkenstock sandals: multicolored stones in perfect patterned swirls.

Sylvie thought of Emma and Cleo: After reading the picture book *Eloise,* they had loved playing a game they'd conjured called "The Plaza." The young Peacock sisters had never been inside a hotel, but they'd pretend that Emma was a room-service waiter and Sylvie was the nanny and Cleo—always—the rich and pampered hotel guest, Eloise. As Cleo made up outlandish requests—a sandwich with the crusts cut off or an animal to keep her company—her sisters would scramble to comply (making simulacra of fancy foods and even sneaking a frog into their room to please "Eloise").

Now, Sylvie gazed around the lobby of Brown's Hotel. She loved the mint-green and blue wallpaper, which featured images of wisteria blossoms and birds. A skylight made the chandelier beneath it glitter. Sylvie took in dove-blue velvet chairs; riots of fresh flowers; a faint smell of cigar smoke; and the sounds of piano notes and low laughter.

A sharply dressed young person materialized, offering gin lemonades from a bar cart, which Sylvie and Simon declined. "Welcome to Brown's," said the woman, her heels snapping against the floor as she led them to an elevator, then down a hallway. "The Kipling Suite," she said, turning her wrist like Vanna White on *Wheel of Fortune.*

"Is there a monkey right there or am I hallucinating?" said Sylvie, pointing to a white sculpture hanging overhead.

"A bit of fun," said the woman, allowing a tight smile.

The woman unlocked the suite and entered. Shelves of antiquities lined a wallpapered hallway. Sylvie tried to follow as the woman talked about the eleven Georgian apartments that were connected to one another to make up the hotel. "Brown's was the very first hotel in London," she said.

The living room of the suite was—quite simply—the most luxurious space Sylvie had ever seen in her life: lush silk curtains; giant couches with a dozen pillows each; elephant sculptures; two duck decoys; and an enormous blurry painting of a seahorse. A glass-topped coffee table was piled with books and hydrangeas. The woman mentioned original paneling; fabric from Lewis & Wood that "gives a touch of today." She hoisted books aloft:

P. G. Wodehouse, and Kipling's *The Jungle Book,* which she explained was, in fact, written here.

In this room.

By Rudyard Kipling.

"Brown's has two entrances," the woman continued. "One on Albemarle and one on Dover . . ." Sylvie's eyes began to glaze over. What time was it in Florida? Simon, noticing Sylvie's spaciness, thanked the woman and bid her goodbye. When she was gone, Simon opened a door to a beautiful bedroom. He lifted Sylvie's *New Yorker* tote from her shoulder and gathered a robe for her from the closet while she undressed. She slipped from her sandals, pulled on the robe, and climbed into the enormous, cloudlike bed. Simon tucked her under the goose feather duvet.

When Sylvie woke, she turned to her naked fiancé, who was watching her sleepily. "What time is it?" she said.

"I have no idea," said Simon. He brought his face to hers, paused as she went liquid. He ran his palm down the side of her body—her rib cage, her waist, moving his fingers to her stomach and down. Sylvie closed her eyes and sighed, letting her head fall into the perfect hotel pillow. Simon brought his mouth to her throat, and then he pulled the bedding over their bodies.

Simon moved forcefully, passionate, greedy for her, but he never forgot Sylvie's pleasure. He knew how to use his fingers and tongue to bring her to abandon, and only when she was verging on climax would he enter her (and always with a condom), pushing impossibly slowly, sometimes stopping until she pressed her hips down to feel all of him inside her. She felt feverish with desire. Sylvie barely recognized herself, and in the best twist of fate, she wasn't ashamed. She wanted Simon and she took him. Afterward, they tossed the bedding aside, breathing heavily, skin cooling, Sylvie lying open but unafraid—a miracle.

"I love you," she said. Simon wrapped around her, and they fell, again, into heavy slumber.

After her nap and a soak in the suite's Italian Arabescato marble tub, Sylvie put on her robe and found a room-service spread in the living room: scones, tiny glass jars of jam, pastries, eggs, bacon, fresh juice, pots of coffee, and a pitcher of cream.

"Tell me everything about our wedding weekend again," said Sylvie, accepting a China cup of coffee and a saucer, sitting cross-legged next to Simon in front of a fireplace. She tossed off the hotel slippers and held her feet toward the warm fire.

"So as your family arrives, Nolan will meet them outside Baggage Claim."

"With the sign," Sylvie said with a sigh, "like my sign, with my name."

"Correct. And their luggage will go straight to the castle."

"I've read about rich-people vacations like these in Agatha Christie mysteries," said Sylvie. "And she really stayed here?"

"Not in this suite, but yes, she used to write here, and meet friends for tea."

"I have to tell you something, Simon."

"Go on."

Sylvie selected a scone, broke it apart with her hands, then spread clotted cream and rhubarb-ginger jam. She took a bite. "I've never read *The Jungle Book,*" she confessed. "But I have seen the movie! And I've read every Agatha Christie."

"Of course," said Simon. "And it's OK about the Kipling."

"Phew."

"So as your family arrives, Nolan takes their luggage and puts them in a taxi to the train station."

"It's like my sisters are Ripley in Highsmith's novels! But hopefully no one disappears, gets poisoned, or has a mental breakdown."

"No one will disappear or get poisoned," said Simon.

"My mom is in a constant state of mental . . . I don't want to say *breakdown,*" said Sylvie. The topic of her mother was painful. Sometimes, Sylvie saw her mother as the girl Donna had been, abandoned by her parents. Sylvie had a picture of Donna at age six, bereft. She would never be adopted, never chosen; she would grow up in a Missoula orphanage for girls.

But other times, Sylvie knew that her mother caused her and her sisters real pain, regardless of what she, Donna, had survived. Donna was a selfish and cruel person—maybe Donna's own mother had been the same.

"Why did you invite your mom?" said Simon.

Sylvie considered his question, which was a good one. "Yearning," she concluded. It was one word, but said so much. She yearned for Donna to be someone Donna was incapable of being. Sylvie still yearned for a mother: She hoped to be seen and loved, embraced. She also knew that Donna had lost these capabilities long before she ever had her daughters.

"I get it," said Simon. He put down his teacup and pulled her close. Sylvie rested her cheek on his chest, kissed the skin there.

"Tell me about the train," she said.

"It was built in the 1920s," he said. "A seven-car, luxury Pullman train, the one used by Queen Elizabeth. Wait until you see how they've restored them—vintage lighting, silk upholstery. We'll have a fancy lunch and sleep in cozy bunks and by morning, we'll be in Mumberton. But I want to take you to Harrods before we head to the station," said Simon.

"Where your grandmother bought the bears," said Sylvie.

"Regrettably, yes," said Simon. He had told Sylvie about the castle's Asiatic black bears that had been purchased at Harrods in London, which had once contained a department called "Pet Kingdom." Pet Kingdom sold lions, alligators, elephants, and bears. In the year Simon was born, the last bears at Mumberton Castle—sisters Pearl and Ruby and Pearl's daughter, Zinnia—were sold to Dudley Zoo.

"I want to get your sisters peacock feather fascinators," said Simon.

"Emma will love that," said Sylvie. "Cleo, who knows?"

"And I have a surprise," said Simon.

"Tell me."

"Sylvie!"

"And then we have the rehearsal dinner, and on Sunday, we get married."

Sylvie felt a shadow pass over her: It was Alexander's ghost. Alexander and Sylvie had created goody bags for all their friends and family who came to Miami for the wedding, filled with local treats.

Sylvie made herself focus. "When does Penelope get here? She should have flown with us, Simon."

"Thisbe said she couldn't miss her last week at camp." He pressed his fingers to his eyes. "Thisbe's in Greece. Or maybe France. Anyway, Penelope's nanny is bringing her, and she'll arrive in Mumberton soon after we do."

There was a heavy pause. Sylvie wanted to give Simon space to say what he needed to say. Beside Simon was Alexander's ghost, wearing his Williams College T-shirt and a skeptical expression. Alexander had not always been nice; he raised an eyebrow now, as if to say, *What did you expect?*

Sylvie had met Penelope before her engagement to Simon, on a day she was exhausted from the Scholastic Book Fair. The Scholastic Book Fair was everyone's favorite event of the year and Sylvie just hated it. She spent all afternoon setting up the various sections: "Kittens," "Chills and Thrills," "Unicorns," "Pirates." She had to handle parent volunteers and instruct them about how to use the red Scholastic cash registers.

When the final poster was hung, Sylvie opened the library doors and kids streamed in like forces attacking a medieval castle, buying up the smelly markers and bookmarks and "BFF pens" and unicorn pens and jellyfish pens and "Mystery Balls" and "Goop," leaving most of the carefully arranged books untouched, except the diaries, which kids fought over between the stacks.

The previous year, a child had drawn penises with an invisible-ink pen all over the school so now Sylvie had to write down the name of every child who bought an invisible-ink pen. The book fair brought out the worst in the kids: They stole erasers, so Sylvie had to keep them behind the checkout desk and spend hours fetching them instead of shelving books! It was complete mayhem and despite prevailing beliefs, it barely raised a cent for her library.

Sylvie got a text from Simon asking her to call him at the same time she was breaking up a fistfight over a strawberry-scented journal with a lock and strawberry-shaped key. She confiscated the "Plush Strawberry Milk Gel Patch" journal (it was the last one available) and said no one would have it, and both of the brawling girls began sobbing.

Sylvie sold out of erasers shaped like video-game consoles and "floating ice cream" pens (each looked like a mini lava lamp) and a book about how to make "Cat's Cradle" with colored string included. They sold out of "Dainty Donut-Scented Markers." There was another fight, this time over *Battle Dragons: City of Speed,* a paperback book that came with a metal dragon necklace attached. One six-year-old, Francis, had bought the book, but another boy, Robert, had stolen the necklace and was caught wearing it brazenly, gleaming on top of his "Go, Gators" T-shirt. Robert had arrived in school the week before speaking three words of English (*I thank you*). Sylvie broke up the fight, returned the trinket, then bought another copy of *Battle Dragons: City of Speed* for the library, removed the necklace, went to find Robert in After-Care (which was held in the cafeteria), and secured it around his neck.

"I thank you," said Robert.

As a treat, Sylvie bought a third copy of *Battle Dragons: City of Speed,* removed the dragon jewelry, and put it on herself. The dragon's stomach was made of a green stone, and she thought it looked great against her buttoned-up pink cardigan.

When Sylvie got home, Simon's truck was parked in her driveway. And on the porch swing, where she'd once whiled away the evening with Alexander, was Simon. He stood when he saw her, grinning.

She loved his height, broad shoulders, and sleek muscles. He was dressed in khaki shorts and a pastel-blue T-shirt. "Sylvie!" he said.

Simon came forward and hugged her. She snuggled in, filled with a calm joy.

A child's voice pierced Sylvie's lovestruck daze: "Your dog wants to get out!"

From the far side of Sylvie's house, next to Willie's outdoor pen, a girl appeared. She was eleven years old, her hair long and tangled. She smiled, exposing buck teeth. She wore sequined pants, a SpongeBob T-shirt, and Adidas sneakers that matched her father's.

"Your dog wants to get out," repeated the girl. Behind her, Willie whined at the gate. Alexander had built a dog door that allowed Willie to access a gated dog run even while Sylvie was at work.

"Penelope," said Sylvie. She felt tears behind her eyes. This girl was *more* than Sylvie had imagined. She was *real;* she was *here*. The freckles! The too-big sneakers! The way she said of Willie, who was wagging her tail and quivering with excitement, "I think maybe she's too hot out here? Or maybe she just really wants to meet me."

"Her name is Willie," Sylvie told Penelope. "She sometimes bites people, so be careful."

"Hold on," said Simon. "Did you say she *bites people*?"

"Once," clarified Sylvie. "She bit someone once. That's why she was at the shelter. But it's never happened again."

"Are you scared she'll bite you?" asked Penelope.

"She is how she is," said Sylvie. "It's not her fault what's happened to her. If she bites me, I'll get stitched up. But I don't think she will."

Penelope thought that over for a moment, then nodded. "Well, come on!" she said. "We need to walk her!"

"We do," said Sylvie.

"Well, where the heck is her leash?" said Penelope, putting her hands on her hips, looking just like Simon. Simon met Sylvie's gaze with an expression that said, *Didn't I tell you she's the greatest child in the world?* Sylvie nodded.

Penelope's fingernails were painted green and gold.

Now, Simon tightened his Brown's Hotel bathrobe. "Goddamn Thisbe," he said. His eyes flashed and his shoulders tensed. If Sylvie believed in perfect, happy endings, Simon's unresolved divorce drama would derail their love story. But Sylvie was good at pretending things were fine when they were not fine.

When Alexander had left his Alcoholics Anonymous books untouched for a week or two and seemed moody, Sylvie had avoided bringing up the topic of his sobriety. Sometimes, to preserve her sanity (or because she was just fucking *scared*), she allowed herself to ignore painful truths. And so, she saw Simon's fury and anguish, but did not invite him to share it.

Sylvie could not go on after her father died. She could not survive in the house with her wounded mother. She could not bear Alexander's death, or moving on from his death. So she stood, and went into the bathroom, brushed her teeth, and rubbed her hands with Brown's Hotel lotion that smelled of rosemary and pears. When she returned to the living room, Simon looked even more haggard, more tortured by his hatred of Thisbe and what she had done to him . . . a hatred so intense, it could be love.

Was Sylvie's method of bearing the unbearable—the method of *forced ignorance*—her greatest strength or most damning weakness?

Regardless, it was her way. She didn't try to fix Simon or to win him. She got back into bed and opened *Murder on the Orient Express,* which she was rereading. Eventually, Simon's demons retreated, and he joined her. He was rereading *4:50 from Paddington*.

"Do you think it's strange that we're preparing for a train journey by reading books about murders on trains?" said Simon. "Or in my case, a murder on a train platform?"

"Is it the same train station we're going to?" asked Sylvie, not really in the mood to talk, her finger marking her place.

"No," said Simon. "My murder happens at Paddington Station and we're going to Victoria."

"Not strange, then," decided Sylvie.

"Oh, good," said Simon.

They would trade books when they had finished.

2
CLEO

Cleo and Danny's flight from JFK to London was smooth. When they landed, Cleo turned on her data, clicked whatever she had to click to get a connection in the UK, and sighed as her phone filled with texts and emails. There was, however, only one voicemail, and it was from Isaac:

> Cheerio, my pet. That actually sounds creepy, sorry. Just calling to see how your flight was and to let you know that . . . well . . . I wish I was there. Give Sylvie a hug from me. It's Isaac, by the way. In case you were fooled by my British accent. OK, bye Cleo. I'm here if you need me. Good luck with your mom.

"Well, here we are," said Danny. "London town!"

Danny had never before been on an international flight. He'd come prepared with a neck pillow, eye shade, moisturizing spritzer, and prepacked healthy snacks. He'd purchased a leather notebook and had dutifully jotted notes in it before taking a pill and falling asleep with his head on Cleo's shoulder. She'd worked throughout the flight.

At one point, Danny totally zonked, Cleo gingerly opened his notebook and read his "novel notes" with dismay: He had written, "Plane to London same as planes in America. Odd smells."

At Heathrow, Cleo watched Danny as he handed his crisp, expedited passport to the customs agent. He was trying to be nonchalant, but Cleo could tell he was absolutely thrilled. Danny had come from poverty, poverty way beyond the middle-class coupon-clipping lifestyle Cleo had known back in Montana. His parents drove from their Iowa farm to a town nearby once a year, ordered a bucket of KFC, parked somewhere and ate it—and called this experience the annual family vacation.

Danny smiled as the guard stamped his passport. He stared at the stamp for a moment and then grinned at Cleo. His unshaven face was appealing to her in a way his overly groomed perfection was not.

"I don't know if I can *not work* for a week," said Cleo as they walked toward Baggage Claim. "I honestly don't know if I can do it."

"I don't know either," said Danny. "Do you even want to, Cleo?"

"What?"

"Do you even want to spend time with me?" said Danny, his voice tentative. "Sometimes I feel like the reason you're so successful is just . . . you don't want to be home."

"Oh, Danny."

"I think I used to be more interesting," said Danny contemplatively.

Cleo didn't know what to say. His allure had always been the impossibility of winning him. But now he was hers, and her desire for him was waning.

She felt a swell of empathy. Danny was terrified to lose her, or to lose her money, anyway. Here he was: a smart guy, his body and face honed to flawlessness, rushing to the carousel to get their bags, which he had packed. Danny was her trophy wife: She'd always detested the term, but was grateful for his assistance in keeping her fed and sharp.

She'd been able to rise to the level of her colleagues because she, like they, had a partner who handled everything else. If she wanted her success and children, a partner like Danny was what she needed.

Cleo had friends who would pay top dollar for a handsome man's sperm alone, and Cleo got the sperm and the attentive licking. Danny *always* made sure she had an orgasm, *always.* It was a point of pride for him. Their chemistry had once been powerful, but had dulled, which was normal. Wasn't it normal?

Outside customs, a man wearing a top hat held a placard that read CLEO PEACOCK. "Where's my name?" said Danny.

3
EMMA

-$35,510.12

"Will you look at this marquetry paneling?" said Rich, touching the wall of the Pullman train carriage where an artist had fitted mahogany veneers together to create glossy images of ocean waves and clouds above. "I've never seen anything like it."

"Where is Sylvie?" said Emma, feeling apprehensive.

Rich shrugged, stretching out in a plush chair upholstered in a vibrant art deco pattern. A man in a white tuxedo jacket hurried to fill a tiny teacup. Rich sipped, then said, "Whoa! This is not tea, Em!"

"It's strawberry wine," clarified the steward. "Would you prefer champagne? We serve Veuve Clicquot, as is served on the Orient Express."

"No, thank you," said Emma at the same time as her husband said, "Yes, please." Emma couldn't possibly enjoy herself. She hadn't been together with her sisters in *ten years*. They'd only known Guinness as a toddler, and had never even met Jameson in person—only in FaceTime calls.

The boys began picking up and commenting on every silver utensil, china salt and pepper shaker (lavender colored and emblazoned with the train's insignia), and napkin. The steward returned with a tray of canapés. Jameson popped caviar canapés in his mouth as if they were his favorite food, Tater Tots.

"This is Albert Dunn," said Rich, gesturing to the paneling. "He did the walls of the *Titanic.* Unbelievable. It looks new. Now *this* is what I want to do." Rich traced the edge of a delicate wave with his fingertip. "Four more years and I'll have enough money to do this," he said.

Emma's stomach clenched. How was she going to tell Rich that she had spent all the money he had saved to make his wonderful dream come true?

"Maybe one of you will want to work with me," said Rich. "What do you think, guys? Catalfamo and Sons custom woodwork and cabinetry?"

Jameson pursed his lips and nodded amiably, chomping the last canapé. "How do they make different pieces of wood look like they're one piece of wood?" said Guinness.

"It's incredibly thin layers cut perfectly and fit together," said Rich. "They use fish bones in the glue."

"That's sick," said Guinness admiringly.

A jazz band began playing on the platform in front of their train car. "Things are happening," said Rich, smiling at his wife.

"I'm so nervous," said Emma.

"It's going to be OK," said Rich, taking her hand in his. "No matter what happens, I'm going to be right here next to you. OK?"

"I don't deserve you," said Emma.

"You certainly do," said Rich.

Emma's awful secret was hot inside her.

"Look, Em," said Rich, touching the wooden wall. "If you look closely at the sky here, you can see tiny, tiny stars."

"There she is!" cried Emma. "There's my sister!"

4
SYLVIE

Sylvie stood in Victoria Station and gazed at the British Pullman, a glamorous train like the ones Sylvie and her sisters had imagined on the nights they packed what they could find in the refrigerator and took what they called "night picnics" into the backyard to imagine ways of escaping Donna: jets to Paris, hitchhiking to the Plaza; trains across Europe.

Donna's parenting had run the gamut from screaming to disappearing for days. The hours Seamus, their father, was home were the only hours the girls weren't wary and scared. When Donna was "in a mood," as she called it, they night-picnicked in the backyard until the light in her bedroom went off and the house wasn't dangerous anymore.

Seamus worked the night shift until he died, when Sylvie was fourteen. Soon after his death, Sylvie opened the book he'd always read to her, *The Bed Book,* by Sylvia Plath. ("Sylvia wasn't all doom and gloom," Seamus told Sylvie, trying—in his way—to undo damage Donna had already done.) Why had their father agreed to naming his daughters after doomed women? He was gone, and Sylvie would never know. Once, Cleo had asked Donna what she had been thinking and Donna had said, "They're beautiful names! Why do you have to be so dramatic?"

When she was a teenager, Sylvie had opened *The Bed Book* to remember her father, and had found a note in his handwriting, jotted on the first page: My Sylvie: You're too old to read this with me anymore, but someday you will open this book, and know that you are beloved.

"Sylvie!" cried Emma now, from her train window. "All aboard, Syl!"

"Emma!" Sylvie ran up the steps and into the train. She was embraced by her nephews and sister. Emma's kids smelled like a long travel day (dirty socks) and Emma carried a complicated, spicy scent in her clothes and hair, likely one of her artisan perfumes. "And you must be Simon," said Emma over Sylvie's shoulder, pulling him into their hug.

Rich stood and joined them. His beard was going gray and he looked exhausted. He enfolded Sylvie tightly, saying, "Little sister, I've missed you."

Sylvie's nephews appeared to be energized, rather than worn out, from their jet lag. "Where's Penelope?" said Jameson.

"She's meeting us at Mumberton," said Simon.

"Mumberton is a CASTLE!" screamed Jameson.

"There's AUNT CLEO!" cried Guinness.

Cleo! She entered their private car, striding up the stairs as if she were entering the Met Gala or a New York Fashion Week runway. She was so glamorous, clad in couture, whittled down to almost nothing. Sylvie felt intimidated, but reminded herself that this glamorous creature was her own big sister.

Behind Cleo, carrying her purse, was a man who looked like a movie star. "I'm Danny," said Cleo's boyfriend, sliding his arm around Cleo.

Sylvie didn't often encounter men (or women) who were so . . . symmetrical. Danny's brown eyes were hooded, the very definition of "bedroom eyes." Even his wrists were gorgeous, not to mention his leather shoes, which would have looked like elfin slippers on an ordinary man. (On Danny, they looked impossibly cool.)

"It's nice to meet you," said Sylvie.

"This is fabulous," said Danny. "Just fabulous. It's my first time on an original Pullman."

Cleo had told Sylvie this was Danny's first trip out of the United States, and his second trip on an airplane, but he sounded blasé.

"Mine, too," said Sylvie.

"WHAT DID YOU BRING US, AUNT CLEO?" shouted Guinness.

"What *did* we bring them, Danny?" said Cleo, who had not seemingly considered her nephews until this moment.

The movie star pulled three new Nintendo game consoles from his bag. The boys cheered, Danny said, "Let's do this, boys," and the three ran into the dining car to begin gaming.

Sylvie walked to her big sister. Hugging Cleo for the first time in years, Sylvie felt only muscle and bone. It was a completely different feeling from hugging Emma, who was yielding and soft.

"Hey, hey," Cleo said, patting Sylvie's back instead of returning her embrace. Sylvie felt like a kid again, burrowing in, seeking comfort and warmth, but everything left of Cleo was cool and hard. Even her hair, which had once fallen loose—as a kid, Sylvie had loved to wrap Cleo's hair around her fingers—was conquered, tamed into a sleek bob. "Thanks for coming," said Sylvie, wiping her tears with the palm of her hand.

Sylvie scanned the grand train car for her mother, but Donna was nowhere to be found. It occurred to Sylvie that you could have all the money in the world, you could have a fiancé (he was walking toward her now, arms outstretched to escort her on this magnificent journey) and a glass of the world's finest champagne, and you could still feel bereft and alone.

As dinner was served—scallop carpaccio, spice-braised lamb and ewe crème cheese with lemon thyme, a trio of bell peppers with artichoke, potato gratin, and spinach—Jameson and Guinness climbed over their mother as if she were a sofa. Emma did seem squished, even defeated. Maybe it was motherhood or maybe just a long journey, but the mischievous flash in her eyes had dulled to a blank stare, her eyebrows raising when she was spoken to as if it were hard for her to pull herself from a worrisome daydream. Emma's lips were chapped and her hair was messy until, halfway through the meal, she gathered her curls into a plastic claw clip and affixed them to the back of her head. Rich was trying to be jovial but seemed similarly strained. Was something wrong with the Catalfamos? Even the boys' chatter appeared anxious, reminding Sylvie of the way she had talked and talked when trying to cheer up her father on the nights he acted depressed, smoking Winston cigarettes at their kitchen table. (The kitchen table that now belonged to Emma.)

Sylvie excused herself. In the bathroom, she put her hands on either side of a marble sink. There were fresh flowers in silver vases on either side of the mirror. Her mother had not shown up.

Beneath Sylvie's feet, a mosaic floor displayed a giant bird. The toilet seat was smooth mahogany; from its perch, Sylvie could admire a circular stained-glass window. Sylvie didn't want to leave the bathroom and wondered for a moment why she had invited her family here at all.

Oh, but she had missed her sisters. Cleo and Emma had shielded her from Donna and consoled her after their father's death. They had celebrated at her first wedding and mourned at Alexander's funeral. But then . . . what had happened? Sylvie didn't understand how they had drifted so far apart. Obviously, the dream of fixing whatever was broken between them by uniting at a massive castle was stupid and misguided.

There was a tap at the bathroom door. "Sylvie?"

Sylvie turned the lock and opened the door. Simon stood in the hallway. The train tracks thrummed beneath their feet. Sylvie leaned in for a kiss. His hands moved around her waist and pulled her toward him. She put her hands on his strong shoulders and they tumbled into the bathroom. Sylvie bolted the door behind her fiancé. Simon, kissing her deeply, lifted Sylvie and placed her on the marble counter; she wrapped her legs around his hips. She was on fire; he slid her underwear down and knelt before her.

Sylvie gasped, trying to keep herself quiet. She opened her eyes and realized that the mosaic bird depicted on the floor was, of course, the mythical phoenix. Simon stood, unbuckled his belt, unzipped his pants, found a condom, and slid it on. His warm hands positioning her hips, his groan as he entered her, the bliss of him moving inside her, gently and then faster. Sylvie felt as if she were made of flames, wings spread wide, exploding into someone new, someone who believed in the possibility of joy.

5
CLEO

At some point, deep into the evening, Cleo found herself in the bar car with Florence and Rashid. Cleo had met them both at Alexander's funeral, but barely remembered Sylvie's best friends from those hazy days. "Isn't this train *stupendous*?" said Florence, refilling her glass of champagne.

"Flo, you are very tipsy," said Rashid, beaming. He was tall and pudgy, with hair long enough to tuck behind his ears but not long enough for a ponytail. His smile was goofy and sweet, and he had a hoop in one ear.

"This is kind of our honeymoon," said Florence.

"Oh," said Cleo. "But I thought you were . . ."

"We've been married for twelve years," said Rashid. "What she means is that we could never afford a . . ."

"We went camping the weekend after our ceremony," said Florence. "But now we're headed to a castle!"

Cleo smiled. Florence's enthusiasm was infectious.

"So, your Danny's a novelist?" said Florence.

"Yes," said Cleo. "I mean, he's working on a novel."

"Rashid tried to write a novel," said Florence.

"Yeah," said Rashid. "But it just never ended. And then I started hating it."

Florence nodded. "Remember, hon? You set up the whole table in the hallway? It made me so sad to see you there, staring at the coatrack."

"Yeah," said Rashid. "I hated it so much." He sipped his champagne. "I wanted to, like, *be* a novelist, you know? I wanted an author photo and a book tour. But actually just typing all day—wow, that sucked."

They both laughed ruefully. Florence hugged her husband. Cleo watched them as if they were strange animals in a zoo: partners and friends who supported each other, not seeming to have anything to prove. Cleo could not imagine saying to Danny (or anyone) that she regretted her choices. She wondered for a moment if Danny, too, hated trying to write a novel . . . and just didn't know how to tell her.

Later, next to Danny in their suite, Cleo closed her eyes and listened to the train as it made its way toward the Lake District—a place made famous by Wordsworth and Beatrix Potter. She was soothed by the low clattering, the sound of wheels against the tracks. She wished she was home, but when she thought of the word *home,* it was Isaac's apartment she envisioned. His mismatched dishes and thick, carpeted floor, and the spicy candles his mother bought him at Bed Bath & Beyond.

It was strange to think of her sisters asleep in adjoining suites. They had shared one room until she had gone to college—Emma and Sylvie in bunk beds and Cleo in a twin bed by the door. Oftentimes (especially when her parents fought in the living room) her sisters would end up in Cleo's bed, where the two older sisters would sleep on either side of baby Sylvie, who loved to have her head scratched.

Cleo had been so homesick during her first days at NYU. She had shared a dorm room with three other girls, two from Manhattan and one from a New York suburb. (Cleo would learn the names of the suburbs and sections of Manhattan quickly, as well as what they meant about a person's past and future prospects: A "bridge and tunnel girl" felt deeply inferior to a "Nightingale-Bamford girl"; a "boarding school girl" was more likely to smoke pot than a "Maidstone Club girl," who might dabble in gin, cocaine, or both.)

"Scholarship girls" like Cleo inspired prurient interest (how poor *was* she?) and begrudging respect, but Cleo worked valiantly to obfuscate her status.

She had painstakingly prepared for her arrival in New York with a chic bob and expensive clothes she'd begged her mother to buy her. Within a day, though, she understood that the most popular girls dressed as if they made *no* effort: long hair and baseball caps, flannel shirts and loose, tattered pants, Birkenstock sandals that made Cleo's leopard-print booties look absurd.

Cleo had copied wealthy tourists who came through Missoula on their way to ski vacations, who paired fur vests with slim pants and leather boots. But she had not noticed that the rich women's kids dressed like (as her mother would call them) hoboes.

Cleo had arrived late to her NYU dorm after taking a bus from Newark, and all that had been left was one of the least-desired bottom bunk beds. Late into the night, the girls complained about other people. Like Cleo, her roommates hated their parents, their siblings, and everything about the places they'd come from.

Eventually, her roommates fell asleep, and Cleo was surprised to feel an unbearable sadness welling inside her. She bit her lip to stay quiet. Then she heard a shuddering exhalation. She turned to see that Cecily, the suburban roommate, was crying. Cleo almost got out of bed to comfort Cecily, but felt paralyzed.

In the morning, one of the Manhattan roommates said, "Oh my God, who was *crying* last night? I felt like I was in a fucking daycare!"

"Right?" said the other top-bunk girl.

Cleo had looked at Cecily. Her eyes were wide and terrified. "I don't know," Cecily whispered.

Cleo thought of her weak sisters, so scared of their mother and of the world. Cleo had taken care of them and she would always take care of them. They needed her to be strong. Cleo, too, had yearned for comfort during her first night away from home, but she wanted to banish the part of herself that was needy. She would do whatever it took to become invincible. And what it took was shutting down the defenseless little girl inside her. The last vestiges of needy Cleo almost reached across to Cecily to take her hand. Instead, she balled her fist and dug her nails into her palm until it hurt.

"It was Cecily," she said, trying on the East Coast girl drawl, a flatness that sounded stoned whether or not you were high. "Pathetic," she'd added.

Cleo and her new friends laughed.

Copying her haughty "city girl" clique, Cleo waltzed into five-star hotels, private events, restaurants with waiting lists. Manhattan became her playground. One roommate even taught Cleo how to open secret gates to private gardens around the city using bobby pins—you could pick any lock by making a "key" from two hairpins, visualizing the mechanics of the lock, pushing up the tumblers with one bent pin while turning the barrel with the other.

From her first night away from home, Cleo understood the two futures available to her: Be the victim, or win. Her choice had served her well.

PART FOUR

WELCOME TO MUMBERTON CASTLE

1
EMMA

-$42,005.30

"Oh my God!" cried Jameson, pointing out the window of the car. Emma peered over her son's shoulder and gasped.

Mumberton Castle!

The building was massive, crenellated, astonishing—a castle from a fairy-tale storybook, rising toward the clouds, making a pattern against the sky. Emma felt tiny as they approached the Visitor's Parking Area of the hulking behemoth, which Sylvie had told her contained a few dozen bedrooms. A few *dozen*! Emma had never been inside a house that held more than four bedrooms in her life.

"Whoa," said Rich, as their car passed underneath a charming stone gatehouse, a narrow passage, and into a courtyard. Mumberton Castle was built on a rocky outcrop; rolling hills spilled down toward interconnected rivers, encircling the entire domain in water.

"My stomach hurts . . . but also, I feel like I'm in *Game of Thrones*," said Guinness, chomping on tablets from his large bottle of Tums.

"We're going into a castle," said Rich, with wonder.

A ten-foot-tall wooden door reinforced with metal bars marked the entrance to a three-story stone tower with a parapet. Emma could feel ghosts here—not only Simon's mother and relatives, but the people who had lived here during King Henry VI's reign, and the Tudors who came after them. Emma had read that King Henry VIII had visited with Anne Boleyn, in the happy window after he had annulled his marriage to Catherine of Aragon and before he had ordered Anne beheaded at the Tower of London to make way for his marriage to Jane Seymour, and later Anne of Cleves, Catherine Howard, and Catherine Parr.

Their driver stopped in front of a side entrance, and they disembarked, seemingly the first car to arrive from the train station. Emma stood before the castle and imagined the women of Mumberton dressed in layers of muslin and silk, their hair braided in elaborate styles, and the men in capes, always on guard.

An elderly woman burst through the door, clapping her hands. She halted in front of Emma and searched her face. Emma had not been considered in so long. She ran her fingers through her unkempt hair and patted her pockets in search of her hair clip. (There had been no time to shower on the train.)

The woman was standing too close. Her breath smelled of stale coffee. "Greetings, love!" she said, in a high-pitched, reedy voice. "Now which one of the wedding guests are you?"

"I'm Emma, the bride's sister. And this is my family." Emma lifted her hands to show off Rich and her sons, who were curious, ready for adventure. She had felt ashamed about Sweet Nothings for so long that she savored a momentary rush of pride.

"What a pleasure to meet you, dear! My name is Louisa Freck," said the woman. "I am the Mumberton Castle librarian. I've been here since before Simon was born! I know absolutely every fact about this place, so if you need anything—anything at all—I'm the one to ask."

As always, Emma's sense of satisfaction was ruined as her

inner Donna began to berate her: *Why didn't you take a few minutes to learn more about the history of medieval England? You had time to watch reality TV, didn't you? You're so lazy and nonintellectual!*

Sure, Rich had made them all watch bloody battles in muddy forests when it was his turn to choose on "Family Movie Night." Was it OK for youngish boys to watch grown men decapitated by antiquated swords on TV? Rich thought it was fine, though he made them close their eyes during the steamy sex scenes in dim castle bedrooms, as women in multilayered dresses disrobed, their crazy headpieces removed to reveal lush manes of hair that hunky men would plunge their hands into.

They had even watched a movie that featured Mumberton Castle: *The Wars of the Roses.* In medieval times, King Henry VI had abdicated the throne, gone insane, and wandered the countryside, somehow ending up at Mumberton, where he was allowed to hide in a tiny space, hidden from view, built into a Mumberton wall for this exact purpose. (The spaces were called "priest holes," but apparently, a mentally unwell king was also welcome.) While he was holed up in a baggy loincloth at Mumberton, his angry wife, Queen Margaret of Anjou, stormed their enemy's castle in chain mail with her army, wielding torches and shooting fire arrows.

"Fire arrows!" Jameson had cried, when Queen Margaret of Anjou started shooting onscreen.

"She is *badass,*" Guinness had acquiesced.

Emma tried to silence her inner Donna, who was now berating her for not *being in the moment* as she stood before the building that contained so many stories and precious artworks—Van Gogh's *Sunflowers* had even been stored here to protect it from the Nazis! It was gone now, but there were several "tatty but valuable items and such" in the castle, as Louisa put it.

"Follow me," said Louisa. Emma's inner Donna was hard on

strangers: The voice in Emma's mind disparaged Louisa's lavender eye shadow and carrot-colored lipstick. *Someone went a little wild in the makeup aisle,* said Donna, in Emma's mind.

They approached a side entrance to the castle, which had a sign over the door reading TICKET OFFICE. Louisa opened the door and led them directly into a huge room dimly lit by low sconces. "*This* is the Great Hall," she said, theatrically. "You don't have to pay the twenty-nine pounds, of course."

Emma looked around, awestruck. The Great Hall was a giant rectangular space—it must have been two hundred feet long. Guinness walked to the center of the room. "I see you looking up, son," said Louisa. "That's called a *hammer-beam* roof. See how the short, horizontal beams are attached to the wall, and can support the curved support beams and wooden struts—so the room can soar open without columns or anything marring the grandeur."

Emma smiled, delighted by how Louisa pronounced the word with a French accent: grand-*eeuuur.*

"It's *lions,*" said Jameson, rushing to touch the legs of a massive table, which had—indeed—been carved into lions. The table was flanked by a stone fireplace, a fire blazing despite the July date. "There are thirteen scary portraits on the wall," Jameson continued, "and the wall is the color of blood!"

"Some of the Mumberton line were handsome, some less so," commented Louisa.

They walked across the Great Hall to enter the library, an octagonal room with another roaring fire. Emma craned her neck, bowled over by the high ceilings, chandeliers, leather-bound books, threadbare carpets, velvet couches, and what seemed to be ten zillion tchotchkes, from marble statues to family photographs to saucers, teacups, baskets, and clocks.

"I cannot believe I am standing in this place," breathed Rich.

"And here is where I make my home," said Louisa, gesturing

to an alcove where a desk filled with papers and dirty teacups was lit by an old lamp. An electrical cord jammed with plugs seemed an obvious hazard in a wooden room filled with flammable objects.

"The ceiling of the Mumberton Library was painted to resemble the night sky on the date in 1205 when a deed from King John gave this land to the family," Louisa said reverentially.

Emma tried to take it all in. A medical kit was left open to display cut glass bottles, a mortar and pestle, and an old syringe. One table was covered with a velvet tablecloth, various coins, blue eyeglasses, a red velvet crown lined with dingy ermine, and what seem to be an ashtray holding a photograph of a king.

In the dining room, Louisa told them that the wallpaper was actually leather; the fruit in crystal bowls was wax; and one of the old men in a portrait had been killed by a tiger in India.

"This drawing room," said Louisa, striding ahead of them, "was once called the *with*-drawing room. It's where the ladies used to go, leaving the men at table to enjoy rum and cigars."

More porcelain. More clocks. More wooden furniture and portraits and vases and candelabras and a tufted velvet stool. Louisa was a very eager tour guide who seemed to have been waiting for some time for an audience to come her way.

The castle smelled of ash from the many fireplaces, but Emma closed her eyes and sniffed, recognizing a base note of myrrh and middle notes of pine and coriander. Did she detect neroli, a top-note floral Emma loved and made from steaming orange blossom petals? Perhaps, but whatever it was exactly, she loved the castle smell and couldn't wait to try to re-create it.

Louisa's tour showed no sign of stopping. "The billiard room," she declared, "has inlaid paneling from a navy ship that fought in the Battle of Trafalgar!"

Rich walked toward one of the stunning tapestries lining the walls. "These tapestries were woven during Tudor times and are incredibly valuable," noted Louisa. "See the gold embroidery? A king would travel *with* his tapestries. If he left them unguarded, they'd be ripped from the walls! Also, they served as insulation. No central heating in medieval times!"

Rich and Emma caught each other's gaze over Louisa's head as she spoke at length about the Tudor Revival plasterwork ceiling. Guinness touched a marble statue of a bear, and looked at his mother with wide, excited eyes, a childish expression she hadn't seen in a while. Finally, they climbed a staircase, which was lined on one side with marble panels depicting nymphs and on the other side, horse portraits.

Halfway down a long stone hallway, Louisa fumbled with a circle holding tarnished metal keys. She turned the lock in one door and it made a low creaking noise as she swung it open. They all crowded around the passageway and then stepped, one at a time, inside.

The room—a bedroom suite—was incredible. The walls were made of hand-placed stones except the far one, which was lined with dark wooden panels. An ivory ceiling with a hexagonal pattern made of wood was lined with deep blue paint, a glittering chandelier hanging in its center.

Louisa approached arched windows, where brass curtain rods held thick golden curtains edged with tiny tassels made of gold thread. "The shutters are just the way they would have been in Tudor times. As you can see, you'd close the shutters to keep out the arrows."

"Arrows," repeated Jameson, nodding reverentially.

"Please call me to light the fire and don't do it yourselves," said Louisa.

"Many thanks," said Rich. "We appreciate your knowledge, Louisa. I think we're about ready for some downtime now if you don't mind."

Ignoring Rich's polite query, Louisa remained with them, pulling the door shut behind them using a circular-shaped metal pull. The lock clicked firmly into place. Wind buffeted the castle, making a rushing sound.

The bedroom smelled of cold stone and rain, with mineral notes that reminded Emma of a fragrance called Terre d'Hermès, designed by the talented Jean-Claude Ellena, the first "nose" (a term used in classical French perfumery) to combine shiso leaves and flint. Emma began sketching a perfume brief in her mind. She would call the fragrance "Mumberton" and use orange, vetiver (to smell like the stones), and a base note of benzoin, sap from cuts in the trunks of trees. How would she evoke the antique feel of the castle? Amber? Beeswax?

"Your sister will be in the Gatekeeper's Cottage, also known as the Honeymoon Cottage . . . you probably saw it driving in—that arched building over the road into the castle. Simon himself helped with the interior renovation. There's one room for a bride, an upstairs arch with a terrace overlooking the castle, and down the stairs on the other side, the groom's rooms. So romantic. They can meet in the treetop archway for a stolen kiss."

Guinness met his mother's eyes and made a face. Perhaps Louisa Freck needed a stolen kiss of her own.

"But back to your abode!" said Louisa. "You can see where the soldiers would have lived in the barracks," she said, pointing out a window. "Despite them, the first Lord Mumberton was beheaded."

The boys crowded Louisa, wanting to hear more. "This room, aside from the witch marks on the window paneling, does *not* appear to be haunted," said Louisa.

"Witch marks?" cried Jameson.

"Can we live here forever?" said Guinness.

"Who knows, lads? Maybe your Auntie Sylvia *will* let you live here forever!"

Louisa halted next to a chamber pot and marble washstand

underneath a beautiful tapestry. She put her hand to her breast. "It's as we always dreamed," she said. "Little Simon finding the right bride and coming home to stay. It's a fairy tale, truly."

Emma's boys were staring at her. "Hold up," said Guinness. "Is Aunt Sylvie going to *live* in this castle?"

"No," said Emma. "No, I don't think so. . . ."

"Come, lads!" said Louisa, who had walked into an adjoining bedroom. "Now this room *is* haunted. It's the ghost of a dead little girl."

"Pardon me, Louisa," queried Rich. "Are you saying this castle belongs to Sylvie's fiancé?"

"Soon it will belong to them both," said Louisa. "Isn't it wonderful? Another Lady Rampling, at last!"

2
SYLVIE

Simon had told Sylvie about Mumberton Castle, had even shown her pictures, but nothing could have prepared her for the moment the citadel came into view. It was breathtaking, an imposing structure made of pink granite. The castle held a rare portrait of King Henry IV, an Elizabethan banqueting table, and a library shaped like an octagon with eight thousand books where, in three days, their wedding would take place.

Like many privately owned castles in England, Mumberton had leaking ceilings and awkwardly sinking floors. Simon called it "the old pile," commenting drily that the medieval men who had scavenged stones from Roman fortresses to build the castle's unassailable walls could hardly have imagined that their descendants, strapped for cash, would host "Haunted Halloweens" and children's birthday parties (one hundred pounds for three hours) during which local kids could joust with foam swords, pose with owls, and eat cupcakes on the hills where once warriors had battled to the death with gruesome weaponry.

Simon's father, Mac, had been tireless in his efforts to keep Mumberton in the family: medieval cookery classes, royal boudoir photo shoots, castle-themed weddings, "Tough Mudder" races, and rock concerts. Sloe gin tastings. Clay pigeon shooting lessons. Glamping tents just past the rhododendrons. "Meet the Ghosts" tours. Croquet, the Vulture Experience, archery lessons—even "Dinner with the Family," during which, for a price, Mac would join tourists and drink too much and "spill the family tea."

"Did King Henry VIII and Anne Boleyn really honeymoon at Mumberton?"

"So goes the legend," said Simon.

"And now you can rent their room on Airbnb?"

"The Royal Love Suite," said Simon, explaining that the room required a two-night minimum stay, but a bottle of mid-level champagne and a fruit tray were included. You could also add on the "Dress Like a Tudor" package, which included velvet gowns, silk robes, and fur-lined crowns. "I think my mom would like to dress like a Tudor," said Sylvie. "If she even shows up."

"If she shows up, I'll arrange it," said Simon.

Various parts of the castle, Simon went on, had been restored to different time periods, trying to appeal to a wide range of tourists, from Tudor obsessives to medieval armory experts, to those who just wanted a commemorative tea towel or a quick coffee for the long drive back to London after a Lake District sojourn.

The house where Beatrix Potter wrote *Peter Rabbit* was nearby; a popular day tour began at Hill Top, stopped in Grasmere for gingerbread, then parked at Mumberton for the afternoon Hawk and Owl show. Mac even rented out the castle for filming, although Mumberton (said Simon) wasn't nearly as regal as Belvoir or Buckingham. "They filmed a Waitrose butter commercial in Penelope's room," he noted.

"Did you ask Penelope's mom about her coming to Miami for the summer?"

"Thisbe said no," said Simon.

"But . . ."

"I'll work on her," said Simon, "or go through the lawyers."

"OK," said Sylvie.

In a few short weeks, Sylvie and Penelope had forged a relationship that was both profound and easy. Penelope was bookish and curious, smart and so *open*. She was willing to give her heart. It made Sylvie feel a bit ashamed of her own reticence, but Penelope asked for nothing in return, and this selflessness made Sylvie want to be around the girl. Penelope had asked Sylvie, during a game of Uno, if she could stay on Hibiscus Street for the summer, and Sylvie had told her she'd love it. But Thisbe—though she left her daughter with a nanny when she traveled much of the time—had said no.

They drove up a rocky outcrop, drawing closer to the castle, and Simon pointed out the River Esk and the Irish Sea below. "The Romans chose this area because they could use the sheltered estuary as a harbor," he said. After a low bridge, they reached a street of charming stone cottages along the vast estuary of tidal flats. A few boats had tipped sideways in the mud, waiting for the ocean to return. "And here is the town of Mumberton," said Simon. "It was once part of the castle grounds. There's a huge wall around everything, but now it's a bit collapsed."

There was a pleasing, briny smell to the air, a swampy fragrance from the mud. Sylvie inhaled, staring at Mumberton Castle. "It's beautiful," she said, though she felt a shiver of apprehension. Looking at Simon, Sylvie could imagine him at age ten, his mother gone, stuck in the castle with only hawks, owls, and a vulture named Penny for company.

"Before we go in," said Simon, "I have something for you." He reached into the glove box of his Land Rover and removed a parcel with a return address of Christie's auction house in London, handing it to Sylvie. He placed his warm palm on her knee.

"If you kiss me here, will people see?" said Sylvie. They were parked in a private lot on the east side of the castle. From up close, the building was even more imposing.

"Kiss you where?" Simon leaned toward her, smiling, inching his hand to reach her thigh. Sylvie set her present on the dashboard and leaned in. His lips were soft but lingered. She opened her mouth and tasted the coffee on his tongue.

"Kiss me here," said Sylvie, exposing her wrist.

Simon kissed up the length of her arm, pulling off her cardigan to move his mouth to her breast. Sylvie's breath caught; she took his shoulders in her hands, pushed him to a seated position, and straddled him, unzipping and positioning and following his directions to get a condom from his wallet. Her large fuzzy sweater from Target covered them like a blanket as they moved together, breathing heavily. Sylvie had never orgasmed in the traditional positions and she didn't now, but as he moved her hips up and down, thrusting, she used her fingers to bring herself to climax and then they hurriedly put themselves back together.

"What if your father saw us?" said Sylvie.

"His rooms are on the other side of the castle."

"Who's behind those windows?" said Sylvie, gesturing.

"Paying guests," said Simon.

"We can say we were reenacting the moment Anne Boleyn finally slept with King Henry VIII."

"But in modern-day dress."

"A contemporary interpretation."

"Open your gift!"

"Didn't I already?"

Simon shook his head, blushing and grinning. Sylvie loved embarrassing him. Simon grabbed the present and used the Land Rover key to slice open the packaging. He handed Sylvie a white cardboard box.

In the box, Sylvie found a glassine slipcase holding a tiny

book, which was stitch-bound with silk cord. "*A Happy Pair,*" she said. "Simon, it can't be." The cover was illustrated with two rabbits—one in a suit with a blue bow tie, and one wearing a crimson cape and a white dress, holding a picnic basket. The rabbits were nestled together under an umbrella. "Illustrated by H.B.P.," whispered Sylvie. "Beatrix Potter."

"It's her first published book," said Simon.

"There's only one edition."

"Yes," said Simon. Sylvie looked at him in amazement. "Don't they remind you of us?" said Simon. Sylvie nodded, speechless. This tiny book was the most precious thing she'd ever held in her hands. Sylvie, by training, knew how to protect and preserve rare books. But she'd never had one of her own.

"I might get a case," said Sylvie. "I could bring it to school and show the kids!"

"Whatever you want," said Simon.

"A happy pair," said Sylvie.

3
CLEO

Cleo and Danny walked through a long passageway lined on either side by ten-foot-tall shrubs of rhododendrons, their flowers bursting into blooms ranging in color from pale pink and apricot to vibrant fuchsia and blue-lavender. Cleo moved quickly, eager to lie down and take some Advil, but instead of reaching a doorway to the building's interior, she found herself surrounded by higher and higher hedges, until she had completely lost her bearings. She stopped, reaching a dead end. Cleo looked around. She was trapped inside a box of yew trees with daffodils and crocuses planted at her feet.

"Where the hell are we?" she said.

"I see a sign," called Danny, who was behind her somewhere.

"What does it say?" yelled Cleo.

"You want me to read the sign?"

"Yes, Danny," said Cleo, squeezing her eyes shut with exhaustion and irritation.

"'Welcome to the Wilderness,'" read Danny. "'Mumberton Castle's wilderness is an English version of a French "bosquet." Hardly uncultivated, this wilderness spans a quarter-acre and is planted with over one million bulbs. Hornbeam hedges, yew, and elm create interstices.' In-ter-stic-es . . . I wonder what that even means?"

"Is that all?" said Cleo. "Does the sign say how to get out?"

"Sorry, let me finish: 'These winding paths, secluded benches, and pleasure gardens make the Wilderness a place where members of the court could find privacy, especially gentlemen seeking a place to entertain ladies in private.'"

"Yes . . . ?"

"That's all," said Danny. He soon appeared beside Cleo and wrapped his arms around her from behind, kissing her neck.

"Oh, hell no, Danny," she said.

"No lovemaking in the interstices?"

"Please, honey, get off of me."

"Love amongst the yew trees and daffodils?"

"I'm sorry," said Cleo. "I'm just *not* in the mood."

Danny pouted. "You used to be *fun*."

Ignoring him, Cleo said, "So the guy who took our luggage said to take a *right* at the knot garden."

"My mom had a vegetable garden," said Danny. "In Iowa."

Cleo was focused on trying to determine which direction to move in order to find a bed where she could conk out. "I feel like I'm in *The Shining*," she said.

"And I'm the crazy novelist who's going to chase you with an axe?" said Danny.

"I didn't mean that."

"Sure."

"Let's not fight," said Cleo. "We just need to find our way out of this . . . maze garden thing." She pulled out her cellphone, but couldn't connect. "Let's go back the way we came," she said.

"Good idea," said Danny.

But neither of them moved.

"Which way is the way we came?" said Danny.

"I don't know," Cleo said, despairingly. Eventually, they found a sign: WELCOME TO THE MUMBERTON CASTLE KNOT GARDEN. A KNOT GARDEN IS A SQUARE SPACE PLANTED WITH AROMATIC PLANTS AND HERBS.

"Ooooh," said Danny, distracted. "Rosemary! Look, Cleo, every herb is labeled. And what is hyssop, I wonder?" said Danny.

Cleo ignored him as he meandered behind her, *enjoying himself.* After what felt like hours, Cleo located the Visitor's Entrance of the castle, and a bellhop walked them back past the rhododendrons, took a right at the knot garden, and explained to the still-curious Danny that hyssop was an herb in the mint family, historically used medicinally for treating cancer, herpes, and ulcers.

"Hm!" replied Danny. "Well, isn't that interesting!"

Was it interesting? Was it? Was something wrong with Cleo that she did not care one iota about what hyssop was used for in biblical times? Was she depressed? Was Danny a complete moron? Was this what people meant by "going on vacation"—wandering around foreign places, suddenly fascinated by random bits of trivia?

Cleo could remember studying things in elementary school—how to churn butter, how to make beaded bracelets. She taught herself to cut out and bake Shrinky Dinks in their oven just so she could watch the way Sylvie colored them so carefully, catching her tongue between her teeth. To tame Emma's long hair, Cleo learned to make French braids from a book she found in the Missoula Public Library called *The Big Book of Braids*.

Once, a colleague of Cleo's informed her that on his vacation in Belize, he had learned how a chocolate bar was made on a "Bean-to-Bar Tour." How had her colleague transformed into a vacationer, someone who genuinely wanted to understand how a cacao bean made its way into a chocolate bar? Because Cleo was not interested—not in castle history, not in cacao. She had loved learning once—what had happened to her?

Cleo plodded up a stone spiral staircase to reach their room.

The bellhop opened the door and Danny said, "Now that's more like it!" as he surveyed their suite. Its walls were stripped back to stone and the bellhop informed them that they were *inside a turret.*

Danny and Cleo beheld a ten-foot-wide bed with velvet curtains ("quite probably the largest four-poster bed in England," said the bellhop), arrow-slit windows, and a fireplace the bellhop asked them not to use without assistance. A lush gold carpet stretched from wall to wall. The furniture was dark mahogany, intricately carved and upholstered in gold-and-rust-colored velvet. Each door featured a stone archway and a thick wooden door. The bellhop handed Danny a metal key ring with a leather circlet attached, the words *The Golden Suite* embossed on the loop in (what else?) gold.

On a coffee table near the fireplace, a plate with two square chocolate cookies was placed next to a cream-colored envelope. Danny grabbed both of the cookies and opened the note. "Breakfast is being served now," he noted, checking his iWatch.

"Oh, good," said Cleo. "I'm starving."

"Grab me a banana, will you, babe?" said Danny, diving through the velvet curtains into their massive bed. "Silk sheets!" he exalted.

Cleo stared at the empty plate where a cookie meant for her had been.

Danny had left her just crumbs.

4
EMMA

Emma wanted coffee. She *needed* coffee. After a quick change of clothes, she left her family in the Indigo Suite and walked toward the staircase. But the stairs were obstructed: A door had been shut and seemingly locked, trapping her in the labyrinthian warren of upstairs rooms. Emma tried the hallway in the opposite direction, but it, too, ended at a door that was locked from the other side.

"The women were kept, like animals," said a familiar voice behind her: Louisa Freck. Did the woman spend her days lurking around the castle hallways?

"You scared me," said Emma, hand to her chest.

"The men didn't want the women and children to get out. It was dangerous beyond the castle walls. Also, they wanted to keep tabs on them."

"Um, might I be able to get some coffee?" said Emma.

"Breakfast is being served in the Tudor Kitchens."

"Oh, OK," said Emma. She wasn't the least bit hungry, but she followed Louisa to a bookcase. Louisa slid the case aside, unlocked a wooden door with an old metal key, and opened it, revealing a dark, round hole. "Go ahead, dear," she said. "This will take you directly."

Emma peered down the hole, making out the rungs of a wooden ladder in the dim light. "Can I just take the staircase?" she said.

"It's much less direct," said Louisa.

"That's fine," said Emma. As she followed Louisa, she asked, "Do you . . . live here?"

"Oh, no!" said Louisa. "No, I'm a commoner. I reside in town, but I help Simon's father keep track of his pills and make sure everything's ready for visitors."

"I haven't met him yet."

"All will come with time," said Louisa. Nothing about what she said was creepy, yet Emma felt a chill of foreboding.

5

SYLVIE & SIMON

Welcome, one and all! We are so thankful you are here. Please find a wedding weekend schedule attached (organized by the lovely Louisa Freck, Mumberton Castle Librarian and Social Media Correspondent and a great help to us over the last few weeks). Hope you enjoy these Kendal Mint Cakes (a local treat). We can't wait to see you all and celebrate together!

Love,
Sylvie & Simon

DAY ONE

Arrival

Breakfast and light lunch served in the Tudor Kitchens

4 TO 6 P.M.

Welcome Reception, Great Lawn

Dress as a Tudor Experience and Family Portrait with Owls

DAY TWO

SIMON'S SURPRISE ADVENTURE

6 P.M.

Rehearsal Dinner, Great Hall

DAY THREE

Wedding Day!

11 A.M.

Wedding Ceremony in the Castle Library

Reception Immediately Following

6
CLEO

Cleo felt strange in the company of her little sisters. She had cooked breakfast every morning of their childhood until she left for college—Cleo had actually made pancakes *on the day* she left. She'd cleaned up afterward, then boarded a bus from Missoula to Billings, Minneapolis, Chicago, Cleveland, Newark, and finally the Manhattan Port Authority Terminal.

When her sisters were under ten, Cleo made them "egg-in-a-hole" (cutting a hole in bread, cracking an egg in, frying the combination) or blueberry muffins from the box. Donna could not be counted on for groceries, and she was usually asleep or in her room as they prepared for school. Cleo loved shopping with bills her father left her, relished placing folded napkins on the table, pouring juice in matching glasses. So much of life was impossible to solve, but breakfast was simple to fix.

All three Peacock girls were together again, but this time they sat in the middle of a kitchen that had been restored to its former Tudor glory, featuring an enormous fireplace on which a hunk of meat impaled on a metal spike was cooking and perhaps had been cooking for five hundred years. Two hapless women in flat felt hats were hand-turning the spit intently. "See the mutton fat there on the left," said one of the women. "Be sure to get that bit over the flame."

It was 10 A.M.

"Is there, like, maybe a diner? A Starbucks nearby?" said Emma. Cleo looked—really looked—at her sister. Emma's face was lined, her hair squished from sleep and tangled. She had a strange, sad complacency; all the feisty spark Cleo associated with Emma—her cigarette-smoking, wild sister—was gone. Spending so much time apart made Cleo see Emma, who had once been completely known to Cleo, as a middle-aged stranger, a mother, no longer the person she had been. This transformation made Cleo anxious: Was Cleo the wild one now, if Emma was the motherly one?

"I just want a fucking cup of coffee," said Emma. "What is even *happening* here?"

Cleo laughed, relieved to hear the old Emma inside the depleted woman sitting across from her.

"I probably should have been more involved in the wedding planning," said Sylvie. "I left it all to Louisa, and I wasn't really paying attention when she talked about breakfast in this historical kitchen or whatever it is. I think Simon said they're filming in the Great Hall. They rent the palace for movies and TV shows, like *Bridgerton.* I actually think they may be filming *Bridgerton,* or a spin-off. I've never seen it. Have any of you guys seen it?"

Sylvie was high-strung, chittering and thrumming with a nervous energy. She'd always been this way, swamped in big sweaters, face framed by the hood of her boyfriend's sweatshirt, eyes darting, seeking a way out. She'd traded high school hoodies for Simon's overlarge Barbour coat. Her hair was twisted atop her head and held with . . . was Sylvie's hair held up with two pencils? She looked like someone who belonged in a library, and only in a library, defenseless if not hidden amongst her organized shelves of books. Cleo felt a familiar panic for her weak and innocent sister, cut with the urgency and thrill of saving her.

"No, I haven't seen *Bridgerton,*" said Emma. "The boys are up later than we are, and they only want to watch YouTube videos."

"Where are they?" said Sylvie.

"They're all fast asleep. Our room is amazing! A two-room suite! I mean, did members of the royal family *actually live* in my suite? I can't believe I'm here, Syl. This is just surreal."

Cleo was also bowled over but tried to play it cool. "Who decided the rooms?"

"We chose them together," said Sylvie. "Simon and I. It's funny, actually, we went out to dinner in Little Havana, and he drew the layout of Mumberton on a napkin. We made little napkin people of all of you and placed you all over the castle, imagining this day. And now it's here!"

"That's so romantic," said Emma.

"Kind of weird," muttered Cleo.

"Cleo . . ." said Emma in a warning tone. Cleo and Emma had discussed being supportive of Sylvie no matter what happened with Simon. They were both hoping the secret they kept from Sylvie could remain deeply buried, allowing Sylvie to retain a bit of innocence, some hope that love and honesty were possible. Emma and Cleo both feared, too, that if Sylvie discovered the truth, she'd stop speaking to them entirely. Emma had seemed unfazed by the sketchy origins of Simon's fortune, but then Emma had always been optimistic.

"What? Napkin people? That's not a bit odd?" asked Cleo.

As if summoned by the word *odd,* three men in Tudor costumes entered the room carrying jugs. "Who might fancy a bit of mead?" said one.

"Is there any coffee?" said Emma. She rubbed her face with both of her palms.

"Ah, no, milady," said a man wearing a voluminous coat over a small, fitted doublet jacket and hose pants tied to the jacket with string points to keep them up. He also sported a wool hat that looked like a giant beige beret and a leather codpiece. "We have ale, as the Tudors did, or a hot cup of posset!"

"Posset," chimed in one of the meat-roasting women, "is milk curdled with ale and spiced with star anise."

"And sometimes cinnamon or cloves," added the woman on the other side of the spit. Her face was crimson and she also wore a wool coat.

"I'm sorry, but no," said Cleo.

"This is SO FUN," said Emma anxiously. Cleo's heart ached for Emma, their mother's apologist, a steadfast devotee of ignorant, toxic positivity. Jesus, Cleo was exhausted. Hiding painful truths was exhausting, and so was remaining alert for danger. She didn't want to be negative! It wasn't fun to be the naysayer! Yet—alas—it was her fate, her role, her destiny.

"Mom's not coming, I bet," said Sylvie. "I know she won't be here for my wedding. She wasn't there for *A Chorus Line,* and she won't be here for my wedding."

"Sylvie, *A Chorus Line* was eighth grade," said Cleo, trying to be gentle.

"Yes," said Sylvie, tucking a strand of red hair behind her ear. "And I had a solo, 'What I Did for Love.' And she never came."

"I'm sorry," said Cleo, touching her sister's hand.

"You weren't there either," said Sylvie. "None of you were there. And dad would have come but he had died."

"We're here now," said Emma.

There was a silence. Cleo wished she could open up to her sisters—if not them, who? *We always fail one another,* thought Cleo. She wanted to just *talk,* the way she had as a kid, just start speaking and let it all spill out. . . . *I don't love Danny but I'm scared to be alone. What if breaking up with Danny means I'll never be a mother? Who am I supposed to save if you two don't need me anymore?*

It had once been as easy as breathing to communicate with her sisters. In their shared bedroom, they had never stopped talking—rivers of thoughts and responses and love.

But now Cleo was struck mute.

You can always tell a kid who raised herself. She enters a room and scans—first thing—for the escape route. She watches adults a bit too closely, second-guessing every move. Her stomach clenches around tangled desires: wanting to please, wanting to be invisible, wanting to be seen. She is sure of only one thing: There is nowhere she is safe.

Sylvie was an adult, but as she bent her head to try the posset, Cleo saw her at age six, hunched over, reading picture books in their childhood living room. Sylvie's terrified eyes snapping to the doorway when someone entered—was it their mother? Was she drunk or angry . . . or both? Would she cry or punish them for an impossible-to-guess mistake? Might she possibly be . . . kind?

While Sylvie had been clearly scared of Donna, Emma had seemed more besotted than afraid. Even before defiant Cleo had left for college, Emma had become Donna's right-hand accomplice and confidante.

Emma and Donna would lounge on the couch, whispering and giggling. Cleo was excluded when Donna applied makeup at the ornate, glass-topped table in the master bedroom, but Emma was allowed to help Donna select which perfume she'd wear for their private "stargazing" walks. Emma's closeness to their mother filled Cleo with envy, longing, and eventually rage.

Years later, Emma told her sister the terrible truth about Donna's affair—that "stargazing" had actually meant that Emma was forced to cover her ears to keep from hearing their mother fucking a neighbor—and fucking over her husband and the girls' father. If only she had known, Cleo would have fought for Emma and put a stop to the cruel nights in the dark. But Cleo hadn't known.

* * *

Simon entered the medieval kitchen. Simon was *built,* maybe even more muscular than Danny. Cleo had to admit that Simon was very attractive. Too bad his cabled cashmere sweater and expensive haircut were all bought with dirty money.

Sylvie stood to greet her fiancé, shoulders relaxing, the strain on her face erased. Cleo hadn't seen her baby sister like this in a long time—since the days before Alexander's death had crushed her like a crystal vase thrown out of a New York skyscraper to the pavement below.

Cleo didn't want to tell Sylvie who Alexander had really been.

She didn't want to expose the source of Simon's wealth.

But she did relish the idea of being the savior, of holding Sylvie's hand as they departed Mumberton in a hastily summoned Uber, Sylvie wrecked but nestled close to her big sister. Did Uber even come to Mumberton? Cleo would have to check on that.

"Simon," said Sylvie. She brought his hand to her cheek.

Emma leapt up to hug Simon. He seemed flustered but happy, definitely not used to sisterly attention. Both Simon and Sylvie were glowing. "My boys are still asleep," said Emma, a sparkle in her eyes as she spoke the words "my boys." And perhaps emboldened by the thought of her "boys," Emma said, "Is there any way I could get some coffee?"

"Of course. There's a café by the barns, and also a more formal dining room with gorgeous breakfasts, pancakes and such," said Simon.

"Ah, Simon!" said a man in full velvet Tudor getup—fur-lined hat, deep blue velvet gown, a shawl of dead animal carcasses around his shoulders, fastened with chains made of silver medallions. "Honor to have you here, mate," said the man.

Simon grinned, embracing him, and clapping him on the back. "This is incredible," he said. "You've done great work, Felix."

"Completely true to the time period," said Felix. "You're about to have the same meal Henry VIII would have had for breakfast! Minced suet pies, spiced with grains of paradise, raisins, and dried prunes. Mutton haunch being roasted right there on the spit, as you can see."

"What year was coffee invented?" whispered Emma.

"Cup of posset, my friend? It's not so rancid once your taste buds adjust."

"Thanks so much, mate," said Simon. "But I need to get these American ladies some drip coffee. Sylvie and sisters, shall we?"

"Aw, Simon," said Felix. "I lit that fire myself this morning with a Tudor tinderbox, flint and steel and a bit of char, then made myself a flame with wood shavings."

"As I said, I'm sorry," said Simon. "Follow me, Peacock women."

"Would you like to see me boil water in a cauldron?"

"Incredible work, mate," said Simon. "We'll be back for the full experience."

Cleo was impressed by Simon's take-charge demeanor. Even she—who read from the Codependent No More app every morning—would have made herself sit through a historical breakfast to appease the staff. She *hated* letting people down. Yet here was the fur-hatted Felix shrugging, and Simon leading the way out of the Tudor kitchen.

They did seem to be filming a period TV show in the Great Hall of Mumberton Castle. A woman and man in gorgeous costumes were helping themselves to a buffet table of fruit and pastries. The woman, wearing a foot-high, elaborate wig, lit a cigarette, and a guy in cargo pants with headphones around his neck rushed to make her put it out. "Oh, *come on,*" said the actress.

They walked past a group of tech people sipping from Styrofoam cups and peering into a camera. The man in period costume walked toward the main door and Cleo realized with a start that he was famous: She'd last seen him in an action movie and fantasized about him for months afterward. His name was Phil Rosen; Cleo checked out his tight-fitting velvet pants appreciatively.

Past horse stables, a coffee shop had been conjured out of a barn. Behind the counter, a young woman stood between a coffee urn and an espresso machine. "There's a patio out back," said Simon. "What would you all like?"

"Just coffee," breathed Emma. "God, thank you. And can I get it to go?"

"Americano with two shots and oat milk," said Cleo.

"Plain coffee, thanks, sweetheart," said Sylvie. "I need a shower and to sleep for a long time."

"Head over to the patio," said Simon. "I'll bring everything over with some scones and fruit."

"Perfect," said Sylvie. She pressed her lips to his, lingered a bit. The chemistry between them was palpable. "I can't believe you're all here," said Sylvie, when she came up for air.

"I miss you guys so much," said Emma, growing teary.

"Yeah," said Sylvie. She paused, seeming nervous. She asked, "Why don't you guys ever answer when I call you?"

Emma looked at Cleo. Cleo gave her a look that said, *Zip it; this is NOT the time to tell her about Alexander.* Emma sighed, raised an eyebrow, responding: *If not now, then when?*

About Alexander: A decade and six months before, Alexander had relapsed. He'd been arrested for drunk and disorderly behavior, and had called Cleo for legal advice. Cleo had insisted Alexander tell Sylvie about his relapse and arrest, but he'd refused.

Cleo could still replay her final conversation with Sylvie's husband to the syllable. Alexander had texted Cleo to set up a time to chat, and she'd agreed. Apparently, he'd told Sylvie he needed *some air.* He'd started their shared car and gone for a drive, calling Cleo as he merged onto Route 1 going north.

"Of course I can help you," Cleo had said. "But you need to tell Syl. We can work on this together."

"Are you fucking kidding me?" Alexander had said. "Cleo, it was a dumb mistake. Please. She'll leave me if she knows I'm drinking. If she knows I was drinking. Just that once."

"You need to tell Sylvie and then I can help you," said Cleo.

They found out later that Alexander was passing Magic Hands Marine Detailing when he lost control of his car. A boat cleaner named Elijah, who was at work late detailing a Wellcraft 242, called the ambulance when he saw Alexander's accident.

"Jesus, Cleo!" Alexander had said, before there was an awful sound, the worst sound, a shrieking of metal-on-metal.

"Alexander?" Cleo had said. "Alexander? Hello?"

"Don't tell her," Alexander had said. "Please don't tell her, Cleo!" And then he started screaming.

Alexander was consumed by flames, and it was Cleo's fault. She tried to avoid feeling her disgrace by burying herself in work and keeping her distance from Sylvie. Instinctually, she believed that her work exposing darkness was building a path away from shame. She just kept moving, researching, calling, typing . . . looking for people who needed her, so she could somehow earn another moment away from herself.

They settled at a patio table. Sylvie said, "I text you guys, and I know you're busy . . . but no one never calls me back."

"We're just busy," said Cleo. She could hear Alexander: *Don't tell her! Please don't tell her, Cleo!* And then Alexander had started screaming.

"It's nothing personal," Cleo said, wanly.

"Oh," said Sylvie, looking down.

Cleo knew that Sylvie knew she was lying.

7
EMMA

-$45,034.81

Emma felt sad after breakfast with her sisters. She walked inside the castle, her mind troubled. Was it possible that *Emma,* with all her debt and humiliation—that she was the happiest one of the Peacock girls? Cleo seemed brittle, hollowed out. Her Botoxed face was a marvel—Cleo didn't have a line on her visage and her severe haircut was very flattering against her chiseled cheekbones—but she didn't seem confident, just tense. It was hard not to take her radiant anger personally, but Emma tried to tell herself that was just how New Yorkers *were*—strident and opinionated—and maybe that could come off as . . . mean.

Had Cleo always been this way?

She reminded Emma of Donna, which was horrible.

Sylvie was shining, her adoration of her fiancé obvious. Emma wished Simon weren't a felon, or whatever Cleo had found out about him in the Private Investigator game she was play-acting with her best friend, Isaac.

Emma was lost in thought as she climbed the creepy staircase lined with nymphs and horse paintings. Upstairs, she was disoriented, wandering dim hallways for a while until she found the

Indigo Suite, slipped in, and shut the door behind her, wishing there were an interior lock. Why did these doors only lock from the outside? Emma shivered. She sat on a regal chair opposite the four-poster bed.

"I'm naked under here," whispered Rich from behind the velvet curtains.

Emma laughed. "I thought you were asleep," she whispered back.

"Join me under the royal coverlet, wife," said Rich.

"Is that how the Tudors spoke?" said Emma.

"Come here, you wench," said Rich.

Emma slipped under the covers, feeling giddy. Rich reached for her and she slid out of her clothes. Rich, her love, kissing her chest, her stomach, going down farther with his warm mouth.

"Oh," said Emma, reclining on silk sheets.

"Shhh," said Rich.

Emma's thoughts—her whirring tabulations, self-castigations, lists of kid-related things to do and worry about—slowly dissipated. She was a body delighted, her mind languorous as she melted toward the blissful movements of her husband's tongue.

8
SYLVIE

"I see what you mean about your sisters," said Simon, as they walked through the castle gardens on the way to their "Honeymoon Cottage."

"What?" said Sylvie, though she was utterly rattled—both Emma and Cleo had whispered that they needed to speak with her later: Emma saying, *Syl, I have a giant favor to ask you—in private;* and Cleo saying, *We need to talk as soon as possible—without Simon around.*

They passed the entrance to a maze of yew hedges and the knot garden, which was planted with vegetables and herbs. Simon looked at Sylvie with mild concern, then seemed to understand she couldn't voice negative thoughts about her sisters; not yet, maybe not ever. Sylvie craved being as close to her sisters as they'd been when they were kids. She ached for that connection, yet it seemed to have vanished.

"I always wanted siblings," said Simon, understanding her and, as always, turning the focus to himself so she could reflect until she was ready to share her thoughts. Simon paused by his mother's rhododendrons. "I prayed every night for a long-lost sister to rise from the moors," he said, waving his arm toward the hills beyond the flowering bushes.

"A sister? Not a brother?"

"No, I had enough male aggression in my life," said Simon. Sylvie waited for him to elaborate, but he did not. He had mentioned that his father could be hard on him. Sylvie didn't mind giving him space and time to tell more . . . or not.

"I wanted a big sister and a little sister. But now I can see that real sisters are more fraught than the ones I imagined as a kid."

"I love them so much," said Sylvie mournfully.

"Yes," said Simon, kissing her. "And I love you." Sylvie noticed that he didn't walk back his comment about sisters being "fraught." For some reason, Sylvie needed to complain about her sisters, but she couldn't bear Simon bestowing anything other than praise.

"Nobody's perfect," she said, defensively.

"What do you mean by that?" said Simon, his voice sounding alarmed. Sylvie's radar sensed that something was up; she swiftly changed gears to avoid conflict.

"I just mean I'm glad my sisters are here. I wish I knew how to make it easier between us. I *know* they love me so much. We never . . . I guess we just never had a chance to be normal around each other. Mom used to pit us against each other. She got off on us fighting or something; it made her the star, I guess. I don't know."

"That must have been hard," said Simon.

"Yeah, but then sometimes . . . it was perfect. We had a game we played called 'Once Upon a Time.'"

"Once Upon a Time?"

"We played it when we were supposed to be asleep . . . it was telling fairy tales, but about each other. Like, 'Cleo, once upon a time you'll be a famous movie star living in a penthouse on Broadway. And . . . Emma, you'll open a perfume shop and Cleo will bring all her famous friends to shop at Peacock Perfumery.'"

"What was *your* Once Upon a Time?"

"Oh, I'd be an astronaut. Or a writer. Always something introverted."

Simon laughed. "What about getting married in a castle?"

"That is the *ultimate* Once Upon a Time," said Sylvie, squeezing Simon's hand. She could remember playing the game in the rocks behind their house, or in their shared bedroom. The murmur of her sister's voices, always soothing, giving one another happy ever afters. They knew, even then, that their best years would happen once they grew up. What Sylvie could never have predicted is that they'd become adults, but not together.

"I'll show you around our secret clubhouse," said Simon, "and then you can rest." Sylvie stopped, closed her eyes, and inhaled, leaning against him. When she opened her eyes, she saw an enormous bird fly overhead, tea-colored wings outstretched. The morning sun was warm on her shoulders.

The garden path Simon had chosen led to a stone building that arched across the main entrance to Mumberton Castle. Wide wooden doors could be closed to seal off the archway. On either side of the central arch were towers, each topped with battlements. Sylvie took in the meticulous stonework and Tudor-style windows.

"The gatekeeper once lived here," said Simon. "Keeping an eye on the drawbridge that was the only way into Mumberton. See? He could shoot through those battlement indentations without being exposed."

"Whoa," said Sylvie.

"I can stay in my old room tomorrow night, if we believe in not seeing the bride the morning of the wedding. . . ."

"We do," said Sylvie. "Maybe Flo and my sisters can stay over here? A slumber party?"

"Of course; I'll have it set up."

"My hen party in my nest," said Sylvie. In her own ears, she sounded a bit drunk—drunk on love.

Simon led the way inside the gatehouse cum Honeymoon Cottage, stepping into a room with a vaulted ceiling and stone arches. Sun was sliced into geometric shapes as it fell through casement windows. A fireplace was set with a perfect pile of kindling and four logs—even the *logs* were charming. Opposite the fireplace was a set of Eames chairs like the ones in Simon's Miami house, and the room had an ivory-colored shag rug, antique tapestries on the walls, and elegant standing reading lamps next to each Eames.

"I'm never leaving this room ever," said Sylvie. She moved to the bookcase, which housed what must have been Simon's own books mixed in with older, leather-bound nonfiction. Sylvie smiled to see some English major standards, in addition to well-read copies of mysteries, thrillers, and (surprising Sylvie) a wide range of short story collections. On a side table she saw a book open and resting on its face. "*Possession?*"

"Have you read it?"

"It's about two academics studying the letters of long-dead poets, right?"

"You cannot beat a timeless love story," said Simon as they moved through the sliding glass doors.

"Agreed. I love epistolary novels. I wish more people wrote letters."

"Noted," said Simon. "What's your favorite point of view for a novel, do you think?"

"I'm really just in it for the story," she said. "But revolving, limited third."

"I like the first person," said Simon. "More immediate. And always, first person inside the mind of the killer if there's a killer."

"Of course," said Sylvie.

"You know when there's a prologue of a killer and he kills someone and you don't know who and then it's everyone arriving at the creepy island?"

"You really do love the dark stuff, don't you?"

"Don't you?"

Sylvie laughed. "Yes," she said. "But I also love the sparse, literary ones, and the Updike, and remember the Kingsolver about the foster kid?"

"*Demon Copperhead,*" said Simon, sighing. "Talk about a first-person *voice.*"

"I need to go to sleep," said Sylvie.

"Oh, Syl, I'm so sorry! You must be knackered."

"I am," said Sylvie. "I am knackered. We don't have as good a word in American-ese."

"Come, you," said Simon. He led Sylvie up a narrow spiral staircase with a few nooks and doorways visible as they climbed. "Those rooms are used for storage now; all my childhood junk, but we could make them anything," said Simon. "Hidey holes or . . ." He didn't say "a nursery," and Sylvie was glad.

"Does Penelope just love this place?" said Sylvie. "And . . . are some of the books . . . Thisbe's?"

"No, this was rubble before the divorce," said Simon. "I renovated it in the depths of ex-husbandly despair. After I got . . . money."

Sylvie paused. "Do you want to talk about the money?" she asked.

"I don't know."

"Well, you can," said Sylvie. "We've all made mistakes, Simon."

"Have you?"

Sylvie considered the question. "I feel more as if mistakes have made *me.*"

They reached what had once been the guard chamber, Simon explained, above the entrance arch. Its window offered a panoramic view of rolling hills in all directions, the river, and the castle grounds. "Maybe," said Simon, as Sylvie took in the view and leaned back against him, "I was making this nest for you."

Sylvie tried to stay in this British wonderland of blooming flowers and green lawns and quiet spaces. Simon walked ahead of her, leading her down another staircase into the room on the opposite side of the archway, saying she had to see the kitchen, the bathtubs, the small patio. The second side of the gatekeeper's house held another den with stone walls and Tudor windows, but it had been furnished in ocean tones: a beautiful, sage-green sectional couch with pillows patterned with lemons, warm wooden side tables, and floor-to-ceiling bookshelves. The shelves were empty.

"Do you see the wall art?" said Simon.

A large canvas opposite the bookcase was impressionistic, but Sylvie recognized her mountains right away. "The Bitterroots," she said, naming the range she'd grown up in. "I don't know what to say."

"I mean, who knows, I got it off the internet, but I wanted to make you feel at home. Bigcanvas.com; I was impressed!"

"Come here," said Sylvie. She hooked his belt and pulled him toward her. They kissed and she felt the length of his body against her. She placed her hands on either side of his face and kissed him more and more deeply.

"Syl," Simon groaned. He pulled himself away. "Wait, I want you to see what I got for you."

"I know what you've got for me," said Sylvie, trying for sultry. She was aroused, hot, wanted her body to be devoured instead of her mind running away. Sylvie reluctantly stopped kissing Simon and turned her attention to a pile of books on the coffee table. She picked up a fragile copy of *The Tale of Mrs. Tiggy-Winkle*. "My favorite Beatrix Potter," she said, touching the drawing of an adorable hedgehog on the cover.

"Cleo and Emma used to read them to you, right? Beatrix was a strange one. She and her brother boiled dead animals to see how their bones fit together."

"Oh my," said Sylvie.

"I also got Sylvia Plath's *The Bed Book.* Not the one your dad left a note in, of course, but a copy, anyway. *The Bed Book* is the best book ever written, Sylvie."

"Isn't it? With the snack bed that gives you snacks like cake and chicken? And the bed on the back of an elephant? The jet-propelled bed, and the submarine bed . . ."

"So that's the start of your library, but you've got a lot of work to do over here."

"This is my library?" said Sylvie. "This is for me?"

The bed of a couch, the books, and Simon kissing her again . . . It felt as if her new world were a great sun, bright but too hot. Simon: his warmth, his smell of woodsmoke and soap. She wanted all of this—so much—but she felt herself leaving.

"Sylvie?" said Simon.

He knew, of course he knew. From above her body, she watched her body and thought, *That person is very lucky*.

"Sylvie?" asked Simon.

"I need to sleep."

Simon took her by the hand and led her into a sunny bedroom that did not look unlike the Escape Room in her mind. She got into the bed and he lay beside her, curled around her, in the cool space.

So this was love.

PART FIVE

WHAT I DID FOR LOVE

1
CLEO

The sun over the Eskdale Valley painted the fells in lemony light. In front of Cleo, a magnificent goshawk was perched on the glove of a ruddy-faced man named Angus. The bird was enormous and terrifying, able to tear apart its prey with its razor-sharp feet and beak, according to Angus. "She loves hare and grouse," Angus explained, "but she'll eat anything she can get in her mouth, really. She could eat my face if she wanted to."

There was an uncomfortable murmur amongst the attendees who had risen early to attend the lecture titled "Large Birds of Prey: Meet Barbara the Goshawk." After flaky and delectable black currant scones in the barnyard coffee shop, Cleo's sisters had headed back to their rooms, but Cleo didn't want to deal with Danny. Instead, she headed to the aviary to learn about birds.

Isaac would be impressed. He loved wandering around Central Park with his ridiculously dorky binoculars trying to spot an owl or a falcon, but happy to see a chickadee. Cleo met Isaac in the park with bagels sometimes but departed when he went on and on about avian topics. Now, she tried to pay attention.

"Right now, Barbara's all dressed up. As you can see, she's got leather anklets with jesses, which are like tiny leashes," explained Angus, pointing to the bird's talons. Angus was cute, thought Cleo, with his long mullet hairdo and tight-fitting jeans. Danny had originally had the same outdoorsy appeal as Angus, but then he had stopped . . . spending time outdoors.

"Babs's got her bells on. When she flies off, her job is to take a pheasant down, and if she does so, we'll need to find her. Hence, Babs's bells." He looked at his audience, smirking at his joke. The three other attendees to his lecture seemed extremely serious, nodding intently. Cleo laughed, finding Angus's clear love of his bird enchanting.

"I've got my gauntlet here—that's my glove so she doesn't tear up my arm—and Babs is wearing her leather chaps, so animals like pesky squirrels don't tear her up. I'll remove her tail guard, but we'll keep her cloth hood on."

"Is that hood cinched around her neck?" said a woman with an American accent. "Seems cruel to me!"

"Yes, we keep it on so Babs won't get overstimulated. The nerve pathways from her eyes and ears go to the motor neurons that control her muscles with much less rational thinking than we have. Babs here reacts so fast, she can't consider whether she's making the right move. She needs a break from herself, hence the hood."

The American woman seemed somewhat appeased. Cleo thought about sensory deprivation tanks that she had read about on *Elite Daily*. Maybe that was what she needed in her life: a hood once in a while, a break from herself.

"So I'll remove her hood—it's about time to let her find some breakfast," said Angus.

Cleo felt a quickening in her chest, excited to see the powerful bird in action. "Wait a minute," said the American woman, furrowing her brow. "What if she doesn't come back?"

"Babs loves him," said a boy at her side. "She'll come back!"

"Has nothing to do with love," said Angus. "Might seem that

way, but that's wrong. I feed and protect her. Keep her hungry so she'll return to eat. We weigh her every day. If she's too fat and happy, we don't let her fly. Wait til she's hungry again."

Cleo sighed, realizing that her relationship with Danny was about two hungry people returning to each other for meager sustenance. Who could Danny be if he felt satiated? And for that matter, what would Cleo dream of if she didn't have to think of Danny and his problems? If she had a partner who took care of himself, had his own interests and work that had nothing to do with her?

Someone like . . . Isaac.

"Let a hawk fly when she was above weight," said Angus. "Only once."

"What happened?" asked Cleo.

"What do you think?" said Angus. "That bird never came back."

2
EMMA

-$45,414.52

Emma was falling for Mumberton Castle. After she and Rich made love behind the velvet curtains of their four-poster royal bed (using pillows in silk pillowcases to slide under Emma's body and achieve just the right slippery, perfect angles, oh my goodness), Emma had sauntered to their en suite bathroom. Some genius had decided to skip the historical accuracy in the bathroom renovation, installing a walk-in shower for two *and* a giant soaking tub with views over the garden. There was a tray across the tub with room for a cup of tea.

Emma had read about medieval fragrances. As she donned her plush robe with the castle insignia and ran a hot tub, she imagined a "Make Your Own Bath Salts" set for the Indigo Suite. She'd include perfume vials from medieval days, like "four thieves vinegar"—made from rosemary, wormwood, mint, and camphor—and nutmeg, pepper, amber, sandalwood, and myrrh. (The latter scents, she'd read, were introduced when trading routes opened up. Emma found this fascinating.)

Sinking into a bath and adding salts she had made and brought along—lavender, lemon, a touch of marjoram—Emma imagined living at the castle, walking her boys to school wearing a dowdy outfit like Louisa Freck, then hiking the fells, maybe with a corgi like Queen Elizabeth, may she rest in peace. Emma had thought she was a Fergie type, even a Diana, but now she realized, stepping gingerly into her sweet-smelling tub, that she had been hiding her inner Queen Elizabeth.

Emma stretched out. She'd promised the boys they could visit the aviary as soon as they woke up. From her perfect bath, Emma could see a hawk in flight, so elegant against the cloudless blue sky. Post orgasms, Emma's body was unspooled, relaxed. What a blessing: to have a moment without worry. In this regal place, it seemed impossible that she had spent her husband's hard-earned savings on Sweet Nothings vibrators and panty sets. She felt safe here in the castle—which was its purpose, after all.

Simon seemed kind and he was gorgeous. Emma knew that Cleo had dug up incontrovertible dirt on him, but Emma wasn't outraged. How could she judge Simon's desire for financial security? She'd be happy—more than happy—to pay off Sweet Nothings with corrupt money and start again.

There was a tap at the bathroom door. "Your boys are awake and hungry," said Rich.

"I'm in Heaven," said Emma.

"No worries, I'll handle them," said Rich. "Take your time."

Emma sighed and sank even deeper into her bath.

"Moooom," said Jameson through the bathroom door. "Come with us to meet the birds!"

Emma started to rise, to please Jameson, to do what he wanted her to do. But she stopped herself, hovering halfway out of the water, which was still hot. *You've had your time,* she told herself. *Now go and be the best mom.*

Instead, she lowered herself back into the water, even turned on the tap for a bit more warmth. What was happening to her? She felt nervous and thrilled.

"Moooooooom?" whined Jameson. Emma remembered trying to get her mother to notice her. Emma knew the pain of feeling unseen. It had hurt so much that she'd been willing to do anything to get her mother's attention. Even being an accessory to her mother betraying her father was better than being invisible.

"Please, Mom," said Jameson, knocking at the door. "Come out, Mom."

Emma remembered a book the boys had loved called *Five Minutes' Peace,* in which an elephant mother tries to escape her elephant kids by hiding in a bubble bath. (She fails—they follow her into the bathroom and even get into her tub.) Emma had tried to be like the mom in the book, sighing and laughing while ignoring her needs. Emma remembered her mother brushing her off, saying she'd show up and then never showing up. Had Donna ever intended to come to Sylvie's wedding?

"Please?" said Jameson.

But Emma was not Donna. She was kind and warm and her boys knew she loved them. She could take a few minutes for herself; she deserved it, and she wanted to be calm and happy for her family. Emma realized she'd been overcompensating for a long time.

"Honey, I am staying in my bubble bath," said Emma. It was the most she'd stood up for herself in a very long time. She braced herself for Jameson to start crying, crumpling to the floor. She hated hurting her son. She waited. The bath was so wonderful.

From outside the bathroom door, she heard a sigh.

"OK, queen," said Jameson.

3
SYLVIE

In the Gatekeeper's Cottage, Sylvie dreamed of Alexander on the day he got sober. He'd returned to Hibiscus Street after his first Alcoholics Anonymous meeting, his dark, curly hair still a bit mashed from spending the previous night in jail. "I promise I'll never drink again," he'd said, clutching a white poker chip, which he said represented the desire to change. He had cried, holding Sylvie on their brown couch, his big body around her, his hands in her hair. "I'm so sorry I fucked up," he said. "Please don't leave me."

"I will never leave you," said Sylvie. "But we're done with the drinking, OK? This is the end."

"I promise," said Alexander. And he had kept his word, and his job as choir director at Coconut Grove Elementary. They had adopted Willie and made sober friends who invited them to raucous dinner parties full of laughter and stories of regret, the nights precious because many of their sober friends had lost so much.

By the time Alexander died, he had four bronze coins, each earned from a year of sobriety.

"I will not leave," Sylvie said.

"You're talking in your sleep, my Sylvie," said Simon.

Oh. She was in England. Alexander was not holding her on their brown couch. Alexander was dead.

Sylvie did not open her eyes. She knew it was wrong but she wanted to go back to her dreams. Alexander! Christ, she missed him. Almost every morning, before she got out of bed, she wished she could go back in time to one hour before he said, "I need some air." Tears gathered behind her eyes as she imagined grabbing him and making him sit down. How could he be gone?

Simon opened the window shades and afternoon light poured into the room.

Sylvie rolled to her side. Her pain still felt so raw. Her friends told her to move on, but honestly she didn't *want* to move on. She wanted to go back.

Alexander had found the strength to stay sober—that was his end of the bargain. And even though he was buried in a graveyard in Miami, Sylvie did not want him to be dead. She wanted to feel Alexander next to her, even just for a moment when she was half-asleep. She missed Alexander and she felt she owed him. She could—at least—have his ghost.

Sylvie sat up. Simon watched her. He waited for her to speak, and when she didn't say a word, he went to her side. "Is it your mom?" he asked.

Sylvie shook her head. "Alexander," she admitted. "I miss him. I miss . . . who I used to be. I was so hopeful when I was young."

Simon exhaled. "I miss who I used to be, as well," he said.

Sylvie nodded.

"We're supposed to think it's better, that this love means we weren't meant to have the past ones," said Simon. "But you and I know."

Sylvie nodded. "Do you still love Thisbe?" she asked.

"I miss loving Thisbe," he said. "I miss who I was before I knew what she would do."

Sylvie felt her disassociation coming on—the room filled with imaginary smoke. She kissed Simon, pulling him into bed hungrily. Sylvie wanted roughness; she wanted to feel something physical—something that was solid and tangible. Simon's breath, his hardness inside her, where she was wet. Sylvie pulled him inside her, arching her back, her fingernails scratching his skin, her legs wrapped around his back. Simon moved slowly and then forcefully, making a guttural sound. Her heart was beating so hard she felt it in her temples. It was so much. She was crying. Her blood was hot. His lips on her.

Sylvie did not leave; she stayed in her body.

4
CLEO

"I have a question," said Danny, standing naked in the middle of their royal bedchambers.

"What is it?" said Cleo, applying lipstick to match her Hervé Léger bandage dress. She'd been unsure about the bright pink dress against her red hair but her personal shopper had insisted and Cleo was glad. "Have you seen my sandals?" she asked, finishing her makeup.

"Should I get an old-timey typewriter? Someone typed this Welcome Reception Menu card on an actual typewriter."

"Can you put on some clothes?" said Cleo. Realizing she sounded mean and schoolmarmish, she added, "You're too tempting."

"Oh! Didn't mean to tempt you," said Danny, thrilled. He approached Cleo and hugged her close.

Cleo kissed him, leaving bright pink lipstick on his mouth. She'd once craved his body, his skilled hands and lips. But annoyance with Danny had extinguished her lust. He wanted more from her than she could give, and it was tiring to fail him, to wish she was sure about him, to love him less than he loved her.

Cleo took the cream-colored card. "Damson gin made with local plums and Cumberland Ale," she said, reading aloud.

"And mini Cumberland meat pies," said Danny. "How mini are we talking? How big is a full-sized meat pie?"

"Yum, though, Grasmere gingerbread. And oooh, caramel sticky toffee pudding!"

"Pudding at a cocktail party?" said Danny.

"Sounds messy," said Cleo.

"I'm on a sugar fast, anyway," said Danny, admiring his biceps in the bathroom mirror. Cleo touched his chest. He was perfect. His body was perfect. His adoration of her was perfect. His desire to have a family with her was perfect. So why had she just popped a birth control pill and swallowed it down with pink rose lemonade from the minibar?

"I need to shower," said Danny. "Wait til you see my welcome reception outfit, babe." He reached into his leather dopp kit and began removing tinctures and toiletries and skin-care serums. "By the way, you look amazing," said Danny, looking at his own face and not at Cleo.

"Thanks," said Cleo. "Do you mind if I head down?"

Anger flickered on his face, but he hid it within seconds. "Of course not," he said. He hesitated before turning on the shower. "Should we have a quickie?" he said. "First fuck in the UK?"

"Maybe later," said Cleo.

In retrospect, she would wish she had taken advantage. She would never have sex with Danny again.

5
EMMA

-$47,805.15

“Jesus,” said Rich, “I keep getting calls from the Bank of Missoula. How do I turn off data? I am *on vacation in a castle.*”

“Must be some mistake,” murmured Emma. She could only imagine what checks were bouncing while they lounged around in swanky robes. There was the mortgage check, the various credit card minimum payments, that damn dentist. . . .

When she had first started with Sweet Nothings, three years before, Cassidy Rose had helped Emma open credit cards in Guinness’s and Jameson’s names to buy the Start-Up Package. When Emma had filled out all the forms, Cassidy Rose held her hands and they sent an intention to the universe together. “OK, picture it,” said Cassidy Rose. “Picture what you want.” Emma was supposed to close her eyes but kept them open, looking at Cassidy Rose’s face, thinking, *What I want is to be like you.*

At that point, Emma believed she would never touch Rich’s retirement account. Three years later, she had cleaned out fifteen years of savings. After the Big O Package, there was the Next Level class series, the software required to take orders, the Life Xtra Seminars, the monthly “Oh Oh Special” you needed to buy, and Exclusive Fuchsia Level fees. Now everything was gone, including the money she'd borrowed from a few mom friends and the fortune she'd taken from Cleo.

Emma was trying very, very hard to believe that her sex toy ship could still come in. Manifesting success, Cassidy Rose and the Sweet Nothings seminars had taught her, was the only way to attain greatness. She had to *believe to achieve.*

Emma closed her eyes and tried to do as she'd been trained, imagining the *tactile details,* making her dreams *reality:* When they got home, she would recruit some new ambassadors and the money would flow. Doubting this vision, said Cassidy Rose, was Emma's problem. Emma imagined the bank pen in her hand—plastic, warm—imagined filling out a deposit slip. She manifested walking out of the red brick Bank of Missoula, feeling like a Boss Babe.

"Should we get ready for the picnic thing?" said Rich.

"Rich?"

"Yes?"

Suddenly, Emma wanted to tell her husband about her desires, her debt, her worries that she was in big, big trouble. He looked right at her. How could she say, "Everything is gone"?

"What?" said Rich. There was an edge to his voice. Some part of him must have known the truth. She had tried to be a serene Montana mom. For *fifteen years* she had tried. But something about watching Sylvie grasp for happiness . . . it made Emma's secrets unbearable.

This feeling was familiar—it was the way she'd felt before she'd met Rich. Holding her mother's disgusting secrets had broken her, worn her out. One night, she'd been alone with her father, eating meatloaf Cleo had made. Emma could remember the sound of their ticking kitchen clock. (The same clock now ticked in her own kitchen.)

Something in her overflowed that night, and she spoke. "Dad," she said.

"Em?" he looked up from the meatloaf. His light blue eyes were so kind and trusting. She didn't want to cause him pain but couldn't stop herself.

"Mom is . . . Mom is having . . ." Emma said, bile rising into her throat. "When Mom says we're going for walks . . . at night . . . it's not true, Dad. Mom is having an affair!"

Her father's face contorted, colored; he stood and ran for the bathroom and Emma heard him gag. She started sobbing. But when her father returned, he said, "Don't you dare, Emma." His voice was hoarse and final.

"What?" Emma was aching for thanks, or just acknowledgment.

"I don't *ever* want to hear you tell *lies* like that again about your own *mother*." Seamus grabbed his jacket and slammed the door on his way out for the night.

Her father's lesson was clear.

Emma never told the truth about Donna again.

"Em?" said Rich now. "I'm listening, Em."

If there was any person in the world who could save Emma, it was her husband. But he was also the one person she couldn't ask for help, because it would break his big and tender heart. "I just . . . love you," said Emma.

"Love means you can tell me whatever you need to, you know," said Rich.

"There's nothing to tell," whispered Emma.

"I believe you," said Rich. He looked at Emma steadily.

"Good," said Emma.

"What choice do I have?" said Rich.

PART SIX

PLUM GIN

1
SYLVIE

Sylvie and Simon walked across the lawn to the castle. Sylvie was happy but nervous. The power of their connection was overwhelming. Sylvie wasn't sure why she felt filled with butterflies—emotional leftovers from childhood? Guilt over betraying Alexander? General cynicism and comfort with being alone? Sylvie was a wounded animal who wanted both to take refuge and to run. And she knew Simon, too, had complicated emotions. Could the two of them possibly make it?

She grabbed his hand and he squeezed back. "I love you," she said quietly.

"I love you, too," said Simon.

The welcome reception was set up on the Great Lawn, with a full bar manned by Simon's friend Angus. The two men hugged and Simon introduced Angus to Sylvie, telling her he was the head falconer.

"And bartender, gardener, jack-of-all-trades," said Angus. He had an angular face, slight stubble, and a mullet hairdo that Sylvie was pretty sure was not ironic. (Somehow it worked on him.) Angus wore an old man's outfit: green wool vest over a white shirt;

a navy silken fringed scarf tied at his throat like an ascot; a tweed flat cap. Canvas work pants and boots belied his elegant upper half.

"Nice scarf on you, mate," said Simon.

"Miss Louisa made me wear it, you arse," said Angus. "You're the one in a straitjacket."

Simon thumbed the lapels of his elegant suit and laughed.

"I'm so glad this one's finally got himself a bird," said Angus. "I can have one of the sisters, innit?"

"Both taken, my friend," said Simon.

"We'll see about that," said Angus.

"Aunt Sylvie! Aunt Sylvie!" cried Emma's boys, racing toward her. Sylvie admired her nephews' finery: Emma had somehow wrangled them into button-down shirts and ill-fitting pants. "I've never seen you so dressed up," said Sylvie.

"It's the *worst,*" said Jameson, pulling at a wrinkled tie.

Penelope came running and encircled Sylvie's waist tightly. "Sweetie, you're here!" said Sylvie, moved by Penelope's vulnerable adoration. Penelope wore a smocked dress but her hair was wild. "Can you help with my braids?" she whispered to Sylvie.

"Of course," said Sylvie. She knew Penelope could do her own hair and was felled by the fact that Penelope preferred Sylvie to do it for her. "Go get your brush and barrettes," said Sylvie.

"Syl," said Rich, approaching. He, too, looked uncomfortable in a button-down shirt. At his wedding to Emma, Rich had worn a rental tuxedo with a paint-spattered cummerbund that had matched Emma's paint-spattered shoes. Now, Rich looked tired. He pulled Sylvie close and she breathed him in.

Sylvie loved Rich—he was like a brother, the only man in their family who'd known Alexander at Sylvie's wedding and known him in a closed coffin. Sylvie had once thought he was too lowbrow for her sister, who she'd imagined trapped in the Missoula valley. But Rich and Emma had built a full life. Sylvie had been wrong.

"Boys!" cried Penelope. "Wait here and when Sylvie's done my braids I'll show you the ghosts."

"She's very bossy," said Guinness.

"But I do want to see ghosts," said Jameson.

"Bet," said Guinness.

Cleo swept toward Sylvie and Simon, decked out in a tight, bright dress that showed off her toned body. Her makeup was expertly applied, and she narrowed her eyes. "Do you want me to do your face?" she said.

"Maybe I could just borrow some lipstick?" said Sylvie.

"You didn't even bring lipstick for your wedding?" said Cleo. Sylvie remembered how as girls, she and Emma would go to Cleo's make-believe "beauty salon" when Donna was out. Cleo would curl Sylvie's hair with Donna's hot rollers, apply foundation to her cheeks and shadow to her eyelids. Cleo would take Sylvie's hand and pull her in front of Donna's mirror, saying, "Ta da! America's new supermodel is *Sylvie Peacock*!"

Sylvie had felt so special and beautiful in Cleo's imaginary salon.

"Please don't be mean," said Sylvie now.

"Sorry," said Cleo. "Here, take this tube. I can do your whole face before the ceremony."

Sylvie followed Penelope into Mumberton's massive library, where Sylvie braided the girl's hair and applied lipstick with the help of her phone's camera.

"I love your tiny diamond earrings," said Penelope, touching Sylvie's earlobe.

"They were my grandmother's," said Sylvie. "She came from Ireland with nothing, and when she turned sixty, her husband and son gave her these earrings. Her son was my father, Seamus."

"Where is he? Why didn't he come to the wedding?" said Penelope.

"He's in Heaven," said Sylvie.

"Do you believe in Heaven?" said Penelope.

Sylvie swallowed, deciding to lie. "Yes," she said.

"Can I have the earrings when you go to Heaven?" said Penelope.

"Yes," said Sylvie.

"Thank you for marrying my dad," said Penelope.

Sylvie stared at Penelope. She felt the familiar dizziness. What would happen to Penelope if Sylvie couldn't marry her father?

"You're welcome," she managed.

"Don't forget to put in your will that I get the diamond earrings," said Penelope.

"I won't forget," said Sylvie.

"Everyone always forgets their promises," said Penelope.

"Not me," said Sylvie.

Penelope stared at Sylvie. Her eyes went blank and then bright again. Sylvie could tell that Penelope, also, knew how to fly in her mind.

When they returned to the reception, Penelope headed off with Emma's boys and Sylvie ordered a glass of champagne and took in the scene: Simon chatting with Angus; Rich and Emma holding hands and investigating the cheese table; Cleo's boyfriend, Danny, who looked like a contestant on *Dancing with the Stars* with his flawless body and artfully styled hair.

Danny met Sylvie's gaze and she walked to him. His expression looked as if he were stoned, though Cleo had told her Danny was against all drugs: With his heavy-lidded, bedroom eyes, he was impossibly sultry and cool. As she approached, though, his surfer dude persona seemed to crack. "Sylvie," he said, his voice wobbly. He grabbed her and pulled her into a hug, clinging so strongly Sylvie couldn't inhale fully.

"Danny?" she gasped.

Danny released her. "I'm so happy for you," he managed.

"Are you . . . all right?" said Sylvie.

"No," said Danny. "No, I'm not all right."

Sylvie struggled to react. Where was Cleo?

Danny pressed his eyes shut and then opened them. "I'm going to go," he said. "I'm going to leave this beautiful castle. But I just want you to know . . . I just want you to know that I loved your sister." He blinked while Sylvie struggled to figure out what to say. "She was probably the love of my life," added Danny.

He held Sylvie tightly again, then turned, took a deep breath, and walked purposefully to the castle maze, pulling out a pack of cigarettes as he approached the high hedges.

Stunned, Sylvie went to search for Cleo, and discovered her chatting with Simon and Angus the falconer-slash-bartender. "I think Danny's having some sort of situation," said Sylvie.

"What?" said Cleo. She pulled Sylvie away from the bar and said, "What do you mean? He was fine a few minutes ago."

"He's smoking in the maze," said Sylvie.

"He doesn't smoke," said Cleo. "Must be bad." She jogged toward the topiaries and disappeared from view. From behind the hedge, Sylvie could hear her sister's raised voice and Danny's fraught response. Their words, thankfully, were indistinguishable, but Sylvie's stomach ached as it always had when her parents fought at night.

"What's going on with Cleo and Mr. Wonderful?" said Rich, after ordering a bottle of Jennings Cumbrian Ale from Angus.

"No idea," said Sylvie.

"Is Cleo OK?" said Simon, joining them.

"Life with the Peacock sisters is never boring," said Rich. "Welcome to the family, brother. Or is it brother-in-law?"

Simon grinned at Rich, and Sylvie felt worried—worried about the damage she would cause if she just couldn't let go of Alexander.

"I'm very glad to join the family," said Simon.

"Let's just say brothers," said Rich.

"Let's," said Simon.

"I could use a brother," said Rich.

"As could I," said Simon.

2
CLEO

"Danny, please," said Cleo, bumming a cigarette from him. He took out his S.T. Dupont bronze lighter (he'd bought it for himself when she forgot his birthday the year before—he'd even wrapped it passive-aggressively and put it on the dining room table with flowers he'd bought for himself and a card reading *Happy Birthday to my Honey*).

Cleo lit her cigarette and took a deep inhalation. Wow, she'd missed smoking. No one could see them behind the bank of trees. "This is my sister's big weekend, Danny. What's going on?"

Danny wiped his eyes and played with his two-thousand-dollar lighter, turning the flame on and off. "I think you know what's going on," he said.

"Where did you even get cigarettes?"

"One of the falconers gave me a ride to the Ratty Arms, in town. It's a pub."

"Are you drunk?"

"No, Cleo! I'm not drunk. I'm . . . I'm heartbroken."

Danny could be emotional, and Cleo was never sure how seriously to take his proclamations. Two puffs of the strong Marlboro made her nauseous, not to mention the image of rotting teeth on the British package. Cleo dropped her cigarette to the lawn, rubbed it out with the toe of her Prada sandal. She summoned her love for this man, who had grown up in poverty and wanted only Cleo (and her money). "What is it, Danny?" she said.

"What is it?" said Danny. "*What IS IT?*"

Cleo bit her lip and said nothing. When he lost his temper, it sometimes frightened her.

"I found your birth control pills, is what it is, Cleo," said Danny.

"You went through my bags?"

"Cleo," said Danny. "I got a new vial of La Mer in case you ran out. I was putting it in your toiletry kit. Did you ever notice that you never run out of La Mer?"

Cleo hadn't actually noticed.

"Or lipstick? Or coffee, or ziplock bags, or soap or shampoo or rice or your favorite yogurt or clean clothes for work?" said Danny. "Did you ever wonder why you never run out of *anything*?"

"Please don't yell," said Cleo. She did feel ashamed, but just a bit. She *paid* for everything, after all.

"I'd been telling myself it didn't matter, since we were going to have a baby, and that was who I'd be."

"What? Telling yourself *what* didn't matter?"

"I'm a failure," said Danny, drying his eyes with the heel of his hand. "I'm never going to write a novel. I'm just your fucking housekeeper, Cleo. But I was trying to convince myself that once we had a kid . . . it would all add up. I would be a dad."

"I didn't know how to tell you," said Cleo. "I'm just not ready."

"I've been keeping track of your fucking fertility cycles," said Danny. "I know it sounds like I was trying to trap you, but I just love you. I thought we both wanted this. You told me you wanted this. You told me we were a family."

Cleo's anger petered out. "I just . . . I don't know," she said. "That's the truth, Danny. I don't even know what I want. Sometimes, I feel like maybe therapy can make me ready. But sometimes, I think I'd just fuck a kid up. I like my life the way it is."

"You do?" said Danny. He seemed genuinely interested.

Cleo thought about her clothes, her office, her endless haircuts and nail appointments and Botox and filler injections. The *purposefulness* of her life felt good. Was it false purpose? Her mother had hammered home to Cleo and her sisters that getting a husband was paramount. A woman needed a man—her entire self-worth should be predicated on being thin, maintaining looks that awed and made others feel inferior, and being seductive to men.

"*Do* you like your life the way it is?" said Danny.

Cleo leaned toward Danny. She loved his smell. They knew each other. "I don't even know how I feel," said Cleo.

"Is it Isaac?" said Danny. "You know he'll never take care of you, Cleo. He's a workaholic like you. He's a mess."

"You're right," said Cleo.

"But you love him."

Cleo felt tears in her eyes. Maybe she wasn't capable of love. She only knew how to avert disaster; how to fight. Love required vulnerability, and Cleo wasn't going to let down her guard. Yet Isaac made her feel calm. His messy apartment was home.

"I don't know," she said.

"You should have told me," said Danny.

"You're right. I should have told you."

"What do you want, then, Cleo?"

Cleo shook her head. When she asked herself the simple question—*What do you want?*—all she saw was Isaac's living room and a Hamburglar glass next to a takeout container of noodles.

Danny's gaze moved over Cleo's shoulder and he straightened, setting his shoulders back. His expression morphed from sad and confused to the smarmy visage he put on when he wanted to seduce. He did something with his eyelids, dropped them to half-closed so he looked sexy and drugged.

"I'm going to figure out what I want," said Cleo, suddenly panicked at the idea of losing Danny. "Can you give me a chance?"

"There you are, Cleo!" said a familiar voice. "And who is this *beautiful* young man?"

Cleo saw her mother's hand first, an old hand with a new manicure, gripping Danny's bulging bicep. In slow motion, as if she were in the midst of a harrowing accident, Cleo followed the arm (clad in bright blue fabric) to a set of massive shoulder pads.

Donna was wearing a double-breasted blazer dress with shining gold buttons, matching blue pumps, and (Cleo forced her eyes to travel to her mother's face) a chapeau with wings.

"Mom?" said Cleo.

"I see you both admiring my hat," said Donna, lifting her chin to show off her wide-brimmed white hat with an aqua band.

"Is it the same one Princess Diana wore?" said Danny. "Her royal visit to Egypt, right? Was it 1992?"

"Mmm, I love a man who understands fashion," said Donna. "No, it's not the same one, silly, but it is an exact replica."

"Chanel," said Danny. "I've seen all the documentaries. I've watched *The Crown* three times."

"Good for you," said Donna. "Princess Diana did adore Chanel, may she rest in peace."

"Yes, may she rest in peace." Danny and Cleo's mother shared a moment of creepy connection while Cleo watched, shell-shocked. "Of course, Diana didn't wear *this* hat with *this* dress," said Donna. "I took artistic license."

"Somehow you make it work with the aqua," said Danny. "Gorgeous." Cleo swallowed. Danny loved to charm.

"Wait til you see the rest of my Princess Diana–inspired outfits," said Donna. "I have a suitcase full. And by the way, Cleo, where's the butler?" Donna gestured to a giant red suitcase with wheels that was certainly *not* inspired by a princess. In fact, Cleo realized, it was the suitcase she herself had bought at Dillard's to take to university.

"There's no butler, Mom," said Cleo.

"I'd be happy to help you with your luggage," said Danny.

"Ooooh, and you look strong enough to do the job," said Donna. She simpered at Danny, then turned to Cleo and spoke again in her creepy whisper. "If this hunk *isn't* your Danny, do tell," she said, raising her eyebrows and gripping Danny tight, as if he were going to attempt to escape, which—judging from his expression—was a distinct possibility.

"I'm not *anyone's* Danny," said Danny.

"Well, that's good news," said Cleo's mother. "I'm not anyone's Donna!"

The two laughed, and Cleo was filled with fury and despair for herself and for the world.

3
EMMA

-$48,005.03

"Penelope's mother, Thisbe, is a *witch,*" said Jameson, flopping into the Adirondack chair next to his mother. Emma, who was very much enjoying her time talking to no one and sipping a plum gin and tonic while eating some sort of tiny meat pie, did not reply. Emma rarely drank alcohol—after overdoing it a few times while the kids were young (and remembering Donna's cruelty when she drank), she'd switched from booze to tea years ago but did enjoy a tipple on special occasions.

"I mean, she's not a *real* witch," said Jameson. "I just didn't want to say the other word."

"Did Penelope say the other word?"

The side of Jameson's mouth twitched. "No," he lied.

"What *did* Penelope say?"

"OK," said Jameson leaning in, finishing the last of his Shirley Temple and placing his crystal glass precariously on the lawn. "So Penelope's mom is *never* home. Penelope has a nanny, like a person who lives with them, and this lady, from, like, Russia, takes care of Penelope, but she doesn't even like her. And Penelope's mom, Thisbe, is just, like, MIA! That means *missing in action.*"

Emma frowned. Across the lawn, she saw Penelope doing cartwheels in a very fancy smocked dress, her frilled underwear visible as she went around. Penelope had abandoned her shoes and lacy socks and the tight braids Sylvie had made for her were falling out. No one was taking care of this sweet girl? Emma was horrified, her righteousness perhaps enhanced by her cocktail, which maybe Angus had made a teeny bit strong. "Well," she said, "some kids have nannies. Especially in New York City."

"And the maybe Russian lady just watches inappropriate television all night and Penelope's mom is *who knows where* in fancy clothes, and Penelope is all alone in her room and she held up a sign saying hi to the man across the alley or whatever it's called but the man didn't write a note back!"

"Like the Taylor Swift video," murmured Emma, "but with a grown man. Oh, dear."

"And Thisbe, the witch, she once had to stay in bed for a month because a doctor vacuumed out her stomach fat!" reported Jameson. "*And!*" said Jameson, his tattletale-with-a-tale energy rising. "Also the *dogs* just sit inside all day! The maybe Russian lady, her name is Vladma, she literally takes the poodles down in an elevator to a lobby in a building and walks ten feet outside and makes them poop on the pavement and then goes *back inside*!"

"Vladma?" said Emma.

"Something like that. Maybe Velma?" said Jameson. "Anyway, we want to stay here, at Mumberton Castle, and then we can keep Penelope here, too. It's *her castle*!"

"Oh, sweetie," said Emma. "We can't stay here. But I'm glad you're having fun."

"Mom," said Jameson. "Guinness says his stomach doesn't hurt here. I can learn about falcons and become a falconer. There's like hundreds of rooms and Penelope said I can pick whichever I want, even though some are reserved for tourists, and she knows which ones are haunted and she needs a real mom."

Emma felt a rush of gratitude. How had she thought everything was lost when she had this boy? "Oh, honey," she said.

Guinness loped over, saying the lawn games were about to start. "Jameson!" he called. "Time to get in a burlap bag!"

Jameson stood. "Just think about it, Mom?" he said.

Guinness, already in a sack, hopped to Emma's Adirondack chair. "Did you tell her?" he asked his brother.

"She said she'd think about it," said Jameson.

"Jameson," said Emma, "I did not—"

"WHAT DID SHE SAY?" cried Penelope, who was having trouble maneuvering her own sack. "WHAT DID SHE SAY?"

"Jameson—" said Emma, but he'd run to join his brother and Penelope. As a threesome, they hopped across the lawn to join some other children and Louisa Freck, who held a silver cup in one hand and a megaphone in the other.

4
SYLVIE

Across the manicured lawn of Mumberton Castle, a bright blue figure moved toward Sylvie. Just the sight of her mother's trademark stride made Sylvie feel dizzy, her blood going hot in her veins, scalding her from the inside.

"Darling!" called Donna.

"Mom," muttered Sylvie.

Each sister reacted differently in Donna's presence: Emma softened into a fawning, childlike servitude—always worried about Donna, tending to her. Cleo got steely and hard—ready to fight. And Sylvie froze, overwhelmed by her contradictory emotions and terrified heart.

Donna reached her youngest girl and hugged her. When Sylvie smelled her mother's musty skin and a strong perfume she didn't recognize, she softened. Donna held Sylvie, then stepped back and looked over Sylvie's shoulder to the assembled guests. "Where's the Face Man?" said Donna. "Hmm?"

"What?" said Sylvie.

"Where's Simon?" said Donna.

"Why would you call him the Face Man? I don't understand. . . ." Sylvie stammered.

"I'm *joking,*" said Donna.

"But what does that mean?" said Sylvie. "Are you insulting him?"

"You're always so serious, Sylvie. It's unbecoming," said Donna dismissively. "So? Where is he?"

"I don't know," said Sylvie.

"Runaway groom!" said Donna. "Just kidding. Anyway, I am exhausted. You know you could have had a wedding in America; they do weddings there," said Donna.

"Uh . . ." Sylvie faltered, lost.

"And a second wedding at that," said Donna. "Usually, second weddings are a bit understated. But not for my girl!"

Sylvie took a deep breath. "Mom, thank you for coming," she said. "It means a lot to me. I'm really—"

"OK, no need for theatrics," said Donna. "As I said, I'm exhausted. Not an easy trek, but what Sylvie wants, Sylvie gets, right?"

In Miami recently, Sylvie had grabbed an Uber back to her place after a night out with Florence. She'd ended up chatting tipsily with the driver, who was from Barbados. Sylvie told him all about her Donna issues—that her mother was toxic, able to ruin any and every interaction for no discernible reason. Because Donna could. Because she was most comfortable when others were upset. To exert power. Because . . . who even knew? Serotonin?

Jim from Barbados drove through the streets of Miami listening to Sylvie go on and on and when she was finally silent, he said, "In my country, we laugh at old people and wish them well."

Well. That hit Sylvie pretty hard. Why couldn't she laugh at her mother and wish her well? She resolved right then and there to try to laugh if her mother was mean. And then Jim proceeded to tell her that in his opinion, many things were better in Miami than in Bridgetown, but that American families were strange as hell.

Remembering Jim and his wisdom, Sylvie tried not to let her mother's jabs hit their mark. Her mother was old and disoriented; maybe Donna was being rude because she felt nervous. "Have a nice nap, Mom," said Sylvie through gritted teeth.

"Cleo's boyfriend is bringing my bags up," said Donna. "What a dear."

"Oh, great," said Sylvie. "Is everything OK with Danny?"

"I doubt it," said Donna, dropping her voice conspiratorially. Donna loved to insult one daughter to another. "A man like Danny isn't going to settle down with a career gal, believe me. Beauty only goes so far. I should know."

And with that cryptic but sinister comment, Donna sauntered off toward the castle, straightening her hat. Sylvie sighed, feeling as if she'd just been beaten up. She touched her grandmother's diamond-chip earrings, wishing for the strength it was going to take to hope for a fairy-tale ending.

5
CLEO

Cleo sat in a lawn chair for a while, feeling maudlin. She watched Angus bring one bird after another out of the aviary to show Penelope, Guinness, and Jameson: an owl, a hawk, a vulture, something Cleo didn't even know how to identify. Angus was so appealing in his British cap. What would it be like to take care of birds as your *job*? Unimaginable. Cleo lit another cigarette. She'd slipped a few from Danny's pack when he went off with Donna to help her with her bags.

"Hey, Cleo," said Rich, coming to sit beside her. As he lowered himself, he made a weird *oooof-ah* sound that was exactly like a noise Cleo's father had once made. It was true that they were all getting old.

"Hey," said Cleo. She'd always been fond of Emma's husband. Emma and Rich's solid—if stolid—relationship was just right for Cleo's crazy sister, even if it would have bored Cleo senseless. Emma had survived enough wild years to last her a lifetime. She'd named her sons after beer and whiskey, for Christ's sake.

"I hear your mother has arrived. Has she met Danny?" said Rich.

"Donna has arrived and Danny and I had a fight," said Cleo.

"Oh boy," said Rich.

"I don't know how you guys do it, to be honest, Rich."

"Do what?"

"Stay in love. Turn into parents."

Rich blinked, looking surprised. Maybe there was trouble in paradise, after all. "Yeah," he said, finally. "I don't know how we did it either, Cleo. How we do it."

Cleo smiled. "Have I ever told you I love you?"

"No," said Rich. "I don't think you have. I love you, too, Cleo."

"What if I never get married?" said Cleo.

Rich put his hand on hers. His palm was warm on her skin: a kindness.

6
EMMA

-$49,795.23

Emma lumbered up her dark, circular staircase. She shivered in her summer dress, her shoes making a sucking sound with each step. Up and up she went, clutching the metal rail. Finally, she reached the arched doorway of the Indigo Suite, opened the door, and eased herself into her big, big four-poster bed. Her boys had followed Angus back to work in the aviary, and Emma felt wonderfully woozy. She was about to succumb to a deep nap when she heard someone banging at her door.

As if she were in a dream of her awful childhood, she heard her mother's voice wailing, "Emmmaaaaa! Emma!" Donna knocked and knocked at the door.

A martyr through and through, Emma fought back her sleepiness and rose.

"Emma, my darling," cried Donna, engulfing Emma in a woody, floral scent, which (Emma couldn't help herself from analyzing) opened with sparkling aldehydes and fruity notes and used amber as its base.

"You made it! You smell good, Mom," said Emma.

"Van Cleef and Arpels," said Donna. "Prince Harry said it was his mother's favorite. At least I *smell* OK."

"Oh, Mom," said Emma. This was where she was supposed to say her mother looked beautiful and young and sexy. Yes: Emma was supposed to comment on her mother's sexiness. But for the first time, she could not bring herself to do it.

"I'm hideous, I know it," said Donna. "I'm old."

"No, Mom. . . ." Emma forced herself to respond. She was supposed to add specific compliments here, about Donna's physique, low weight, outfit, or hair. Emma scanned her mother, creating favorable remarks. "Look at your dewy skin," said Emma. "You look very thin, Mom, too."

"Only *you* love me," said Donna, placated. "You've always been the best one."

Whenever Emma spoke with her mother, she felt disparate emotions concurrently: a craving for her mother's praise; understanding that this need was super fucked-up; the desire for her mother to ask about *her;* and the knowledge that this would never happen, because Donna had been diagnosed as a narcissist when she went to see a psychiatrist while Emma was in high school.

(Donna had fired the psychiatrist who diagnosed her, then asked him out to dinner, slept with him, and ghosted him. Emma could remember Dr. Mundell standing on their front lawn, crying. He moved to Billings soon afterward.)

"Look at your castle room!" said Donna, sitting down and making herself comfortable. "It's so much *bigger* than my castle room."

"Where's Noah?" said Emma.

"He said he's too old to travel," said Donna.

"Oh, Mom, that's awful."

"It is! I left Montana because you never had time for me and now I'm stuck in Arizona with an old man and you couldn't care less!"

Now was the time for Emma to insist that her life was meaningless without Donna. She inhaled. "Mom," she began.

"I thought we had our whole lives ahead of us, but now we're washed up."

"No . . ."

"I have a green dress for tonight," continued Donna, as if Emma wasn't there. "And, like Princess Diana, I am going to wear an emerald choker across my forehead! Well, *faux emerald,* of course, because Noah isn't good with finances. And Emma, I am going to need that hundred dollars I sent you."

"You mean the money you sent for the boys' Christmas presents last year?"

"What do you think of Simon?" Donna went on. "Love the accent but he's not nearly as good-looking as Cleo's Danny, now is he?" she said. "Not that *he'll* be around for long," Donna added, darkly.

Donna took off her enormous white hat, set it on a side table, made her way to Emma's king-sized bed, and climbed in. "Mmm, much more comfortable than mine," she said. "Can we talk later about Noah?" said Donna, closing her eyes. "I need your advice, Emma. The spark between us . . ."

"Sure, Mom, later," said Emma, though it had been repugnant for her to hear about her mother's lover when she was a kid and it was repugnant now. "You know," said Emma, "I could also use some advice. You know the company I'm working for? Sweet Nothings?"

Her mother did not answer, and Emma saw that Donna was asleep, or pretending to be. Her hands were folded over her bright dress. Emma had twisted her whole life into a string of lights to impress her mother: marriage, beautiful children, a bungalow on the good side of Missoula. But the object of Emma's fixation was just an old lady whose hair was thinning so much that Emma could see her fragile scalp.

7
SYLVIE

As the welcome reception wound down, Louisa Freck herded the Peacocks into the Great Hall. It was time, she proclaimed, for the "Dress as a Tudor Portrait" package, which included two ladies-in-waiting, a box of truffles, unlimited champagne and mead, three racks of costumes, and live owls who would arrive in time for the photographer.

Sylvie was so tired that her head felt as if it were a lead balloon. Brilliant chandeliers blazed overhead, daggers aimed at Sylvie's aching eyes. As a lady-in-waiting named Ainsley began to dress her, Sylvie shivered in a white linen chemise. A second lady-in-waiting, whose name was Poppy, slipped a black hoop skirt over Sylvie's head. "You might wonder," commented Poppy, "if Anne Boleyn wore underpants."

"Honestly, no, I hadn't wondered—" started Sylvie.

Ainsley cut her off. "We don't know!" she cried. "The Tudor Dynasty ended in 1603—none of the garments have survived. We only know what the Tudors wore from their portraits, and no one painted a portrait of their underpants!"

"So we assume *no,* they did not wear underwear. But they did wear linen and silk chemises like the one Sylvie's got on here," said Poppy. "Poorer folk used rough hemp."

"What kind of weirdo spends their time thinking about Tudor underwear?" said Donna.

"Perhaps historians," said Louisa Freck, defensively. "Ainsley, Poppy, did you hear about the Austrian castle? They found a hidden vault underneath fifteenth-century floorboards! Guess what was in there?"

"Do tell," said Ainsley.

"They found medieval bras, girls!"

"But no drawers?" said Poppy.

"Pity that," said Ainsley.

"Time for the bum roll," said Poppy cheerfully, securing what looked like an airplane neck pillow around Sylvie's waist.

"The first Queen Elizabeth listed *girdles* in her household accounts," said Ainsley, pulling skirting made of white nets over Sylvie's head. "And by the way, we call silk stockings 'silkies.'"

"Ooooh, now the golden corset," said Poppy.

"Is that what you call marriage here?" said Cleo, snickering.

"Please don't laugh at me," said Sylvie.

"Sensitive Sylvie," said Donna.

"I'm sorry," said Cleo. "That was a dumb joke. I apologize."

"Thanks, Cleo."

Poppy and Ainsley yanked Sylvie's bodice tight, making her struggle for breath. They draped strands of heavy jewels around her neck. A deep green "kirtle" dress followed, and then both of Sylvie's arms were encased in detachable gold sleeves, which ran from her wrists to her elbows. A giant bejeweled headband was attached to her hair, then the hair was gathered and shoved into a black velvet bag. Poppy hung some gold necklaces around Sylvie's waist like belts and said "Voilà!"

"Why are you dressing her as a bride who'll be beheaded by her future husband?" said Cleo, an arm crossed in front of her chest.

"You look stunning," said Emma kindly.

"When will it be my turn?" said Donna.

8
CLEO

The "Dress as a Tudor Experience" was supposed to be fun but it was not fun. Cleo felt sick about Danny finding her birth control pills. As Ainsley explained that Cleo's enormous hoop skirt was called a "farthingale," and that the headdress she attached around Cleo's face was the "Spanish style," Cleo tried to pay attention.

"We're re-creating Catherine of Aragon's outfit from Emperor Charles V's visit in 1520," explained Poppy. "Silver lamé petticoat, golden gown lined with violet velvet, pearl necklace with a cross made of diamonds."

"And her hair was red, like yours," said Louisa.

The ladies-in-waiting had wheeled in a full-length mirror. Cleo marveled at her image. She looked iconic, powerful, and brave. "Catherine was beautiful in her youth," noted Ainsley, setting out ugly little Tudor flats for Cleo to slip her feet into.

"But then she was stripped of her title of queen," said Louisa.

"And also beheaded," noted Poppy.

9

EMMA

-$50,391.67

The men had clearly been enjoying free mead. By the time they swept into the Great Hall, wearing enormous velvet-and-fur coats, scabbards holding swords, and the same ugly shoes as the women, the men's voices were loud and festive. Emma had been trussed up and positioned behind a harp for some reason. Rich and the boys had donned floppy, bejeweled hats. A fire roared in the giant fireplace and Emma felt a bit overheated and dizzy.

The photographer arranged the extended Peacock family, settling Donna in a throne-like chair and Sylvie and Simon on either side of her. The rest of them crowded around.

"And here come the owls," said Simon's friend Angus, opening the door and entering with birds of prey.

"Just let them loose; they can fly in and out of the portrait," said the photographer. One of the owls flew directly at Emma and she screamed.

"Always with the drama," muttered Donna.

"I've got you, honey," said Rich.

The bird swooped over Emma, circled around, and flew back

toward her. She was terrified, her mouth open in horror. Donna's expression was beatific. Sylvie looked wan. Cleo looked wary of Danny, who had his hand on his Tudor sword.

"And . . . smile!" said the photographer.

"What a happy family," said Ainsley.

PART SEVEN
SIMON'S SURPRISE

1
SYLVIE

"Good morning, everyone!" said Simon. Sylvie watched her fiancé sleepily. He was giddy, wearing a cashmere sweater, waxed cotton coat, corduroy pants, and wool socks with high rubber boots. (He'd dressed Sylvie in similar birdwatching attire.)

"Is it morning, though?" muttered Cleo. In her defense, it was still extremely dark. Simon had informed them at the end of the Tudor portrait session that he had a big surprise: a birding tour of the nearby Winefride Royal Society for the Protection of Birds reserve (also known as the WRSPB). "And we're going to leave before sunrise," he'd said, "to try to catch the chiffchaff warblers before they leave their mud-and-twig nests to forage for fish."

The Peacock family's reaction to this announcement had been muted. Donna groaned audibly and hissed, "Did he say *forage for fish*?" to her new sidekick, Danny. Apparently, Danny and Cleo had had a fight, and he had asked Louisa Freck to move him to his own room in the castle. When Sylvie had asked Cleo what was going on, Cleo said, "Danny wants to sulk in the pele tower." When Sylvie asked Cleo why he was sulking, Cleo said, "Don't ask."

So much for sisterly confessions.

Sylvie had slept fitfully, inhabiting another disconcerting Alexander dream. In this one, Alexander was pleading with her to help him escape a video-game-like maze. When the front desk (aka Louisa Freck) called to wake Sylvie and Simon for bird-watching, she dressed slowly, still half with her first husband, running through a nightmare Roblox world, and half donning wellies in the chilly Gatekeeper's Cottage.

She knew it was wrong but she'd wanted to get back under the covers and return to Alexander. Remembering him—not moving on—was all she could do for him anymore. It was the last connection to her first love. Giving that up would be . . . free fall.

Sylvie avoided uncertainty at all costs. Control was her salvation, and she could control a situation that had already reached its conclusion. What remained to be seen was if she could leap into a story that was just unfolding, wild with possibilities for joy *and* pain.

Sylvie knew that the Winefride Bird reserve meant a lot to Simon—his first published photograph had been a baby guillemot along the Winefride trail. In the image, the bird was tiny and fuzzy with newborn down, nestled under the wing of his father. It was a bird photograph, yes, but also a portrait of devotion.

Despite her family's lack of enthusiasm, Sylvie respected and adored Simon's knowledge of birds and animals. She'd gone on photo shoots with him, listening as he explained which places could provide interesting backdrops (a bush with bright yellow buds, or tall grasses in front of which a colorful bird would pop), then sitting still and quietly for a long time, hoping an animal would arrive to pose beguilingly.

"Some photographers chase after the animals," Simon told her, "but I like to frame the perfect shot and see who wanders in." He and Sylvie would sip coffee or tea or cold water from a metal bottle, whisper once in a while, but primarily watch. Sylvie found this quiet time soothing and revelatory. She daydreamed, or rearranged her library in her head, or thought about a book she was reading, and sometimes a bird flitted in and Simon shot with his various lenses, and sometimes nothing happened at all and they went home when it started to get dark.

Louisa Freck stood by the side of the hired minibus and addressed Sylvie's family. "Don't mind the rain!" she chirped. "We've prepared breakfast boxes and warm coffees for you. All aboard!"

"I was *not informed*," complained Donna, "that I would be dragged on a muddy excursion in a British *monsoon*." Donna's rabbit fur Cossack-style hat was growing wet, and her cinch-waisted wool coat did not appear to be waterproof. Even her matching muff, though possibly keeping her hands warm, was drooping.

"Princess Diana wore Wellingtons and Barbour coats in inclement weather," said Danny. "Like Simon's. *Exactly* like Simon's."

"Don't worry, Donna," said Simon. "We've got an assortment of mackintoshes and boots for you at Winefride, and binoculars to see the birds in detail."

Donna sniffed, but—seemingly cheered by the thought of a freebie or two—begrudgingly climbed onto the bus.

As her family tucked into gourmet baskets of scones and hot thermoses of coffee (not to mention an array of pastries, fresh jams, yogurt parfaits, meats, and cheeses) Sylvie relaxed a bit. She kissed Simon on the cheek, and he said, "OK, Syl, here goes nothing!"

Simon made his way to the front of the bus, where he stood next to the driver. He cleared his throat and spoke. "We are headed to my old stomping grounds," said Simon, nervously messing with the buttons on his Barbour coat. "The Winefride warden will meet us there and we will walk a short, cliff-top path to see the only colony of cliff-nesting seabirds in North West England."

"Will we see penguins?" asked Jameson, gripping the seat in front of him excitedly.

"Great question, Jameson," said Simon. "One of the birds we might spot is the guillemot, which is actually a tiny British penguin! Since we're going early, we might even see baby guillemots jump from the cliffs into the sea!"

"Yikes," said Donna.

"Some of the other creatures we might encounter at Winefride include kittiwake, peregrine, wheatear, and . . . if we are *very* lucky . . . rare gray seals!" said Simon. "And of course, the chiffchaff warblers."

Emma and Rich were enthusiastic, looking like kids themselves in anticipation of an outing they were not in charge of. "This is so cool," said Emma. "Thank you, Simon."

"Tiny penguins," marveled Cleo, perking up a bit from her Americano with oat milk.

Unfortunately, Simon did not stop while he was ahead. "There have also been recent sightings of a northern bottlenose whale, huge numbers of squid eggs, and sea gooseberries," he said.

"What is a sea gooseberry?" asked Donna. "Sounds revolting."

"They're round, jelly-like blobs," said Simon. "Though we'd have to paddle out in sea kayaks to be sure to see gooseberries."

"No, thank you!" cried Donna.

"I feel like Queen Elizabeth," noted Danny. "Remember, in *The Crown*, when she goes to the Scottish Highlands with her corgis?"

"*Of course* I remember," said Donna. "That show is very complicated, but the costumes are top-notch. Diana's outfits inspired many of my outfits for this weekend."

"Donna, you're an icon," said Danny, which seemed to Sylvie like a bit much.

At Winefride, the owner of a local toggery shop was waiting to outfit them, assuring a thrilled Donna, Cleo, and Emma that, after the hike, the shop would ship all the British outerwear home.

Donna beelined to the Burberry, selecting a check cotton gabardine trench coat with a matching bucket hat and boots. When Simon asked if she'd like bouclé ankle boots and a cashmere wrap to warm her up later, she cooed, "Oh, why not, Simon? And maybe some sunglasses?"

Rich said defensively that his family already had raincoats and boots, but Cleo said she couldn't resist a smoke-blue, full-length coat from an Irish brand called Jack Murphy.

Simon greeted the Winefride warden, an older man named Barnaby, who offered to personally escort Donna along the cliff. Danny looked a bit put out, aggressively ignoring Cleo but happy to accept a new trench, fedora, and pair of Blundstone boots.

They set out along a trail as the sun came up, going single-file at times so no one would fall down the cliffside. The ground was wet and muddy, but the Irish Sea below was breathtaking. Simon walked quickly, switching between binoculars, two camera lenses, a pair of glasses on his forehead, and sunglasses around his neck.

"Ha! Bag the poo!" cried Guinness, pointing to a sign for dog walkers.

"So immature," pronounced Penelope, rolling her eyes like a teenager.

"But kind of funny," said Sylvie to her, gently.

"Yes, OK," said Penelope, acquiescing to being a kid for a moment. "Kind of funny. Very British." She ran to find the boys, Emma, and Rich, who were determinedly hiking along in the rain.

"Where's your mother?" said Danny, peering at Sylvie from beneath his waxed cotton fedora. Cleo was hurrying to catch up with them.

"What?"

"Where is Donna? She was walking arm in arm with that old man and they've fallen behind."

"I wouldn't worry about my mother," said Sylvie. "She takes care of herself, I promise you."

"Well, she and I were talking about something important," said Danny peevishly.

Sylvie shrugged politely and moved to Simon, who was crouching down at the edge of a cliff peering intently through his binoculars. "Syl," he said, reaching out with the hand not holding his binoculars to squeeze her knee.

She scrunched down next to him, saying, "Don't fall, Simon."

"I've got you," he said. "Sylvie, look."

She fumbled with her new binoculars. When she peered through them, she only saw black. She realized her lens caps were on, removed them, but still only saw black. "I can't see anything," she admitted.

"Lengthen the eyecups," said Simon. She unscrewed the part of the binoculars that met her eyes, elongating them, then peeked again and inhaled with wonder.

Below them, on the beach, she saw a large gray seal rolling on its back. "A seal!" she said.

"Look in the water."

Sylvie moved the binoculars, refocused, and saw a tiny baby seal swimming, playing in the greenish waves. It paddled to shore, and used its fins to lurch across the sand to the bigger seal.

"It's only three feet long!"

"It's her newborn," said Simon.

The baby seal reached its mother and nestled close. The mother seal twisted her whole body around her little one. Sylvie felt close to tears.

"We never had that," said Simon. "Neither of us, did we?"

Sylvie and Simon watched the mother and baby. Simon put his arm around Sylvie. The rain fell, lightly.

"What is it?" Cleo came close and bent down. Sylvie helped Cleo adjust her binoculars and peer through them. (The Peacock family had not owned binoculars.)

"Do you see?" said Sylvie, pointing.

"Aw, look," said Cleo. "Look at that baby all cuddled up."

"Yeah," said Sylvie.

"Reminds me of us," said Cleo.

"What?"

"Remember? You and Emma used to come cuddle in my bed at night. We were all warm and cozy and it snowed outside. We'd play the Once Upon a Time game."

"Lucky sisters," said Simon.

"Yeah," said Sylvie. She took Cleo's hand. "I wasn't alone. I had you."

"You'll always have me," said Cleo.

2

CLEO

Once Upon a Time, thought Cleo, *Sylvie will fall in love with a kind man named Simon and live happily ever after in a castle . . . and Cleo will become a professional birder and go for long walks with Isaac around the Central Park Reservoir. . . .*

Maybe it was time for Cleo to admit it. She wished Isaac were here. It was *so green* here in the Lake District. And although Cleo spent hours a week toning her physique, she hadn't gone for a hike outdoors in a long time. And this was such a stunning adventure, despite the rain . . . or maybe even because of it.

Isaac would love it here: the wide vista to the crashing waves below, the flocks of birds and the sweet baby seal and its mother, the way the air was chilly and fresh, smelling of mud and grass and feral, outdoorsy things. . . . She'd forgotten about the power of nature. How wild the natural world was, how *vast,* and how nourishing! "Look," said Simon, the perfect guide to this place. He paused and pointed to a pile of rocks on the beach. "Ringed plover."

Sylvie and Cleo raised their binoculars. Cleo laughed, delighted, as she saw baby chicks perfectly camouflaged in a nest—tan-and-white heads that looked just like stones, black masks, little orange beaks jutting out when they popped up to look around.

"What's the teeny one there?" said Emma, joining them. They peered at a round bird with a dark mask around its eyes, hopping and pecking at the ground.

"Northern wheatear," said Simon. "And see the ducks over on the sand, next to the tidal pool?" The sisters swung their binoculars. "Common eider ducks," said Simon. "Aren't they pretty, big ducks? The males are white and black with pistachio on their necks, and the females are barred with brown and black."

"I see rabbits!" said Guinness.

"Indeed you do, son," said Simon.

"Nice eye, Guinness," said Penelope, copying her father's schoolteacher affect.

"What's the one flying, with the red beak?" said Rich.

Simon looked up. "Shelduck," he said.

Rich looked pleased with himself.

"Birdwatching is cooler than I thought," said Guinness.

"Oh? What did you think?" said Simon, playfully.

"I guess I thought it was kind of . . ." said Guinness, going bright red and stammering.

"Dorky," clarified Jameson.

"So American," muttered Penelope, disdainfully. A citizen of the UK and the United States, she considered herself a worldly arbiter of culture. Cleo saw herself in the girl—Penelope was sensitive, watchful, wise, and extremely judgmental.

"In the winter," said Simon, "there are Canadian geese."

Sylvie's family trained their gazes on the beach, helping one another figure out how to use the binoculars and camera lenses, sipping hot tea from thermoses. They gasped when a flock of birds lifted as one. "Oystercatchers," said Simon.

"A group of oystercatchers is called a stew, Rockefeller, or parcel," added Penelope.

Cleo savored watching the oystercatchers; all of the sisters were transfixed, silent, awed.

"There you are!" cried Donna, shattering the magical moment, huffing and puffing her way up the trail. She grabbed Cleo's arm. "This is *so boring,*" she said, "right?"

"I'm having fun," said Cleo.

"Oh, please," said Donna.

"I thought we could take a break in the hide here," said Simon, pointing to a dilapidated wooden shack, "and then head back to the van."

"Cleo, you come with me," said Donna. "We need to talk."

Cleo ached to join her family in the hide, to page through the bird books Simon had brought. But she stayed in the rain with her mother.

"Listen," said Donna, as the rest of their crew moved out of earshot. "It's not too late with Danny. He's ready to forgive you. He wants to *marry you,* Cleo! This estrangement has been a big misunderstanding."

"I don't want to marry Danny," said Cleo.

"Yes, you do," said Donna. "You don't know *what* you want, honey, you never have."

In this statement, at least, Donna was absolutely right.

"Go on," said Donna. "He's waiting for you over there in the mud by the scary cliff. Say yes, and then all my girls will have handsome husbands, and honestly, who knows what might happen to *me* in England!" She turned and waved to the Winefride naturalist, who was bringing up the rear of the group. Barnaby seemed surprised and pleased by Donna's attention.

"No," said Cleo.

Donna stared at her eldest daughter. "What did you say?"

"I said no," said Cleo. "You don't care what's good for me. I didn't want to be an actress and I don't want to get married now, and I'm not your pawn, Mom. I love you, and I always will, but I need to figure out what I want on my own."

"This is the craziest thing I've ever heard," said Donna. "You're not in your right mind, dear. Did you hear me? Danny wants you to marry him and he is going to ask you right now in the rain on this strange and chilly beach. So go!"

"I don't think you heard me," said Cleo.

"The ring he brought is *not* enormous," said Donna. "You're going to need to go to Tiffany's for an emerald cut. We don't really like the round cut, do we?"

In truth, Cleo *didn't* like the round cut. She wore pearl earrings, like Donna. She (like Donna) disparaged Japanese cars, vegans, and cellulite. Until Danny had upgraded their lotions, she'd used Jergens Cloud Crème as Donna did. Every inch of Cleo was ready to be evaluated by her mother. But as she comprehended this, Cleo also realized she could stop.

"I don't have to repeat myself," said Cleo. "You're never going to hear me."

"He also bought *himself* an engagement ring," continued Donna. "Which—I'm sorry, but gauche."

Cleo shook her head. Clarity felt like being doused with freezing cold water.

She had never been golden.

Danny was waiting, as promised, in the mud by the scary cliff. "Cleo!" he cried, dropping his cigarette and extinguishing it under a new boot. He scanned the ground around himself to kneel, but it was all mud. "I love you, Cleo," he said, opening his palms.

"Oh, Danny. You're such an amazing person."

"I want to be a family," said Danny. "I want to be a dad. We can do this, Cleo."

Cleo wished it were true. But even if it meant she would never be a mother, she knew that having a child with Danny was a mistake. She was going to start telling her truth, even when it hurt people, because she couldn't take care of herself and everyone else at the same time.

"Why can't you try?" said Danny.

"Because I'm in love with Isaac," said Cleo.

3
EMMA

-$52,190.55

After the Winefride Bird Preserve, Simon offered to show them around the nearby Lake District town of Grasmere. Florence and Rashid met them at their first stop: Wordsworth's Dove Cottage, which was warm and cozy. Emma followed the tour guide from the parlor to a small writing room where William Wordsworth had composed poetry.

"On the wall is the portrait of the Wordsworths' terrier, Pepper," said their guide. "William's sister, Dorothy, also lived here beginning in 1799. She wrote in her journals and did the washing." In Dorothy's bedroom, the guide said, "You can see the tray of small sticks Dorothy would have used to clean her teeth."

The guide paused by Wordsworth's writing desk and read from a poem composed there called "Ode to Duty":

Oh, let my weakness have an end!
Give unto me, made lowly wise,
The spirit of self-sacrifice . . .

"Easy to write an ode to duty when your sister's waiting on you hand and foot," noted Florence.

"And cleaning her teeth with sticks," added Rashid.

They laughed, and Emma laughed, too.

"Self-sacrifice is a trap," said Emma, testing the words as she said them.

"Right on, sister," said Flo.

4

SYLVIE

The line to enter Sarah Nelson's Grasmere Gingerbread would take about forty-five minutes and the rain was growing heavier. "Please," said Donna. "My neighbor at Margaritaville Retirement Community never stops talking about the goddamned gingerbread at this famous shop."

"I love gingerbread!" chimed in Louisa.

"My neighbor went to England twenty years ago and we never hear the end of it," said Donna. "I just need a package from this one shop, or a T-shirt."

"They also have rum butter and sticky toffee sauce," added Simon.

"OK," said Sylvie, though she was chilly and wanted to climb into a warm bubble bath. "OK, sure," she said. The van driver found a parking spot next to a wide mud puddle. Sylvie wrapped her scarf around her neck and Simon readied umbrellas.

"I'll wait in the toasty bus," said Donna. "Can you grab me some gingerbread and a T-shirt?"

5
CLEO

When a lovely young woman wearing an old-timey bonnet gave Cleo a sample of gingerbread, she jammed it in her mouth and savored the incredible taste—for some reason, she'd expected it to taste like a graham cracker, but it was more like a thin, soft, buttery cake. She bought six squares of Sarah Nelson's Celebrated Grasmere Gingerbread nestled in a sweet little tin box with a purple label, paying with a twenty-pound note and stuffing the change in her pocket.

On the van, Danny was pretending to be asleep. His face was so sad, defeated. Cleo sat next to him. They wound through picturesque streets on the way back to Mumberton Castle. She ate five squares of gingerbread.

Cleo slipped the last warm cake to Danny, who didn't open his eyes but—keeping his face turned away from Cleo—ate the gingerbread, chewing quietly.

6
EMMA

-$53,170.91

Cassidy Rose had been calling Emma's phone repeatedly. Emma didn't answer the calls or follow-up texts. She felt frightened. Maybe it was jet lag. After their bucolic birding sojourn, Rich and the boys settled in for a nap (Rich) and iPad time (Jameson and Guinness), but Emma was wired. She wandered down the main staircase of the castle, locating a quiet room that looked like a sumptuous living room except for an unmanned bar in the corner.

Emma eyed a decanter containing dark red liquid, labeled SLOE GIN. She filled a tiny glass—it was like a crystal thimble with a stem: a glamorous British shot glass, no more than a sexy sip. The aromatic elixir tasted like someone had mashed up and fermented a bush, including the branches.

Emma sank into a yellow sitting chair flanked by a couch made of red-and-gold patterned silk fabric and a red tartan love seat. She leaned against a square-shaped pillow embroidered with an "M" over a "C" in gold thread. Brass side tables and low coffee tables around the room held dainty tea sets. Someone had decorated this room with great care. Castle interior designer—what a dream job!

More elegant than selling sex toys, that was for damn sure.

Emma refilled her little thimble and gazed up at three multi-tiered chandeliers, eyeing endless, shimmering strands of crystals. Metallic petals clasped little lamps, each with its own little lampshade. The multipaned windows held colored-glass family crests. The rain had abated; sun poured through windows and glittered across the wooden floors and five different (but complementary) carpets. Emma was dazzled.

She admired everything, wanting to stay here, wanting *this,* whatever it was. It felt like this room represented the epitome of splendor, of something precious preserved with (she knew) an enormous amount of effort. This room—this castle—struck Emma as a worthy obligation. Such a straightforward and important goal: keep its magnificence intact, make it sparkle and shine. She wished she had such a clear sense of purpose.

For some reason, Lionel Richie was playing loudly through a hidden speaker system: "Oh oh oh oh, sail on! Honey! Good times never felt so good!"

The sloe gin made Emma feel more and more tranquil, so she kept imbibing, turning things over in her mind. What if she took the kids' suggestion seriously and *did* offer to stay on, with her family, after Simon's dad was gone? Rich could design woodwork masterpieces. She could run the various businesses, create medieval fragrance kits, raise the boys amongst lakes and fells and climb Black Combe Peak.

I'm home, Emma whispered to herself, though this made no sense at all. Maybe it was the gin, but she had the glorious feeling that she could be at peace, for once in her life, if she could stay inside Mumberton Castle.

7
SYLVIE

Sylvie sank into a hot bath filled with bubbles. Her birding clothes lay wet on the floor of her opulent bathroom. Simon had kindly installed a wire rack to hold a book and a candle over the tub, but Sylvie struggled to sit up and read—she kept sliding into the bubbles. Finally, Sylvie dropped her hardcover to the side of the tub, savoring the ridiculous extravagance of owning a new book she could splash on. Her brain clanged like an alarm bell, but she tried to ignore it. She didn't need to figure out what was wrong, and she didn't need to find a way to escape. She was no longer a child in danger—why couldn't her body get the message?

Sylvie took a deep breath and let it out slowly. If it was the right thing to keep fighting her panic-fueled disassociation and marry Simon, why did her stomach feel as if it were filled with acid? Why was she still dreaming of Alexander?

Sylvie heard a phone ring. She hadn't known there was a landline in the cottage, but she heard Simon's low tones as he answered. Sylvie closed her eyes. Simon's voice rose in volume and sounded upset.

"Please," whispered Sylvie to no one.

(She didn't believe there was anyone watching over her.)

She wanted her body to be wrong.

Simon's voice went silent. If there were something amiss, he would come and tell her. Sylvie waited. She floated in the water and then she drained the tub and wrapped herself in a robe.

There was a knock at the bathroom door. "Simon?" said Sylvie.

"I'm so sorry," said Simon. He did not open the door but slid a cream-colored envelope underneath. Sylvie picked up the envelope, and she opened it.

8
FROM THE DESK OF SIMON RAMPLING

Dear Sylvie,

~~I just got a phone call from Thisbe that made me realize~~

There are things you need to know.

~~I am so sorry, and I only hope that~~

~~Please understand that~~

~~I will write everything down and you~~

I love you.

Simon

9

CLEO

Danny stood next to his bags at the entrance to Mumberton Castle. He checked his phone. "My Uber will be here in thirty-eight minutes," he said.

"I'm glad they even have Uber here," said Cleo. She exhaled, gazing down the road that led past the Gatekeeper's Cottage to the A6 and eventually, Carlisle. There was a low mist over the lawns. Cleo thrummed with clarity: She was going to clear the air with Sylvie and then return home to Isaac and whatever her confession to him would bring.

"I'd prefer if you could leave me alone," said Danny. "I feel dumb enough as it is." He had packed quickly and efficiently, saying he'd be out of their apartment by the time she got back to Brooklyn Heights.

"Where are you going to go?" said Cleo.

"That's really not your problem," said Danny.

"Well, there's no rush," said Cleo. "We can sort through everything when I get back."

"It's not my brownstone. Nothing there belongs to me," said Danny.

"Your notebooks," said Cleo. "And . . . your guitar."

"Oh yes, my guitar," said Danny morosely. He released a large sigh.

"You can stay for the wedding if you want," said Cleo. "I mean, we can still be friends, Danny."

"As if," said Danny. "Sorry, Cleo, but no way."

"I'll see you back in the city," said Cleo.

"Probably you won't," said Danny. "We don't even have anything in common."

"That's not true," said Cleo, though it was, actually, true.

"Just leave me alone, OK?" said Danny.

"OK," said Cleo.

"I hope I never see you again, and I mean that," said Danny.

Cleo blinked.

"I mean it. Seriously. Leave me alone, OK? Please, Cleo."

Cleo wanted to protest but held her tongue. It was the least she could do. She went back into the castle, leaving Danny to wait for his car. She felt very sad, hungry, and tired. Cleo wandered into the octagonal library and fell asleep on a gold velvet divan.

"Cleo?"

She sat up, startled, and discerned Simon in the arched doorway. He held a beer bottle. "Father and I are watching television in the drawing room. Would you like to join us?"

"Where's Sylvie?" said Cleo.

"Where's Danny?" said Simon.

She met his gaze. They came to a silent understanding—no more questions. "Come have a drink," said Simon. Cleo followed him, her Prada hiking boots thunking on the tile floor, into a cozy den with plaid furniture and a bright fire. Simon's father, in a wheelchair and wearing a kilt, was yelling at a TV show on an old television—*Snooker: World Championship.*

"May I present my father, Simon Rampling, Senior," said

Simon. "He goes by Mac. His original surname was MacLeod. Da, this is Cleo, Sylvie's sister."

"Welcome to the Wild West of England," said Mac, who appeared to be drunk or heavily medicated (perhaps both). His complexion was pallid, but he seemed to be making a valiant effort to charm her.

"I'm happy to meet you," said Cleo. She'd meant to change for dinner, but her cashmere turtleneck dress was warm and comforting, a relief from her usual severe, tight-waisted attire.

"We're so far North you may as well be a Scotsman, which in point of fact, I am," said Mac. Cleo caught Simon's gaze and he shrugged. She noticed that he, too, looked wan. "They tried to keep us out, but here I am, the owner of the goddamned castle!" said Mac.

In truth, the castle was owned by a shell company laundering dirty money, but Cleo kept her mouth shut.

"You'll forgive me for not rising," continued Simon's father. "My legs don't work and I only have days left on this earth. I am—in fact—on many strong painkillers."

"Of course. I'm Cleo." She extended her hand and Mac kissed it. His lips were dry and warm.

"Get this gorgeous creature a drink!" said Mac.

Cleo was wary of lecherous men, but Mac seemed benign. He was remarkably loquacious for someone who was very ill. Could he be pretending to be sick? Cleo shook her head, trying to stop her wary scanning. "Do you have whisky?" she asked.

Simon's father laughed. "Break out the Lagavulin, son," he said. "I could meet my maker any moment and you've been dumped by another American . . . on the eve of your wedding."

"Definitely time for the Lagavulin," agreed Simon. He moved to a bar in the corner of the room and poured single malt Scotch into crystal tumblers.

"What do you mean, dumped by an American?" said Cleo.

"He told the truth, the eejit," said Simon's father.

"Can we have a drink first?" said Simon. "Please?"

"So you told her about Thisbe's money."

Simon dropped a glass of whiskey.

"Och! Son!" cried Mac. "That's the good stuff!"

"How do you know?" said Simon.

"My best friend, Isaac," explained Cleo. "He's an investigative journalist with *The New York Times*."

"I never wanted to take the money," said Mac sadly.

"If it weren't for Thisbe's money, we would have had to sell," said Simon. "This castle was my mother's. We promised her we'd keep it in the family."

"That we did," said Mac. "But who's going to run things when I'm gone?"

"I'll sort it," said Simon tersely.

No wonder Simon hadn't wanted to be honest with Sylvie—this castle was an albatross around his neck. Simon would know that the last thing Sylvie would want would be to inherit an ancestral castle and move to the sticks. From the day Sylvie had landed in Miami, she had never wanted to leave, not even for a vacation.

Cleo heard a voice call "Yoo-hoo!"

"Emma?" Cleo followed her sister's voice into a wood-paneled dining room with a massive stone fireplace that was surmounted by a coat of arms. A table that looked to be seventeen feet long was set with gleaming silver and peach-colored flowers that matched the upholstered walnut chairs. From gilded frames on the wall, the faces of dozens of Simon's male relatives watched them sternly. Emma's boys and Penelope were already seated, tucking into rolls.

"Where is everyone?" said Emma. "It's time for the Rehearsal Dinner!"

"Emma, it's a long story. . . ." Cleo began.

"Also," announced Emma, "I'm drunk!"

PART EIGHT

BADLY BEHAVING GROWN-UPS

1

Rehearsal Dinner Menu

Lakeland Dexter, Smoked Marrow & Caviar

Pickled Cockles & Mussels

Poached Lemon Butter North Sea Cod

A Sauce Made from Nasturtium & Buttermilk

Venison Larb in Baby Gem Cups

Fig, Sweet Cheese & Lemon Verbena

First of the Season Strawberries with Victoria Sponge

Liquorice Parfait with White Chocolate & Sweet Cicely

2
EMMA

-$54,080.12

Emma wanted to hug her big sister. Poor Cleo, standing in the doorway, her face wrinkled on one side as though she'd just waked from a nap. Emma remembered how Cleo could always fall asleep anywhere, even on a picnic blanket or the carpet in front of their childhood TV with the rabbit-ear-shaped antenna. Cleo hadn't changed from her birdwatching outfit; her fancy boots were caked in mud.

Emma stood up from the table to console her lovelorn sister—they'd all heard about Danny's failed proposal—but knocked over her own heavy wooden chair. Emma stared at the chair, then realized she was holding a delicious warm roll in one hand and a silver goblet of red wine in the other. A porter or bellhop or what was he called—serving wench?—rushed to Emma, taking hold of her elbow and tilting her upright. "Thank you . . . sir," said Emma, unsure of how to address a servant.

The man looked annoyed, and Emma felt ashamed. As usual! She always, *always* felt ashamed and she was SICK OF IT. She took another sip from her goblet. It was possible that her sloe gin pregaming (and champagne in her claw-foot tub) had been excessive. Again, here came the shame.

"Oh, gosh, Em," said Cleo, trying to take the goblet from Emma's hand.

Emma yanked her arm free, sending Cabernet all over her thrift-store velvet dress, the white tablecloth, and a certainly priceless rug. Maybe it had once been Anne Boleyn's rug. "I'm just having some *fun,*" she said, leaning over the stained tablecloth to pour herself more wine. "And where the hell is Sylvie?"

Unlike their childhood days, when Cleo's motherly impulses seemed indefatigable, Cleo let go of Emma's arm and sank into the chair next to her sister. When Emma put the wine bottle down, Cleo filled her own glass. "Danny's gone," she said, quietly, while the others fussed with settling the children.

Emma felt so sad for Cleo. "Mom told me," she said.

"Of course," said Cleo bitterly.

"And Mom said you don't want kids?" said Emma.

"I don't know," said Cleo. "I mean, if you look at Mom, it doesn't seem like motherhood is the best idea. . . ."

"But look at me," said Emma, fury rising in her esophagus.

Cleo was silent.

"What?" said Emma.

"You're much more . . . giving than I am," said Cleo. "You've always been."

To keep herself from giving Cleo a piece of her mind, Emma drained her glass of wine and refilled it.

"But I *do* think I love Isaac," said Cleo, changing the subject.

"Isaac is awesome," said Emma, her anger cooling from a full boil to a low simmer—thanks, alcohol! "Remember *Tony n' Tina's Wedding*?"

Cleo laughed.

Emma had visited Cleo in New York while Cleo was in law

school and they had attended the interactive off-Broadway show. Cleo had danced with one of the actors, who was playing a handsy groomsman named Dominic. Isaac had made a big scene pretending to be Cleo's furious paramour. "Isaac said he was a *pro volleyball player.*" Emma laughed.

Cleo shook her head. "Is that even a thing?"

"No idea," said Emma.

"So I'm going to tell Sylvie about Alexander," said Cleo. "It's time. And also about what Isaac uncovered about Simon's money, though Simon already told her, I think. And then I'm going to go. I want to go home."

"Really? Tonight?" said Emma, feeling a bit bereft.

"Where is Sylvie?" said Cleo.

"I don't know," said Emma. She polished off her wine, then narrowed her eyes to see her mother in the doorway. Donna was wearing a voluminous emerald-green dress with what looked like a bedazzled belt strapped around her forehead, tufts of gray hair curled around her face. A waiter in a slim tuxedo pulled out Donna's chair.

"Oh, thank you," simpered Donna. "Well, hello, boys," she said to her grandsons.

"Hi, Gram," said Jameson politely.

"I'm your new granddaughter," said Penelope.

"Nice to meet you," said Donna.

"You look wonderful, Donna," said Rich politely.

"This old thing?" said Donna.

Florence and Rashid entered the dining room. Florence wore a purple minidress that matched Rashid's tie. Simon made sure Mac was settled at the table, then took the spot next to Emma. Emma felt flustered. Sylvie was still missing. Simon smelled as if he was wearing Blenheim Bouquet by Penhaligon's, a scent Emma loved—spicy and clean, it opened with black pepper and notes of lemon, lime, and lavender, mellowed to a pine and musk finish.

The fragrance was a classic—it had been created more than a hundred years ago for the ninth Duke of Marlborough by Walter Penhaligon. Simon's alluring scent made Emma want to lean close to her sister's fiancé.

Instead, she sat up straight and refilled her wine.

"My darlings!" cried Donna. She repeated, weepily, "All my darlings."

"No, that's wrong," said Penelope. "Sylvie's not here. So all your darlings are *not* here."

"Who is this child, again?" said Donna.

"Simon's dazzling daughter, Penelope," said Emma. She moved just one inch closer to Simon to breathe him in. Mmm; Simon's smell made her feel like a guest at a royal banquet.

"Hmm," said Donna. A phalanx of servers swooped into the room, setting down plates of some sort of pâté in a bone with toast points.

"Yummy!" cried Penelope. "It's bone marrow!"

"Gross," said Jameson, grinning.

"It *is not* gross," said Penelope, haughtily. "It's Grandpapa's favorite!"

"Sorry," muttered Jameson.

"Dub," said Guinness, nodding.

"*Dub* means 'W,' as in 'winner,'" noted Rich.

Emma smiled at her husband and gazed at her sons. All of them wore suits and ties, their hair clean and combed but still a bit wild. She was filled with love for them. Rich caught her eye and winked. He never made her feel ashamed, ever. He just *liked* her, as a person and a wife. All the booze she'd imbibed and the Blenheim Bouquet hit her at once, and she was overcome with emotion.

"I took it all for granted," she said, standing again, knocking down her chair again, and causing the same man to tilt her upright again. "So sorry," she said to him.

"S'all right," said the butler.

"Good Lord, Emma," said Cleo. "Sit down!"

"Now that it's all gone," said Emma, making sure not to slur but to punctuate her words carefully. "Now I get it. Rich Catalfamo, you were *everything*."

Rich stood, walked around the table, set her chair to rights, sat down in it, and pulled Emma into his lap. "Shhh," he said, into her hair. His arms were strong and warm. She curled into his embrace, reminding herself that she also loved Rich's eleven-dollar cologne, Old Spice Classic.

"Pass the wine, please," said Donna.

"Eeeeew! Don't kiss!" said Jameson. Rich kissed Emma's neck.

"Dub," said Guinness, smiling.

Simon tapped his glass with a silver fork and stood. He cleared his throat, looking toward his father. "Welcome to Mumberton," he said. "Not all of you know, but this castle has been in my family since the year 1205."

"Why wouldn't they know?" said Mac.

"We're just so glad you're home!" cried Louisa the freaky librarian, who had entered the dining room wearing a long maroon-and-gold striped gown. She strode to Mac's side. Her eye shadow matched her dress: maroon on the lids, gold above.

"I met Simon's mother in town when we were young ones. I was the new veterinarian. She asked if I could castrate her bears!" said Mac, jarringly.

"What does 'castrate' mean?" said Jameson.

"To castrate is to remove the testicles," said Penelope.

"I'm a simple Scottish veterinarian!" said Mac. "I was not to this manor born!"

"It was an unconventional pickup line, but it worked," said Simon. "My father came to help my mother with the bears, and my mum and dad fell in love, and eventually, he devoted himself to Mumberton Castle."

Louisa produced a pillbox and began counting pills for Mac. "Not *now,*" he hissed at her, and she sheepishly put the medication away.

Mac spoke, his voice weak but audible. "We've been waiting a long time for young Simon to find a bride up to the task of taking on Mumberton," said Mac. "I'd propose a toast to the next Lady Rampling, but . . ." He seemed to deflate. "Where is she, now?" he said. "What's happened? I know something happened . . . but I forget what it was."

"Sylvie didn't know what she was getting into. I should have told her sooner, but I . . . I didn't tell her. But I wrote it all down, and . . . she's reading it, I suppose. Or she's read it, and she's gone."

"Simon, what the hell?" said Florence, getting up.

"Flo," said Rashid, trying to placate her.

"She's been through so much," said Florence, her voice rising as she remained upright. "I told her to believe in you. I told her I thought she could trust someone. I told her to trust *you.*"

"You're right," said Simon sadly. "I was just . . . I was afraid she would give up on me if she knew how complicated . . ."

"You own this castle? Is that where your money comes from?" said Florence.

"My dear," said Mac, "that's where the money *goes.*"

Emma looked at Simon. Instead of anger at the man who'd apparently kept secrets from Sylvie, Emma felt sympathy. She knew what desperation tasted like in the back of your throat. She knew how desire for something false to be true could warp your morals and change you into a stranger to yourself.

"I lied, too," said Emma.

"Shhh," said Rich.

"No!" said Emma. "I lied, too!"

"Christ, she is *wasted,*" said Cleo.

"I lost all our money," said Emma.

"Mom, what?" said Guinness.

"Sweet Nothings," managed Emma.

"That's her business," said Penelope. "It's a line of personal, empowering products for women."

"It's not empowering," said Emma. "Though I appreciate that, Penelope. Thank you."

"Sweetheart . . ." whispered Rich.

"No! If Simon's brave enough to tell the truth, so am I," said Emma.

"More like drunk enough," said Donna.

"Right?" said Cleo. She laughed. "You got that right."

"Cleo, I can't even tell the difference between you and Mom," said Emma. "She made us ashamed our whole lives and now we do it to each other. But you know what? This has nothing to do with either of you. And the fact is . . ."

Everyone was silent, watching Emma. At last, she was in the spotlight, although not in the way she had envisioned. "Sweet Nothings is a scam," she said. "I lost everything. Cassidy Rose . . . Cassidy Rose tricked me. It's a pyramid marketing scheme. We're completely broke." Emma exhaled, finally free of her horrible secret.

"Not true," said Rich. "Honey, it's OK. We have plenty of savings and we're going to—"

"No," said Emma. She shook her head. "I spent all that, Rich. It's all gone. Everything."

Rich stared at her. "Say that again," he said.

"Our savings are gone," said Emma.

Rich was silent for a moment. He closed his eyes and shook his head. And then he stood up and walked slowly across the dining room toward the Great Hall. He opened the heavy door and closed it carefully behind him.

"Oh, Emma, what have you done?" said Donna.

"Leave her alone," said Florence. "You're all terrible people! None of you deserve Sylvie! Where is she, Simon?"

"She's in the Gatekeeper's Cottage," said Simon. "That's where I saw her last, anyway. I'd hoped she'd call me, or come to dinner, but . . ."

"You're all insane," said Florence. "Come on, Rash," she said, taking her husband's hand. "We're packing up, we're finding Syl, and we're going home."

"Fair enough," said Rashid. "Thanks . . . uh . . . for everything."

"This is a nightmare," said Cleo, refilling her wineglass. "What about the loan I gave you last year?"

"Gone," said Emma. She felt loose with relief.

"Well, Simon," chirped Louisa, "at least you're back at Mumberton. Where you belong."

"Ah, Christ, son," said Mac. "You don't belong here. You never did."

"Come on, Da," said Simon in a low and defeated voice.

"More interest in Penny the vulture than your ancestors," said Mac. "I appreciate the money. We all do. But you don't belong where you started, son."

"Dad, I'm here now. I promised Mom I'd keep it in the fucking family."

"Daddy!" cried Penelope. "That's inappropriate!" She and Emma's boys were bug-eyed, taking in the badly behaving grown-ups around them.

"You've done the right thing now, Simon, you've made your Da's day," said Louisa, inanely. "Now, darling, let's get your pills and we can have some marrow on toast."

"Darling?" said Simon. "Wait, Dad, are you and Louisa—"

"It's cold winters here in Mumberton!" thundered Mac.

"No one should be alone on a cold winter's night and that's a fact," said Donna.

"This is such a happy occasion!" said Louisa.

"If we're baring our souls," said Cleo, "I'd better go speak with Sylvie, too."

"Don't," said Simon. "Leave her alone. It's enough."

"As if you have any idea what's best for Sylvie," said Cleo. "Save me some sweet cheese verbena, whatever the hell that is," she said, striding through the dining room and slamming the door on her way out.

"Did you really lose all our money, Mom?" said Guinness.

"I did, yes," said Emma.

"Cassidy Rose is a hustler," said Jameson. "Sheesh."

"That's true, actually," said Emma.

"Her pants are *so tight,*" said Jameson. "And made of leather, which honestly, Mom? That's unethical."

"It's so bad," said Penelope. "Skinning an animal? Barbaric."

"Adults are wack," said Jameson. "Right, Penelope?"

"You're right, Jameson," she said. "You are so right."

"Bet," said Guinness.

"Anyway, Mama Bear," said Jameson. "We love you!" He picked up his warm roll and bit down, his expression rapturous.

"Quite a motley crew you have here, Simon," said Mac.

Emma wanted to run after her husband, to scream and beg, but she was worn out, exhausted, a bit hysterical. She started to laugh.

"Anyone for a beer?" said Simon.

"I should maybe say no," said Emma.

"Truth, Mom," said Guinness.

"Yeah," said Jameson, his expression sad and optimistic at the same time.

"I'm sober," said Penelope. "It's a good lifestyle choice."

"Oh, me too," said Jameson. Guinness nodded.

"My mom is sober," said Penelope. "It's super hard but here's what you do: You can never, ever do anything you don't want to do. Ever again, seriously. Then you don't have to drink! My mom and I leave parties if we're not having fun. It's awesome! OK? You can only do what you want."

"I can't go home," said Guinness, his voice growing loud. "Mom . . ."

Emma turned to Guinness. "Yes?"

He looked down at his plate, unable to speak, it seemed. Jameson spoke for him. "The kids make fun of him, Mom," said Jameson.

"Stop," whispered Guinness.

"They call him a moonpig, because he draws cartoons," said Jameson. "They hit him and they put poop in his locker!" Jameson started to cry.

"Oh, sweetheart," said Emma. "Is that true?"

"Don't make me go back, Mom," said Guinness.

"Doesn't anyone care about my emerald headpiece?" cried Donna.

3
FROM THE DESK OF SIMON RAMPLING

Dear Sylvie,

I am a coward, so instead of telling you the truth while I look in your eyes, I am going to write it down.

I just hung up the phone with Thisbe. In order to explain what she wants, I need to tell you what I've done. I had wanted to be the one person who did not disappoint you, yet here we are, in this bleak castle, where everything always goes to hell.

How can I explain the situation with Thisbe? In broad strokes, Thisbe's father works for dishonest politicians. I don't know the details, but I know he is ruthless. All their money—all my money—is corrupt.

Christ, this is not what I want to be doing right now. Leave it to Thisbe to ruin even this day.

Thisbe and I met in college. She had a boyfriend and I was her best friend—I was not-so-secretly in love with her. One night during a fight with her boyfriend,

Thisbe ended up at my place, and we conceived Penelope. I don't know why she married me; she had many options, but she said she wanted me—us—and so we were married in the Miami Four Seasons Hotel.

My father came to the wedding. He was utterly mystified by the ironic '80s cover band, the bright sun, the enormous guest list, and multilayered cake. He looked so small in the ballroom. At one point, I brought him a whiskey and he said, so quietly, "Who **are** *all these people?"*

I had no idea. Thisbe's family is enormous and influential. They own properties in Miami, London, New York, Caracas, the Cayman Islands, the Bahamas, and Houston. (And that's just the ones I know about.) Thisbe's father bought us a home on Indian Creek Island and we welcomed Penelope. I thought I was happy.

I sent money to Mumberton instead of going home. (Thisbe's father's money, of course: A company he created now owns Mumberton, but the company is willed to Penelope.) My father replaced the roof and refurbished the rooms one by one, completing all the plans my mother had left in notebooks (even completing projects my grandparents had dreamed up). He told me he was proud. I don't know where my mother is but I imagine she is pleased if she is anywhere.

Thisbe told me she was leaving me when Penelope was eighteen months old. She surprised me one evening, appearing with her ex-boyfriend in our home library, declaring their rekindled love. Thisbe wanted a divorce and she wanted to bring Penelope to New York full time. She offered me a lump sum to sign a nondisclosure agreement—she had all the papers ready to go. I would get Penelope for all of her school holidays, including the upcoming summer break, and I would never have to work again.

I did consider telling them I would expose her father and fight for full custody. But there was no doubt I would lose and I didn't want my father to know I'd essentially sold the family property to a man who was using Mumberton Castle to launder money.

I avenged nothing. Sylvie, as they stood in front of me, in my library, I wept. And then I signed the papers, all of them. I left my home that night. Penelope and I flew to England for the summer. I hated myself.

In the fall, Thisbe sent for her daughter. Penelope is not a pawn: I let her go. I began to focus on my photography. I read for hours. Thisbe's father gave me our house on Indian Creek Island and I had it torn down and built my cabin.

Thisbe called this morning to tell me she is leaving New York. The US government is investigating her assets; her father is relocating her, probably to the Bahamas or Cayman Islands. She wants Penelope to move in with me until she can sort out her affairs. So in addition to my filthy money (which may well disappear or land me in jail), I now have full-time custody. I won't lie, this thrills me, but it's nothing you signed up for.

It was never about the money for me—I hope you know me well enough to believe that. I want to sit with you, and read, and be still. I know the wedding is rushed. It was yet another trick my brain tried to play: If I could give my father a new Lady Rampling, he would not die, or would die happy.

I am a liar. Tell me what is next, and I will accept it. My love is yours if you will have me. The front desk can arrange whatever transportation you need if you just want out.

Yours,
(Forever)
Simon

P.S. Attached is a map to the castle, with a star next to a side entrance that leads directly to my room, if you want to talk.

To find this entrance, approach the base of the castle's northern wall. There, you will see a small, ivy-covered door, almost hidden amongst the rocks. The door is unassuming, with no handles or locks to indicate that it is an entrance. But if you push it open, you'll find yourself in a tunnel that winds its way beneath the castle walls.

Be careful not to bump your head on the low ceiling. The floor is uneven. But after a few minutes of twisting and turning, you will see a spiral stone staircase. It's narrow and tight but will lead you to me.

I will be waiting, my love.

4
SYLVIE

Sylvie put down Simon's letter, which she had just read for the twelfth time. Her body, clanging with foreboding, had been right all along. Hope was a hole through which despair could enter her. It was time to go home and heal.

Despite her deep desire to connect with Simon, to love him and be loved, she could not bear it. She did not believe there was a plan, or a point, or someone watching over her. Alexander could no longer surprise her: There was safety and calmness in choosing his ghost and the steady ache of loneliness.

At the window of the Gatekeeper's Cottage, Sylvie watched the castle and she watched the moon. She thought about her sisters, feeling pierced by sorrow thinking of them as kids, just little girls, desperate for an adult to protect them.

Sylvie wanted to feel comfort in her sisters' presence, but being with them just reminded her of how sad she had been for so long. She had reframed their nights under the stars as something beautiful, but they had been desolate girls. Her sisters had nothing for Sylvie.

But she could return to her Miami library, a place where she was known. She had her house on Hibiscus Street. She had Alexander's ghost, who could not hurt her anymore or ask for more than she could give.

In her pajamas, Sylvie sat down at a small desk Simon had placed in the corner of the room for her. She reached into the *New Yorker* tote bag she used as a purse, rummaged until she found a Bic ballpoint.

Sylvie ripped a clean page from a tiny notebook. She wrote,

I'm sorry, Simon.
I'm going home.
It's over.

Sylvie signed the letter and heard the sound of someone banging on the cottage door. Sylvie moved downstairs, unlocking the entrance. "What is it?" she said.

"I've ruined everything," said Emma, stumbling in, reeking of alcohol. "I'm going to be sick," said Emma.

Sylvie helped Emma to the bathroom, then walked her upstairs and put her to bed without even trying to change her out of her stained dress. Emma kept repeating, "I had everything and I lost it all."

Sylvie got a cool towel for Emma's forehead, situated a bucket by her side. She texted Rich that Emma was asleep. Rich gave the message a thumbs-up, then typed: *Thanks. She needs the rest.*

Rich was a sturdy oak; they were lucky to have him in the family.

Emma fell into slumber, and Sylvie heard another rap at the door. It was Florence and Rashid. Flo had changed into sweatpants and her *Coconut Grove Choir* T-shirt, her bags packed in their rental car. After a long hug, Florence said, "Rash, honey, can you wait in the living room?"

"Of course. I love you, Syl," said Rashid.

"I know you do," said Sylvie.

In the other room, Rashid clicked on Simon's tiny television. A newscaster was excited. "Ladies' day is usually synonymous with fancy hats and fizz, but tonight in Penrith, it was all about the racing!"

Florence and Sylvie climbed the stairs to cross over to Sylvie's section of the gatehouse. Sylvie handed Simon's letters to Florence, who read them in silence.

"Well, we knew it was something shady," said Florence.

"I don't want to do this anymore," said Sylvie. "I'm sorry I made you come."

"I don't know, Syl. At least he's come clean."

"It's not the money," said Sylvie.

"Then what is it?" said Florence. "Tell me, just open your brain and talk."

"This was all a mistake," said Sylvie. "I tried . . . you know I tried. But I don't want this. I feel just sick with wanting to be home."

"You don't want your own library in a castle?" said Florence, eyebrow raised.

"I want to go back to my life," said Sylvie. "I changed my mind."

"You don't love Simon."

Sylvie shook her head.

"You *do* love Simon."

"I do love Simon, yes."

"Even now that you know he's living on stolen money."

"This isn't even about love, Flo. I know you don't understand."

"You're scared," said Florence.

Sylvie looked at her hands. She had taken off her ring from Simon. It was so much bigger and flashier than the simple gold band Alexander had placed on her finger (and that she now wore around her neck). Florence hugged her. Sylvie blinked back tears. “I can’t hope anymore,” she managed. “It’s too hard.”

“OK,” said Florence. “I get it. I can understand that.”

Simon’s letter didn’t make Sylvie adore him any less. In his missive, she found the man she loved. But before she even read the postscript, Sylvie felt something in her come to a halt. She had been allowing herself to fall, to be pulled by some exquisite gravity into marriage, into a life without steady sorrow. She was reading letters like a Jane Austen heroine, in a castle in a country not her own. She had been inhabiting an impossible but thrilling dream.

Now she was awake.

As distracting and scary and *fun* as this whole Simon fantasy had been, Sylvie ached to be on her brown couch, Willie asleep next to her. She dreaded the long journey to get there from where she was.

Sylvie respected that Simon had been honest with her. She owed him honesty as well. Simon was saddled with a decrepit castle and ghosts of his own; he did not need a bride who still clung to a dead husband. Penelope did not need a mother figure who had stopped believing in God.

Sylvie would miss Simon so much, especially his kisses.

And days spent in hammocks.

And the way he smelled like pepper and fir trees. And his sense of humor. And how it felt to have someone love her so very much. She would miss that. She would miss the beep of a text from Simon distracting her from shelving, the books he’d bought two copies of, and long quiet evenings reading near each other. Sex, she was going to miss that. And the way he made perfect coffee, every time, and how he called Penelope every day. And watching Penelope grow and maybe Penelope might have wandered the hallways of Coconut Grove Elementary.

When she was finished packing, Sylvie looked out the window of her empty home library. The sun had set over the Eskdale Valley, and Simon had told her that families and couples strolled on the dunes by a nearby estuary. The air smelled faintly salty, wonderful. Sylvie wanted to call Simon and—

No. That was done now. She would not walk with her Simon by the sea.

5
CLEO

Outside Mumberton Castle, it was absolutely silent and cold. The stars were brilliant overhead and the castle was lit up, breathtaking in its magnificence. Mumberton Castle had been waiting for decades for a Rampling to marry inside its walls. Cleo was in the most scenic place she'd ever been, and she was so lonely.

She walked toward the Gatekeeper's Cottage, speeding up to stay warm in the brisk summer air. Her boots pounded on the gravelly hiking path. When she reached the cottage, Cleo stood under the arch and stared up at the portcullis that could be lowered so quickly it would crush her. In an alleyway between the two hanging gates, there was a small door. She knocked, and when there was no response, started hitting the door with the side of her fist. Then she started banging hard. "Sylvie?" she called. "SYLVIE! Come down here!"

Sylvie opened the door. She looked exhausted and was dressed in one of her librarian outfits: a matching cardigan set the color of a cooked salmon, a wide-waled corduroy skirt, and big wool socks with clogs. "What's going on?" said Cleo. "Why do you have a suitcase?"

"Come on in," said Sylvie.

Cleo took in the modern interior, surprised that the historical building opened into an airy foyer. Sylvie led Cleo through a dimly lit library where Rashid was watching the news in an Eames chair, up a set of limestone steps lined with a sleek wooden railing, to a sitting room with giant windows on both sides of the uppermost room, allowing Cleo to gaze over both Mumberton Castle and Mumberton Town. Cleo suddenly missed Montana, the inner quietude that a big view was able to give her.

Cleo followed Sylvie into an enormous bedroom. A California king bed was made up with light-pink linens, framed by a huge velvet backboard. There was a cozy fire lit and two love seats had been made up into beds on either side of the room. Someone (Louisa Freck? Simon?) had fanned gossip magazines on a low table, along with popcorn, bottles of sparkling wine and lemonade on ice, coupe glasses, a bowl of Twizzlers (Emma's favorite) and After Eight mints (Cleo's favorite—she'd imagined, when little, that rich adults ate them). A big television on a wheeled cart had a stack of 1990s DVDs on top: *My Best Friend's Wedding, Ever After, Titanic,* and *The Wedding Singer.*

Cleo shook her head: These had been their favorite movies to watch back on Joy Street—all of this was Sylvie's doing. Cleo's gratitude for her sweet, dorky little sister only made her hate herself more. Sylvie's desires were so simple, a child's dreams: sisterly connection, popcorn.

Cleo saw Emma passed out on the bed, and Florence in hideous sweatpants on a settee. "Nobody told me you were all here," said Cleo. A voice in her mind said, *Left out again . . .*

Florence stood. "I'll be in the other room," she said. "Just tell me what you want to do, Syl."

"OK," said Sylvie. "Can you guys just stay here tonight? Maybe that couch folds out. . . ."

"Of course. Whatever you need."

Cleo crossed her arms over her chest. "I feel like the only kid not invited to the slumber party," she said.

"It was supposed to be a surprise after dinner," said Sylvie, sighing. "But then Simon decided to confess or whatever and I had to read his letter. Then Emma came here really drunk. It scared me. She was acting like Mom used to act."

"Yeah, that's bad. She was a wreck at dinner."

"How's Mom?"

"She's the same. But Syl, there are some things I want to talk to you about. Things I *need* to talk to you about." Cleo lay down on the bed that was made for her, complete with a stuffed frog and a bright purple comforter. (Her favorite animal and favorite color when she was ten; it was a little strange.)

"I know you don't like Simon," said Sylvie. She'd always had a knack for sounding petulant.

"That's not—"

"It doesn't matter. I'm going home with Florence in the morning," said Sylvie. She blinked back tears. This wasn't petulance, Cleo realized: It was heartbreak. The way Sylvie's shoulders sloped forward was the same sad way she'd used to sit in the kitchen, trying to stay out of Cleo's vicious fights with Donna.

"Syl, there's something I need to say," Cleo began. "I've been avoiding this . . . I hate having to make you sad. . . ."

"Do you, though?" said Sylvie.

"What?"

"Sometimes it seems like you get off on it, to be honest. If I'm a mess, then you're the big, fucking savior." She exhaled. "Cleo, the knight in shining armor," she said.

"I never wanted to have to take care of you guys," said Cleo. "I *wish* someone would take care of *me*! Keep an eye out for me, for once!"

"Danny was a terrible match for you," said Sylvie. "OK? You

two were miserable together from what I can tell. You both deserve better."

Cleo nodded. "You're right," she said.

"I know I am."

"Listen, Syl," said Cleo. "Simon's money comes from his ex-wife. Her dad is a crook."

"I know, Cleo. But who am I to judge? You think I shouldn't marry Simon, but truly, I don't even deserve him," she said. She waved her skinny arm, gesturing to the fancy sheets, the fresh flowers, the stacks of new hardcover books. "I do not deserve any of this. And yet, you know what, Cleo? When he hugs me, I feel better. When I cry about Alexander, and I say I miss him, and my life feels ruined . . . Simon listens to me. He doesn't try to change my mind or fix anything. We've both been through a lot. And he says he loves me. And that feels . . . I don't deserve it, but I want it." She exhaled. "I wanted it," she said.

"But now you don't?"

"I'm not going to marry him," said Sylvie. "I wish I could. I can't tell you how much I wish I could."

"I have to tell you about Alexander," said Cleo.

"You don't have to tell me anything about Alexander," said Sylvie. "I'm going to bed."

"Alexander's death was my fault. I'm the reason he died."

"Oh, Cleo, please . . ."

"Syl, I'm the one who caused the accident."

Cleo said it, she just said it. Hearing about Sylvie being held, being comforted, it ripped her open. "I was on the phone with Alexander," she said. It felt as if she were slicing off her skin: raw, sheer pain. "I was on the phone with him when he crashed. When he . . . when he died."

Sylvie stared at Cleo. "What do you mean you were on the phone with him? Why were you on the phone with Alexander?"

"Alexander was in bad shape."

"What? What does that mean?"

"He'd relapsed, Syl. He was drinking again."

"No," said Sylvie. "No, Cleo, he wasn't."

"He'd been arrested, and he wanted to talk to me about what to do."

Sylvie stared at her sister. "What the hell are you talking about?" she said. "He wasn't arrested! *My* Alexander? You were talking to my Alexander?"

"Yes," said Cleo. "I was talking to your Alexander." Cleo's mind gave her a list of ways to spin it, to obfuscate the narrative. But she had to be honest. Cleo had betrayed her sister for years, keeping the truth of her dead husband from Sylvie. Hiding what she had done.

"He was arrested on some boys' night out, Syl. He was arrested for being drunk and disorderly. He was off the wagon. But he didn't want me to tell you. He was afraid he might get fired. He didn't know how to get a lawyer without you finding out. You thought he was perfect."

Sylvie was completely still.

"And he wasn't perfect. He told you he quit. But he hadn't quit."

"Alexander was *arrested*?" said Sylvie, shaking her head, closing her eyes.

"He wanted me to do some legal research to help him," said Cleo. She took a breath. She just needed to speak the truth and then she could leave.

Don't tell her! Please don't tell her, Cleo!

Silencing the sound of Alexander's last plea, Cleo forced it out: "The night he died . . . Alexander called me. I told him I was going to tell you about the arrest and his drinking," said Cleo. "I said I was going to tell you everything and he was trying to talk me out of it and then he crashed. And then he died."

And then Alexander started screaming.

"I don't even understand what the fuck you're talking about," said Sylvie, shivering in her pink cardigan, her knees pulled to her chest on a big bed where Emma slept in her clothes, snoring lightly.

"Sylvie," said Cleo. "I've wanted to go back in time every day since. It was my fault he lost control of the car. It was my fault I didn't tell you sooner. It was my fault, all of it."

"Why did you wait ten years to tell me this?" said Sylvie, anger reviving her. She stood and began pacing, her eyes wild.

"I am so sorry, Syl," said Cleo. "I didn't know how . . . I didn't want to hurt you. And the longer I waited, the more impossible it seemed to say anything." She moved toward Sylvie, her heart cracking. "All I have ever wanted to do was protect you," said Cleo. For a moment, Sylvie was warm against Cleo's chest.

And then Sylvie broke free, took a step back, and then another.

"Go to hell," said Sylvie.

Of course, thought Cleo. It wasn't as if she hadn't known how this would all play out. She was frozen in place. "Please . . ." said Cleo.

"Get out," said Sylvie. "Just go!" She took Cleo's arm and pulled her toward the stairs. She started to sob, hitting Cleo's chest. "Get out! Get out!" she screamed.

Cleo ran down the stairs and outside and the chilling night hit her like a fist. She put her hands to her face but could not cry. She pulled out her phone, seeing that Isaac had sent a text. It was a photo of a brunette woman. *You would be proud of me, met Rebecca on Jdate, she works at the Whitney.*

Cleo deleted the message, pulled a cigarette from her purse, and lit it with a match. She stood outside the gatehouse, not knowing which direction to go, because there was no destination where she would be welcome.

This was what she deserved.

6
EMMA

-$55,120.32

Emma woke up in the middle of the night. She was not in her room in Missoula. She was not in the four-poster bed in the Indigo Suite. Where was Rich? She touched her forehead, pain blooming behind her eyes. She moaned, and a cool hand swept her hair back from her face. She squinted: It was Sylvie.

"Hey," said Emma's baby sister. Sylvie looked washed out and tired, her face inches from Emma's, smelling of mint toothpaste and cherry-almond Jergens Cloud Crème. (Emma also still wore the same lotion as Donna.)

"Where am I?" said Emma.

"The Gatekeeper's Cottage," said Sylvie.

"I need to call Rich."

"I told him you were staying the night. It's fine," said Sylvie. She snuggled next to her sister. "Cleo made Alexander crash his car," said Sylvie quietly. "She was . . . I don't know . . . they were . . . Cleo was on the phone with him. And then he died."

"I know," said Emma. "It was a long time ago."

"You know?" said Sylvie, sitting up.

"You loved him so much," said Emma. "You wanted him to be

someone he wasn't. Cleo told me everything at his funeral. We didn't want to tell you he'd relapsed, Syl. Alexander was an amazing guy, but he . . . you seemed to want to remember him a certain way."

Emma remembered Cleo telling her what had happened in Sylvie's cramped kitchen on Hibiscus Street. They were drinking shitty Chablis that some friends of Sylvie's had brought in gallon jugs. Cleo was haunted, her eyes sunk into their sockets. She was shaking when she told Emma about Alexander's screaming. Rich had been there, too. He had gathered Cleo and Emma in his arms, held them tight. Sylvie lifted her head from across the room and made her way to the scrum, like a magnet. A split second before she joined the fold, Emma said, "Don't tell her today. It's too much."

So they'd never told her.

"I hate both of you," said Sylvie.

"Not more than we already hate ourselves," said Emma.

7
SYLVIE

Emma snored. Just a little, like a small cat. Sylvie couldn't sleep. She remembered a time that Donna had fought with Emma—Emma always seemed to be the focus of Donna's attention, especially after Cleo had gone away to school—and when Emma collapsed into her bed, tearful, Sylvie came to lie beside her, scratching her back until she quieted.

Sylvie missed Cleo. Her anger was short-lived: Lying next to Emma, she just felt cozy and weary. Her sisters had only been trying to protect her, as they'd always done. It was Alexander who'd been at fault, not Cleo and Emma.

Sylvie thought Alexander was an example of a man with a hard-won sober life: He was steadfast, beloved by his elementary school choir, honest. He had sponsees at AA. After he was bodily gone, she'd made her fantasy Alexander into what her fragile heart most desired, in a sick way—an ideal companion she could allow in her life without fear. Only ghost Alexander was safe because he could never surprise her, disappoint her, or abandon her.

The airbrushed version of Alexander—a presence she'd imagined in her kitchen while she read, in her bed while she slept, keeping Willie company when Sylvie was at work—was not real.

Alexander had been flawed, more complicated than Sylvie had known (or maybe she had known, maybe she had). The perfect marriage Sylvie had believed in seemed tangled now, a mysterious entity that had held secrets and disappointments and fears her husband had never shared with her. Drunk and disorderly? Arrested for arguing with a police officer? Not sober, as he'd vowed, proud like a child with a good report card, carrying around his Big Book and doing his daily readings. She felt such sadness, wishing she had been able to understand all the sides of him, even the ones that would disappoint her.

When she listened for him now, for his spectral companionship, there was nothing. She had made him up, had imagined a simple, soothing version of a complex, fucked-up, beautiful man. Now she saw that her ghost husband had only been her imagination all along.

But Sylvie was not alone. She had no Alexander, but she had her sisters.

From the day she was born, she had been loved by her sisters.

8
CLEO

Cleo shivered, hunched up on the steps of Sylvie's cottage without a coat. She could call Isaac, but what would she say? She knew he would answer, and he would listen, but she did love him, and she wanted him to be happy. If he had finally struck gold on Jdate and was curled around a Whitney curator in her sleek apartment, Cleo didn't want to ruin that sweetness for him.

Cleo sighed. At least she was free of her secret, and free of trying to love Danny, a man she *should* want but just did not want.

There were two bicycles leaning against the Gatekeeper's Cottage. Should Cleo ride into town and try to find a warm place to sit, more cigarettes? She could not remember the last time she'd been on a bike. It had probably been in Montana, when she and her sisters had wheeled around town in a pack. How had she forgotten the pleasure of going fast down a hill on a bike?

Cleo startled when a light went on in the kitchen of Sylvie's cottage. She narrowed her eyes and saw Sylvie in the doorway.

Cleo stood. The night was bright with stars. Sylvie saw her, smiled sadly, and waved. Cleo lifted her hand.

9
EMMA

-$56,480.32

“I need Advil,” groaned Emma. “I need Pepto-Bismol and Advil and Excedrin and Tylenol and coffee.” She pressed her palms to her eyes. “I have never been so hung over in my life,” she said. She felt as if she was going to throw up and cry simultaneously.

“You were a wreck,” said Cleo.

Emma opened one eye. Cleo lay next to her on Sylvie’s cozy bed, propped on one elbow. “Where’s Sylvie?” said Emma.

“I don’t know—she was here when I fell asleep,” said Cleo.

“So she forgave you?”

“Yeah,” said Cleo. “Yeah, she forgave me.”

“It was my fault, too. Maybe even more my fault.”

“Damn right,” said Cleo.

Emma could only laugh. She sat up, fighting back a wave of nausea. “I have to call Rich,” she said. “Cleo, I have really messed up this time.”

“Can’t argue with you there,” said Cleo.

“Do you think he’ll leave me?”

“I don’t think he will, Em,” said Cleo.

“I’m too nauseous to call him,” said Emma, snuggling back

under the covers. "I want to live here," she said. "I want to live at Mumberton Castle with Rich and the boys and start over. I want to go back in time and make better decisions."

"You can't go back in time," said Cleo. "But you can have everything else. Why not? Ask Simon if you can stay here. He wants to go back to Miami. Maybe he'll . . . rent it to you. I don't know."

"I never should have stayed in Montana!" said Emma.

"Hey," said Cleo. "It's OK, Emma."

Emma started to cry. "It's my hangover," she cried. "Or maybe it's my hormones!"

"Oh, Emma. You're allowed to want more."

Emma shook her head. "I'm not allowed to want anything," she managed.

"Jesus Christ, Em! Did you hear what you just said? You can at least be nice to yourself," said Cleo.

"I don't let myself want anything, actually," said Emma.

"I know," said Cleo. "Believe me: I get it."

Emma took a deep breath. "I know you get it," she said. "I know you do."

"I mean, the only person I enjoy being with on the island of Manhattan and the surrounding boroughs is Isaac," said Cleo. "I literally dislike everyone else in my life."

"Isaac has always loved you," said Emma.

"Well, unfortunately, he just met someone. She's Jewish, and her name is Rebecca. And for another thing, what if we try to date and then it falls apart. . . ."

"I get it," said Emma miserably.

"I know you get it," said Cleo.

10
SYLVIE

Dawn light lit Sylvie's way as she walked along the trail toward Mumberton Castle. Her clogs were unsteady on the gravel path but Sylvie was filled with a very rare sense of certainty. She could smell cedar and salt, a reminder that the sea was near. At the top of a rocky incline, she stopped to catch her breath, turned to take in the view of the River Esk and the hills below.

Reconnected with her sisters, Sylvie felt strong. When they had fallen asleep on either side of her, she had stayed in her body, made herself breathe slowly in and out. Cleo slept on her back, ever alert, likely scanning even as she (lightly) slept, her breaths slow but shallow. Emma burrowed in, a warm and trusting animal, seeking warmth.

If Simon broke her heart, she would not be alone.

This knowledge helped Sylvie understand the invisible channel she'd used to escape her emotions. When she felt too much, she'd fled into her girlhood self, the one who was protected by Emma and Cleo. Lying between them in the Gatekeeper's Cottage, she felt that girl and her adult self come together. She didn't have to fly. She was a thirty-five-year-old librarian who could marry or not marry, who could love and lose her love. She could abide, because she could return to the place where her sisters' hearts kept time with hers.

Sylvie kissed Emma's temple and then Cleo's cheek. She left them asleep and went into the reading room Simon had made for her. She smelled of Emma's perfume and Cleo's cigarettes. Sylvie sat cross-legged on the couch and opened *The Bed Book.* Of course, there was no note from her father, but Sylvie turned the pages, reading about every bed in Sylvia Plath's imagination. She reached the "Bird Watching Bed," a bed depicting a hammock between trees. In the sky above the children watching birds, she saw a note in Simon's handwriting.

Dear Sylvie, Someday you will find this note, and know that you are beloved.

As Simon had promised, there was a secret door covered with ivy along the northern wall of Mumberton Castle. Sylvie reached the door and pushed—it was unlocked. With the beam of her cellphone, Sylvie illuminated a narrow tunnel. She found her way to a spiral staircase. The stairs were slippery and Sylvie felt claustrophobic. The air seemed dense and dark inside this seldom-used space. At the top of the creepy circle of stairs, she opened an egress with relief, taking a big breath and finding herself in a corridor painted red.

Sylvie rapped at the door to her right.

She heard footsteps; it was Simon's gait.

"Hello?" said Simon. He turned the doorknob. "Sylvie?"

Here he was—Simon, his sleepy eyes, his beautiful body, the mouth that opened hers, that brushed her skin, the tongue that electrified her, that brought her body pleasures she had never thought possible. She wanted to gather him to her, to press him against the wall, kiss him hard. . . . Simon, who had remembered what Sylvie's father had written in *The Bed Book*. Simon, who had made her a library, had given his heart, had trusted her with his most shameful truth. Sylvie didn't want to run anymore.

She slipped off her coat and stood before him.

"I'm here," said Sylvie.

And she was.

PART NINE
SECRETS & SMOKE

1

CLEO

Cleo sat up in Sylvie's bed. She stretched and made her way into the bathroom. On the mirror, Sylvie had left a note in pink lipstick: *See you at my wedding.* Cleo blinked. So Sylvie was going through with it. "Emma!" she called. "Sylvie's getting married!"

"What? What time is it?" said Emma, sitting up in her stained and rumpled dress.

"It's ten—we only have an hour."

"Sylvie's getting married?" said Emma. "Did I dream that she was done with love?"

"I thought I was coming here to ruin everything," said Cleo, borrowing Sylvie's toothbrush and lining it with a British toothpaste called Macleans. "And I was *right.* Simon *does* have dirty money. But honestly? I love him anyway."

"Cleo, do you really think Simon will let me rent Mumberton Castle? How much do you think it would cost? We only need the Indigo Suite. . . ." said Emma, rubbing her eyes.

"I think it's actually on Airbnb," said Cleo. "But I bet Simon will give you the whole thing, including that librarian with the eye shadow," said Cleo. "Maybe if you and your family stayed, he could go back to Miami and live the dullest happy life imaginable with Sylvie and all her dusty books."

"Maybe," said Emma. "Maybe he'll pay off Cassidy Rose, too!"

"Oh God, why not?" said Cleo. "Emma, I seriously can't believe you fell for that."

"I'm ashamed already," said Emma. "Leave it alone."

"I'm sorry," said Cleo.

"More of being a nice sister, please, OK?" said Emma. "Less of being like Mom."

"Got it," said Cleo. "I really am sorry."

"I need to be less like Mom, too. Starting with not drinking, sheesh." There was a knock at the bedroom door. The sisters looked at each other. "Who is it?" whispered Emma.

"Who is it?" called Cleo.

"It's Simon."

Cleo raked her fingers through her hair and opened the door. Emma tried to smooth her wrinkled dress. "Simon, about last night . . ." she began.

"Oh, we've all gotten pissed," said Simon. "No bother. Look what I've brought." He held out two deep green circular boxes.

"Harrods," said Cleo, impressed.

"What's Harrods?" said Emma.

"The most luxurious store in the world," said Cleo.

"I'd love to take you both there," said Simon. "And . . . I've made a lot of mistakes. I know I have. But all I want is to be with your sister. And that dog, Willie, who might bite me."

"She will probably bite you," said Emma.

"Open the boxes," said Simon.

Cleo grabbed hers. She opened the Harrods case, and nestled in tissue was a hat made of peacock feathers. "It's called a fascinator," said Simon. "You wear it like a headband. The feather . . . contraption . . . goes to the side."

Emma lifted her hat from the package: It was deep blue with the same feathers as Cleo's.

"Simon . . ." said Cleo. "I can help you, if you need a lawyer. That's what I do, you know."

"Defend criminals," said Simon.

"Well, alleged criminals. Yes."

Simon nodded. He sighed, without an answer. "Sylvie put your clothes in this suitcase," he said, after a moment, sliding a bag through the door. He grabbed Sylvie's shoes and vanity case. Her dress had been hung in the castle since its arrival. "Well, cheers! I've got to run. See you soon."

"Cheers," said Cleo and Emma.

"These are some fancy hats," said Cleo.

2
EMMA

-$62,511.21

"Hey, it's me," said Emma.

"Hey, Em," said Rich.

"Thank you for answering your phone."

"We're all set over here. I'll see you at the ceremony."

"Rich—"

"Yes?"

"I don't know how to explain what I did."

"You could have fucking tried, Em," said Rich. "How was I supposed to know you didn't want . . . what we had . . . anymore?"

"It's not that I didn't want what we had—"

"Isn't it?"

Emma sat down in Sylvie's empty library. She saw a copy of *The Bed Book,* a childhood story they'd all loved. "I guess, yes," she said. "I'm not happy."

"Why didn't you just *say something*?"

"I wanted to fix it," said Emma. "I knew I should be happy and so I tried . . . to be happy."

"Weird way to fix things," said Rich. "Jesus Christ, Em."

"I love you," said Emma. "I love you and the boys. I can find a way to . . ."

"Nope," said Rich. "You're not finding a way to *anything* on your own. We're in this together, Em. We're a family, for Christ's sake!"

"Oh," said Emma.

"Yeah," said Rich.

"What about England?" said Emma.

"What *about* England?"

"Would you ever consider living here for a bit?"

"What?"

"I thought I might talk to Simon. And maybe we could see about staying in Mumberton."

"Staying in Mumberton?"

"The boys gave me the idea. A fresh start. We could just try it and . . ."

"I mean . . . OK. OK, Em. Whatever you need."

"I don't want you to do it just for me," said Emma.

"Why not?" said Rich. "Why can't it just be for you?"

"Because I . . ." She was about to say, *Because I'm nothing.*

"Because you . . . ?"

"Because my mom made me feel like I'm nothing."

Rich was silent. When she did not say more, Rich said, "You're everything, Em. And if you can't see that I don't know what to say."

"You could say that again."

"You're everything, Em. You're everything to us. To me."

"Yeah," said Emma hesitantly.

"And I can't believe I'm saying this, to be honest, Em, but I'd love a break from teaching. Hell yeah, let's live in a goddamned castle."

"Oh my God," said Emma.

"What the fuck else are we going to do, sell our house to your unsettling friend, Cassidy?"

"What a mess," said Emma.

"Speaking of," said Rich. "Need to get these boys ready for the wedding."

"I'll come help."

"Just get your head together, Em. We'll see you soon. No more lies. I'm never going to leave you, so just tell me the truth. OK?"

Emma nodded, starting to cry.

"I can't hear you," said Rich.

"I said yes," said Emma.

3
LOUISA

Wedding Reception Buffet Menu

Starters

Cucumber Salad with Seasonal Sweet Melon Pearls & Linseed Oil

Handmade Chicken Liver Parfait with Apple & Saffron Chutney

Mumberton Venison Terrine with Prunes, Orange, Juniper & Thyme on Toasted Brioche

Mains

Roasted Sirloin of Local Beef, Horseradish Yorkshire Puddings, Roast Potatoes & Rich Gravy

Roasted Butternut Squash with Sage & Hazelnuts in Brown Butter (V)

Leg of Cumbrian Lamb with a Mint Sauce & Buttered Carrots

Gourmet Lakeland Bangers & Mash with Stout Onion Gravy & Mushy Peas

Desserts

Homemade Triple Choc with Kirsch Cream & Black Cherries

Individual Selection of Local Cheeses, Water Biscuits, Grapes, Celery, & Relish

Warm Homemade Sticky Toffee Pudding, Custard & Chantilly Cream

Assiette of 3 Apple-inspired Desserts

Elderflower & Buttermilk Pudding with Summer Fruits

Mumberton Berry Mess

PART TEN

THE PHOENIX

1
SYLVIE

Sylvie climbed from Simon's four-poster bed, parting velvet curtains, and walked toward the window. The dawn songs of goldcrest and thrush seemed a soundtrack to her joy. She put her wrists to her face and inhaled. Emma had created an original fragrance for Sylvie on her wedding day—it smelled mineral-y and clean, like rushing rivers and snow, reminding Sylvie of Montana.

Sylvie wanted this: a man she desired, nights of reading and sex. And more reading. And sex. Simon called hills "fells" and knew more than anyone needed to know about the migratory patterns of puffins. Was it the dream of every unmarried librarian to find a hot reader to love? Regardless, it had been her dream and it had come true. It was terrifying to have a dream come true.

Sylvie dropped her hands and waited for her sisters to come to her and walk her down the aisle in lieu of her father. She thought about their night picnics in the Bitterroot Valley. The stars, the trail mix they brought to snack on, the smell of the prescribed burns, the climb to the top of Skull Rock. The memory of her backyard playground in the mountains felt so real to Sylvie that she could smell smoke.

2
CLEO

Cleo and Emma, fascinators fastened to their hair with bobby pins, climbed in the car that waited to transport them from the Gatekeeper's Cottage to the castle ceremony. (Cleo appreciated the car; her heels were way too high to hike the damn path to the castle again.) After the wedding, Cleo was going to go straight back to Brooklyn. She was happy for Sylvie—she really was—but there was no reason for her to stay. She wanted to fly home and show up at Isaac's doorstep and declare her love for him, hoping he would let her in. "Call me when you wake up," she had texted him.

Isaac had not responded, but it was early on the Upper West Side. Cleo tried not to wonder if Isaac was alone. She closed her eyes and wished for him to be alone, dead asleep on his couch, *Law & Order* still playing on his old TV, a container from 88 Noodle on his coffee table. Cleo imagined a second set of chopsticks—her chopsticks—and her shoes discarded on his old-but-expensive rug. (His parents had bought it in Israel.) Cleo was ready for Isaac and his love, willing to beg (if needed) for him to enfold her in his arms. She made a list of what she'd bring into her new life, but it was a short list: some clothes, her makeup, a painting of a peacock she'd bought in college.

For a moment, Cleo thought the orange haze engulfing Mumberton Castle was the rising sun. Was she dreaming? The walls were intact, but above the crenellated parapets, Cleo saw orange and red flames and billowing smoke. "What the—"

"Oh my God!" screamed Emma. "The castle's on fire!"

Their driver made an abrupt U-turn, going back the way they had come; Cleo and Emma had to turn around to see the burning building that held their family.

"Go back," said Cleo. "Turn around, goddamnit!"

"My boys!" cried Emma.

"It's a fire, loves," said the driver. "Nothing for you there. Happens more than you'd think, these old castles burning." He shook his head. "It's a shame, but we're not going near that mess."

Cleo remembered her cigarettes, the garden, Louisa's library filled with old books. Angry Danny and his fancy bronze lighter. Had she carefully extinguished every match? Was Danny capable of . . . ?

"No!" said Emma. "Go back!"

Cleo felt as if she were in slow motion: Her mouth went dry, her heart rate increasing. Her phone rang. It was Isaac. She did not answer.

The taxi slowed at an intersection, blinker on. Cleo opened her door and jumped out. "Take my hand," she said to Emma.

"Where are you going?" cried the driver, alarmed.

Cleo didn't answer. She remembered the bikes leaning against the Gatekeeper's Cottage. She ran, with Emma, toward their family.

3
EMMA

-$65,702.10

The firemen would not let Emma inside the castle, no matter how she strained against them, no matter how much she protested. "My husband is inside!" said Emma. "My boys are trapped!" she cried. "Rich! My children!" Men in mustard-colored fire tunics and helmets held her back.

There were so many trucks, sirens blaring, dozens of men erecting scaffolding and aiming hoses at the blaze. The flames were colossal, engulfing everything, growing larger by the second. Paned windows created hundreds of years before were liquefying mouths emitting smoke. Emma shouted and broke free of the men, but before she got any closer to the castle, she was caught by other men in fire suits; she fought and bit, reckless with terror. Where were her boys? Where was Rich?

Finally—surrounded by strangers—Emma collapsed to her knees, pressed her hands together, and prayed. She lifted her head and she prayed. She had not prayed since the first night her mother had left her in the grass and lain down with Noah, not since her mother had used Emma and abandoned her.

God had not saved Emma then, so she gave up on Him.

Eyes closed, Emma heard Sylvie call her name.

Sylvie, wrapped in an aluminum blanket. She wore her wedding dress; it was singed at the hem and her feet were bare. "Emma," said Sylvie.

"They're inside!" said Emma.

Sylvie began coughing, deep and rattling coughs.

"They're inside!" Emma screamed.

"How do we get in?" said Cleo, at her side.

"My boys. My boys—my boys—they're inside!"

"I know a way," said Sylvie.

"Show me," said Cleo. Her authority calmed Emma as it had done since they were small. They passed Mac and Louisa. Mac sat in his wheelchair, staring at the massive fire. Louisa was surrounded by tapestries and works of art she had dragged from the castle. They seemed in shock, unable to do anything but witness the end of all they had known. They would later learn that Simon had followed an ambulance to the local hospital, where Penelope and Donna were being treated for smoke inhalation.

Sylvie, still hacking, led her sisters to the ivy-covered hidden doorway. It opened, but the passageway was ominous. "This leads to a staircase," said Sylvie. "But it might be locked at the top. We could get trapped." She started to panic. "It was hot," she said, starting to cough again. "I thought I was going to die," she said.

"My boys," said Emma.

They looked into the deep space, a path that could lead to Guinness and Jameson and Rich. "You can't go in there," said Sylvie.

"Try and stop me," said Cleo. Before they could, she was gone, forcing herself into the narrow space that led into what was left of the castle. Emma went into the entrance after Cleo. And as always, Sylvie followed her sisters.

4
SYLVIE

Just hours before, Sylvie had been full of expectation, making her way down this same low tunnel toward Simon. Now, the smoke was thick and Sylvie couldn't breathe. She felt her way along, her fingers touching stone and then an indentation. Simon had told her of rooms hidden deep within the castle where persecuted priests or castle owners could hide.

Sylvie tried to shut her brain off, to just move forward. But this was clearly a bad idea; this was such a bad idea. Sylvie felt nauseous and faint. And where was Simon?

Terror had followed joy, as she had known it would.

As her body had known it would.

But Sylvie inched along anyway, not brave exactly, but understanding that there were only two choices: Stay still or take one step forward, steel yourself, then step again.

5
CLEO

There was fresh air in the tight circular staircase. Did this mean it was locked at the top? If it were open, there would not be air.

"We can't go up," said Sylvie.

"Cleo," pleaded Emma.

"I'll go. You wait here," said Cleo.

"You're not going without me," said Emma, and the determination in her face was so familiar, Cleo felt as if she were ten years old again.

"Right, OK," said Sylvie, pressing her lips together and nodding.

Cleo went first.

6
EMMA

-$66,225.87

When Guinness was a baby, he would cry. And every time he cried, Emma was shattered. *Let him cry,* said Rich. Her pediatrician said, *Let him cry.*

Emma knew to go to her son. In her arms, he was serene.

From the horror-movie stairwell in Mumberton Castle, Emma heard Guinness. She did not hear Jameson, did not hear Rich. Cleo continued to climb. Sylvie's coughing sounded in her ears. And Guinness. Guinness was crying.

As she had known when he was a baby, Emma knew now:

If I can stop my baby's sadness, nothing else will matter in this world.

7

SYLVIE

The ceremony at St. Michael's in Mumberton was somber and beautiful, held after a week of mourning, of walking through ruins, stepping over charred remains, searching for anything that could be saved.

Mac was buried next to Simon's mother in a plot they had bought as young parents. The fate of Mumberton Castle was unknown, but Mac had died surrounded by family—his son, granddaughter, and Louisa at his side in the hospital.

Cleo told them, at the funeral reception held at the Ratty Arms pub in town, that what had turned out to be the most important thing she had learned in all her years of schooling had come back to her like a miracle as she stood outside the door of the Indigo Suite.

"I could hear Guinness crying," said Emma, shuddering.

Cleo had taken off her peacock fascinator, leaving bobby pins in her hair. The door to the Indigo Suite was locked.

"The sound of my son," repeated Emma.

Cleo pulled the pins and closed her eyes, trying to recall the skill her freshman year roommate had taught her to enter secret

New York gardens. She focused on the silent snap of the tumblers as they fell into place, turning her wrist precisely to free the lock.

Emma was making her way up the spiral staircase when her prayers were answered and her boys returned to her, all three of them, spilling from the room, terrified but alive.

Together, they escaped. Sylvie and Cleo and Emma and Guinness and Jameson and Rich and Louisa pushing Mac in his wheelchair across the Great Lawn, huddling together far from the inferno. By the time the fire was completely extinguished, eighty percent of the castle was in ruins.

There would be many investigations into who locked which doors and where the fire may have originated. But on the night of the fire, Angus invited them all for supper at the Ratty Arms, his brother Leon's pub. Penelope was kept at the hospital for observation. Simon and Sylvie spent the night in folding chairs next to her bed. She was released in the morning, and they returned to the Gatekeeper's Cottage.

Mac declined rapidly and died in his sleep, knowing his son was returned to Mumberton Castle, or what was left of it.

8
CLEO

Cleo was having a cigarette on the patio of the Ratty Arms pub when a group of shouting children heralded the arrival of a Mercedes G-Wagon. A local drug dealer? A visiting rapper? Cleo, exhausted, watched dully as the driver's-side door opened, the retractable running board deployed, and out stepped . . . Isaac.

"You smoke now?" he said.

"You can drive?" said Cleo.

"Barely," said Isaac.

Cleo stood, and when Isaac reached her, she leaned against him, and his arms went around her, holding tight. "What are you doing here?" she said.

"I love you," said Isaac.

"I'll quit smoking," said Cleo.

"Again," said Isaac.

"I love you, too," said Cleo.

"Danny posted that you were the devil on his Instagram," said Isaac. "I drank a glass of gin and booked a flight. The only rental car they had in Carlisle was this thing. I got here as soon as I could."

"What about Rebecca?"

"She's very nice, but she's no Cleo Peacock."

Cleo pressed her ear to Isaac's rib cage. "I can hear your heart," she said.

9
LOUISA

Items recovered from Mumberton Castle Fire

Number 602
Phoenix Rising

Pre-fire condition: Stored in the basement.
Salvageability: Yes.
Damage description: Minor.
Item description:

"Phoenix Rising" depicts a scene of a mythical bird emerging from flames. It is a part of the tapestry series "The Lady and the Phoenix." In previous tapestries, a woman, clad in flowing robes and with an expression of glacial serenity, has been portrayed as an infant, young woman, and bride, and has now transformed into a bird.

The background of the tapestry features a landscape with trees, buildings, and mountains. The colors used in the tapestry are vibrant and include shades of blue, green, red, and gold.

The tapestry “Phoenix Rising” dates back to the early 16th century and was created in Brussels, Belgium. It measures 12 feet tall and 32 feet wide and is woven in wool and silk.

Signature and date: *Louisa Freck, July 2025*

10
EMMA

DEBT-FREE; $2,500/MO (PLUS HOUSING)

Outside the door of her mother's hospital room, Emma steadied herself. Smoke inhalation was serious and would require monitoring and rest. Rich, Guinness, Penelope, and Jameson had been released by their doctors, but Donna remained. The Catalfamos had already missed their flight back to Montana.

Donna's eyes were closed, her mouth covered by a mask attached to a breathing tube. Her inhalations and exhalations were even and deep with the aid of an oxygen machine.

Emma had never seen her mother weak. It was terrifying. Donna opened her eyes.

"Of course it's you," she said. "And not Noah. Just you."

"I love you, Mom," said Emma.

"I told the doctors to call and say I was dying, but I guess even that wasn't enough to get him off the couch," said Donna. "So much for my love story."

"I'm here," said Emma.

"Of course you are," said Donna. She turned her head away. "All I wanted was to be loved," she said.

Emma was invisible to her mother. Donna had not considered

her—a small, scared girl in the grass—while she made love to Noah; Donna had not thought of Emma when she moved to Arizona. Of course Emma felt bereft and angry and sad as hell. But she was sad for want of a mother who did not exist.

It was possible that Donna's awful parenting had led Emma to create such a close-knit family. Emma's years of misery made her stunned and grateful now. And that was not nothing. Emma remembered a line from Cheryl Strayed, a writer she loved: *You were a dark teacher, but you were nonetheless a teacher.*

"Thank you for everything you did for me," said Emma. "I'll make sure you get home safe."

"It was always you three girls against me," said Donna.

"I'll see you tomorrow, Mom," said Emma. And without regret or acrimony, she left the room.

11
SYLVIE

Emma and Rich approached Simon and Sylvie with a careful plan, outlining how they wanted to spend a year with their boys in the coastal village of Mumberton, helping in any way they could with insurance or restoration in exchange for a loan to pay off their debts.

The week after Mac's funeral, Rich and Emma drove Simon, Sylvie, and Penelope to the airport in Simon's old Land Rover. "Thank you again," Rich said to Simon, and Simon said, "Believe me, mate, the pleasure is all mine."

"You never liked it here," said Rich.

"No, I did not," said Simon.

"I don't get it," said Rich. Louisa had found Emma and Rich a stone cottage in Mumberton overlooking the estuary, and secured spots at the local school. Emma had already outfitted them all in secondhand waxed jackets and wellies from the St. Mary's Hospice thrift shop in nearby Millom. The boys spent their days at the football pitch and field in the village, playing with locals who kidded the boys, kindly, about their accents and the way they kept forgetting and calling football "soccer." For the week he was in town, Isaac gave the boys rides around the village in the G-Wagon, cementing their popularity for years to come.

"Wait til winter, brother," said Simon.

"Gotcha," said Rich, shaking his head but grinning.

Donna had recovered enough to fly back to her Margaritaville Conch cottage. When Cleo called to see if she had arrived safely, Noah told them that her feelings were hurt after they "all ignored her" at the wedding, "treating her like an old sofa cushion," and she refused to come to the phone.

"One of us is going to have to fly down there at some point, you know," Emma told her sisters.

"She *has* a husband," said Cleo.

"Lucky," said Sylvie.

Simon and Sylvie flew with Penelope to Heathrow on a puddle jumper, and then direct to Miami. Florence and Rashid had taken in Wilhelmina, but they were tired of the rescue dog. *She barks a lot,* said Florence, in a text. *Also, the library at school is a disaster! Nothing shelved, overdues all over the place! Come home!*

When they were settled in their plane seats and Penelope had inserted her earbuds to listen to the audiobook of *The Jigsaw Jungle,* Simon said to Sylvie, "There may not be any money when this is all over."

"We have a home," said Sylvie, thinking about the house she had shared with Alexander on Hibiscus Street. The tomatoes they had planted in the garden and the bed they had shared. She didn't want to move, but she could replace some things. She could clean out his side of the closet, and even make some room on her bookshelves. It was time to buy new basil and marjoram.

Sylvie took the book she was reading from her backpack. Simon found his book as well. They leaned against each other, settled in for the long flight. Penelope rested against Sylvie, and put her thumb in her mouth.

"She sucks her thumb?" whispered Sylvie.

Simon smiled. "My girls," he said. Penelope's weight on Sylvie's shoulder made her feel anchored, somehow *necessary.* Sylvie felt, though she still did not believe in a benevolent Father in Heaven, that something, some magic, connected her and Penelope. And belonging to Penelope gave Sylvie an answer to a question she didn't even know she was desperately asking.

Sylvie and Simon began to read silently, entering fictional worlds that made life's sharp edges dissipate like smoke. By the time a steward approached with the drink cart, Sylvie, Simon, and Penelope had fallen asleep, curled together, their books abandoned on their laps.

EPILOGUE

CLEO

Isaac and Cleo liked paper papers; the Sunday *New York Times* was strewn across the bed, along with their bagel wrappers and napkins. Cleo snuggled under Isaac's arm, kissing his neck and then his mouth.

They both had work to do on a Sunday. They both had work to do every day. Isaac and Cleo lived on takeout, gin, and sex. It was wonderful. "I know we have to work, but . . ." said Cleo, straddling Isaac.

"Work can wait," said Isaac. "But not for too long."

"Agree one hundred percent," said Cleo. She licked cream cheese from the side of his mouth.

"Can work wait a teeny bit longer?" said Isaac, when they were showered and dressed, Cleo headed to the office and Isaac to the public library.

"Ugh, why?" said Cleo, trying to close her overstuffed case.

"I thought we could take a quick spin around the reservoir?"

said Isaac, putting his binoculars and his camera around his neck. "Word is we might spot a Cerulean Warbler."

"It's a detour but OK," said Cleo. "I'll have to make it up tonight."

"My parents are coming for dinner anyway," said Isaac. "Just join for dessert if you can."

"I'll try," said Cleo.

"I know," said Isaac.

Cleo grabbed her own set of binoculars. Her sisters had gifted them matching Swarovskis as an engagement gift. Isaac's parents had thrown them a beautiful party, and Hannah had clasped Cleo's shoulders and said, "You call me Mom now, Cleopatra."

"Yes," said Cleo.

"My friends and I have a book club and everybody brings their daughters. First Wednesday of the month," said Hannah.

"I'll be there, every month," said Cleo.

"OK, then," said Hannah.

"Thanks, Mom," said Cleo, surprising herself by tearing up. Her own mother had not made it to her engagement party or sent a card.

"This month the book is called *Choosing a Jewish Life*," said Hannah. "It's my month, and that's the book I picked."

"I'll order a copy tonight," said Cleo.

"No need," said Hannah, handing her a bag from Barnes & Noble.

Isaac took her hand as they left their apartment and headed across Central Park West into the park. It was a bright day, the sky as blue as the Caribbean Sea. Cleo told Isaac about the pro bono case she was focused on: a man in jail who was refusing a plea deal, insisting he had not shot his wife, despite numerous eyewitness accounts that he had been in the room when she died. Isaac suggested Cleo have her client's clothing tested for gunpowder residue; maybe there had been another person in the room. (This advice would free the man from prison; the lack of residue on his clothes inspired Cleo to find more eyewitnesses, one of whom named another shooter, who was convicted.)

They paused when they reached the Jacqueline Kennedy Onassis Reservoir, taking in the Manhattan skyline and the water, the trees, and the sun.

"Cleo, look!" cried Isaac.

Cleo put her binoculars to her eyes and scanned the trees around them. She saw the female Cerulean Warbler, magnificent. "Oh," she sighed, taking in the bird's bluish-green head, the yellow stripes around its eyes. "She's looking right at me," said Cleo.

Isaac lifted his Nikon and focused. He clicked the shutter and smiled—capturing the elusive bird.

EMMA

First, the legal looting. Before the Mumberton Castle fire consumed the roof, firefighters and troops from local army barracks grabbed what they could: precious (and not so precious) artwork, furniture, antiques, swords, and birds of prey, rehomed to a nearby aviary.

Second, the rain and the trash. Rich commandeered crews to remove thousands of bins of debris, which was combed through to make sure no treasures were discarded. In what he would call "the most important job of my life," Rich found locals who knew more than he did, retired men who held priceless knowledge: how to rebuild leaded windows, hand-fit oak roof timber, and re-plaster ornate ceilings. These men—they were all men—trained Rich's younger staff. If the Brits resented an American in charge, they kept it to themselves. Rich's boundless enthusiasm and Simon's deep pockets endeared Rich to the artisans and laborers he relied upon. Rebuilding Mumberton would take a decade, but it would be done, and beautifully. The cause of the fire was ruled undetermined, and every single lock in the castle was replaced. Could it possibly be true that the door to the Indigo Suite was old and locked itself? Emma had never trusted Louisa Freck, but couldn't find a reason not to believe her when she insisted she had never locked the door. Still, sometimes Emma woke in the middle of the night and wondered if Louisa was lying. It was an unsettling idea, and there was no point in dwelling on it.

One morning, Emma found herself with nothing to do. Guinness and Jameson were at school, and Rich spent his days happily shuttling between the castle grounds and his home office. Emma went for a walk in the rain, which had continued unabated for much of the spring, after a winter less dark than Montana's winter but just as cold.

Emma ambled toward the estuary. Her coffee, the salt smell, the rain. She closed her eyes and began to assemble a profile: She would utilize a form of Japanese snowbell oil called benzoin that made a fragrance warm and woody, exuding leather undertones like a brand-new glove out of a Harrods box. Chanel, Givenchy, Yves Saint Laurent, Hermès, and Prada had made fragrances with benzoin; it inspired serenity and made someone wearing it feel elegant.

Emma reached the estuary and gazed at the water. Women in the Middle Ages had carried pomanders filled with rose petals, ambergris, or violet root powder. Emma breathed in deeply through her nose. She would rush home and write down the scent profile she would call "Mumberton." The Mumberton Pomade necklace would be the first product from Peacock Perfumery.

PENELOPE

My family was fortunate to have the Catalfamos in our lives. I visited Auntie Emma and Uncle Rich throughout my childhood—loving long, warm days with my cousins, Guinness and Jameson, but always happy to leave as summer turned to fall. Uncle Rich built bookshelves in my pele tower room, and a desk with an inlaid marquetry surface: two circles depicting the globe, each country I hoped to visit cut out in intricate detail using multicolored veneers.

Auntie Cleo's wedding to Uncle Isaac was intimate. They married at a New York City courthouse and then we all went to Bella Luna for pasta and tiramisu. As promised, Auntie Cleo defended my father in court, and my father did not go to jail. Thanks to Auntie Emma's business acumen and my father's new job at the Miami Botanical Gardens, we got by even after my father's assets were indefinitely frozen.

Sylvie offered to sell *The Happy Pair* to a museum, but my father insisted she enclose it in a rare-book display case. Sylvie ordered a poster of the illustration to hang over their Miami bed and brought the case to her library once a year to show her kids.

Auntie Emma started Peacock Perfumery, and her bestselling product—the Mumberton Pomade necklace, scented with benzoin, amber, and styrax—was so successful that she was able to fund the castle restoration even when my father could no longer do so. (My father's former neighbor on Indian Creek Island, a supermodel, wore the Mumberton Pomade for months and paparazzi photos of the model in Auntie Emma's necklace drove sales into the stratosphere.) Auntie Emma even hired Louisa part-time to attempt to restore the octagonal library.

As for me, my mother moved to Caracas; I never lived with her again. The place that suits me is my home on Hibiscus Street in Coconut Grove, Miami. Some nights, Willie sleeps in my room, when my dad and Sylvie crowd her out of their bed.

I was the flower girl at my father's wedding to Sylvie the summer after the fire. Beatrix Potter's former home, now a museum called Hill Top, did not host weddings as a rule. But Mac had been close friends with Deirdre, who ran the gift shop, and in his honor, she used her connections to secure a half hour in the gardens that inspired *The Tale of Peter Rabbit*. Angus worked part-time for the National Trust and agreed to look away when we gathered at Moss Eccles Tarn, a lake on the Hill Top property. Beatrix had liked to sit at the edge of the lily-covered lake to draw while her husband fished for brown trout.

Sylvie and my father's wedding day was sunny and clear. Uncle Rich, Angus, and my cousins, proud groomsmen, stood next to my dad. Florence, Sylvie's sisters, and I wore lavender dresses.

I opened the latticework garden door (featured in *The Tale of Tom Kitten*) and made my way up a slate path, past the rhubarb patch I recognized from *The Tale of Jemima Puddle-Duck*. I had a basket of rose petals and felt lovely as I tossed them into the air. The rolling hills were so green they almost vibrated; that color is the one I imagine whenever I need a shot of happiness.

The end of this story is many things, but for me it is this: I reached my father and held his hand. Together, we stood in front of the tarn and waited for Sylvie. When she began walking up the path toward us, she was accompanied by her sisters, one on either side—the strong women who would become my bonus aunties. Cleo's freckles had come out in the sun, and Emma's color was high from her daily walks along the Irish Sea.

That morning at Hill Top, Sylvie Peacock became mine—not my mother, exactly; in name she was my stepmother but that hardly explained our connection. She was my one, and one is all you need.

After their vows, my father and Sylvie kissed and fell into a tight embrace. Sylvie understood childhood sadness. As everyone clapped and cried, Sylvie reached out and gathered me close. Look at me: I was a girl in tight braids, being pulled into warmth by my favorite librarian on her wedding day.

I would never be alone again.

The End

ACKNOWLEDGMENTS

Thank you, Michelle Tessler, Beth Howells, Wendy Wrangham, Julia Romero, Mary Pender, Kara Cesare, Jesse Shuman, Jennifer Hershey, Andrew Sean Greer, Claiborne Smith, Emily Hovland, Liz Gershoff, Roz Gillespie, Moyara Pharis, Sam and Remy Shaber, Sarah McKay, Liza Bennigson, Mary-Anne, Peter, and Brendan Westley, the Meckel and Toan families, Meg Gardiner, Mary Helen Specht, Dalia Azim, Christina Baker Kline, Kim Hovey, Kara Welsh, Sanyu Dillon, Taylor Noel, Emma Thomasch, Chelsea Woodward, Tara Ewing, Reese Witherspoon, Jenny Day, Suzanne Wofford, Melissa Atterberry, Stacey Gardner, Tina Donahoo, Robbie Harrison, Priya Pamar, Terry Benaryeh, Julie Berwald, Jaye Joseph, Cory Ryan, Marie Gray, Jenny Hart, Sage MacLeod, Jenny Jackson, Elin Hildebrand, Caroline Wilson, Alexia Rodriguez, Erin Kinard, Heather and Russell Courts, Jardine Libaire, Owen Egerton, Hanoch Patt, Meg Wolitzer, Paula McLain, Ashley Bartram, and Alison Edwards. I love you all.

I will never know how I got lucky enough to share my life with Ash, Harrison, Nora, Neff, Roux, and my main squeeze, Tip Meckel. Thank you, my beloveds, for everything.

ABOUT THE AUTHOR

Amanda Eyre Ward is the *New York Times* bestselling author of eight novels including *The Jetsetters,* a Reese's Book Club pick. She lives in Austin, Texas, with her family.

amandaward.com
X: @amandaeyreward
Instagram: @amandaeyreward
Find Amanda Eyre Ward on Facebook.